# DANGER CLOSE

## The Echo Platoon Series

*Book One*

Marliss Melton

Cover and Book design by eBook Prep www.ebookprep.com

August, 2014
ISBN: 978-1-61417-642-8

*ePublishing Works!*
www.epublishingworks.com

# FOREWORD

*Danger Close* is a full-length novel that was inspired by a short story I wrote for the *SEAL of My Dreams Anthology* in 2011. If the story seems familiar at first, that's the reason. Read on, and you'll find that the rest is exciting and new.

# ACKNOWLEDGMENTS

My projects inevitably end up being the product of a group effort. It is only right that I publically acknowledge my able assistant, Wendie Grogan, and my talented editor and best friend, Sydney Jane Baily (who is also an historical romance author in her own right—you should read her books). In addition, I owe a debt of gratitude to my Beta readers for hunting down typos. Penny, Mellena, Cindi, and Dannielle—your efforts are so greatly appreciated!

would escort them into Matamoros, the lawless town situated across the U.S. border from Brownsville, Texas. There, the SEALs would initiate a forty-eight hour reconnaissance, monitoring the movements in and around the site, before sweeping in to recover their target. If all went well, they'd drive to the exfiltration site and fly off on a Navy Seahawk.

*Easy Day.* Sam simmered as he slipped the phone back into his pack. This whole goddamn op wouldn't be happening at all if the idiot daughter of oil magnate Lyle Scott had left Matamoros when the U.S. embassy issued a mandatory evacuation for all U.S. citizens. If not for her, Sam and his men would be headed for Malaysia on the warpath to killing the arms smuggler who'd injured one of their fellow teammates last year. Instead of Lt. Tyler Rexall's debilitating injury and lost career, Sam had to play nursemaid to a global environmentalist who didn't have any sense of self-preservation. The silver spoon stuck in her mouth must have interfered with her deductive reasoning capabilities. He'd christened this mission "Operation Dumb Broad" in her honor.

"That's our guy," Bronco confirmed, lowering his weapon. The vehicle came to a squeaky stop and dimmed its lights.

"Go," Sam ordered.

Bullfrog, their medic, darted out of hiding first, providing cover for Haiku and then Bronco, who leapfrogged his position. Sam brought up the rear and was the first into the rust-colored taxi, taking shotgun, as was his due as the officer in charge. His three companions squeezed into the back seat, grunting at the tight fit. Cigarette smoke filled the car's interior. The car boasted plastic-covered seats and a working meter.

The DEA officer tossed his Marlboro out the

window and turned his head to glance at Sam. "Welcome to hell," he rasped, his eyes glinting in the dark. Engaging the meter like he meant to charge them by the kilometer, he hammered the accelerator, flinging them all back in their seats as the taxi took off.

Beyond the swinging crucifix that hung from the rearview mirror and the slapping windshield wipers that ticked like a time-bomb, the glow of Matamoros beckoned them into danger.

Sam's resentment bubbled. The spitting sky, the time of year—late spring—and the circumstances of this op reminded him of an incident in high school, one that had formed his opinion of wealthy individuals, women especially. Back then, the source of his torment had been beautiful Wendy—daughter of a real estate tycoon, prom queen, and the biggest tease in the twelfth grade. If he'd known the outcome of his heroics, he would have let her suffer the consequences of her flirtatiousness. Instead, her hoarse screams coming from the bedroom at an after-prom party had awakened his protective instincts and sent him flying to her rescue.

Streetwise, with a private crush on Wendy, Sam had thrashed her two male companions within an inch of their lives. He'd expected her to at least thank him, but she hadn't. Those boys had been her friends, after all. And when her father demanded an explanation for her bruises, she had offered up Sam as a scapegoat.

He'd suffered a month in prison while his stepfather scrounged up the money for a decent lawyer. But even then, being Latino, from the wrong neighborhood, he'd been cast into the role of criminal, and no one would see past the stereotype, so he'd left that life behind and joined the Navy.

Since then, he had broken every stereotype into

which he'd been cast, never quitting, until he'd become a warrior worthy of every man's respect—a U.S. Navy SEAL.

Yet, here he was, as a Navy SEAL, putting himself and his teammates into peril for what?—to extricate the precious daughter of the CEO of Scott Oil Corporation? She'd gotten herself into this mess; she ought to have to figure her own way out.

What the hell was she still doing here in Matamoros when drug lords ruled the city? Or was she just too pampered, too used to being coddled to realize what could happen to her in this lawless realm?

He supposed he was about to find out. Right now, the only certainty was that if he failed in this mission to extract Lyle Scott's foolish daughter from this corrupted city, his career would be over—just like that. He could feel it in his bones. Everything he had fought so hard to accomplish could be stripped from him as if it had never happened. Why? Because the CEO of Scott Oil Corporation obviously had friends in high places, or this ridiculous waste of his time would not be happening.

As water droplets on the windshield grew brighter, Sam's stomach knotted with the fear that history was about to repeat itself.

# CHAPTER 1

The SEALs' instructions were to nab the recovery target when she least expected it. A note in her file had warned that she might resist leaving. Why? Was she crazy or something?

The SEALs had reconnoitered *El Santuario*, the school for girls where she'd gone from testing their drinking water to protecting the students when their teachers up and abandoned them. For forty-eight hours, they'd taken note of routines, personnel, points of entry, and all exits. At precisely oh-four hundred hours, Sam and Bronco made their way through a light rain into the school yard, climbed onto the dormitory roof, and lowered themselves via a nylon climbing rope to Miss Scott's chamber. Haiku and Bullfrog secured the perimeter in the meantime.

The first to arrive at her window, Sam struggled a moment to breach the locked shutter. When it released with a *pop* and swung open, the figure in the bed inside rolled over. Hanging one story from the cobbled courtyard, he waited for the occupant to resume sleeping before easing silently inside the chamber as Bronco made his own descent.

Lowering the NVGs atop his helmet, Sam peered

through them to make a positive ID. Madison Scott's honey-blond hair glowed neon green through his lenses. But the curve of her cheek and the peachy skin of one bare shoulder confirmed she was, indeed, their target. Her fresh beauty had taken him aback the first time he'd seen her while watching the schoolyard the previous morning. It did little to endear her to him; being even lovelier than Wendy indicated that Miss Scott would have a personality which was even more entitled, narcissistic, and downright spoiled.

Bronco had just touched down into the room beside him, as stealthily as a Native American on the hunt, when Miss Scott rolled back over to face the ceiling. The prettiest tits this side of the Rio Grande glowed neon green in his NVGs, and Sam practically swallowed his tongue.

Christ, he hadn't expected her to sleep naked. Bronco assessed the situation, choking back a chuckle while Sam commanded himself to announce their presence. But then a scream erupted out of the alley behind the school and Miss Scott lurched awake.

Maddy stared at the open window, alarm licking up her spine. She was certain she had closed the latch before going to bed.

Beyond the netting draped over her bed, her vast chamber stood quiet and full of shadows. Drug lords prowled the streets of Matamoros preying on girls as young as thirteen. The wall around the school might be topped with broken glass, but it was only a matter of time before the predators found their way inside. Most of the teachers had departed at the mandatory evacuation for American citizens. Maddy, who'd been testing tap water in Northern Mexico, had recognized the students' plight and refused to leave them.

Praying that the latch had simply worked itself

loose, she peeled the sticky sheet off her naked body and scooted to the edge of the bed. She would cross the room swiftly and close it. But the rasp of a masculine chuckle drove a blade of terror straight through her heart.

With a shriek, she scrambled back onto her mattress and away from the sound. The shadow she'd mistaken for her bureau detached itself from the wall. A large man closed in on her, muttering words she couldn't hear over the blood roaring in her ears. As he swiped aside the mosquito netting, she leaped off the far side of the bed, avoiding his outstretched hand.

A squeal of panic betrayed her fear as she sprinted toward the door, plowing into a second man who blocked her path. Spinning about, she issued a full-blown scream when they boxed her in. A large hand clamped over her mouth. A thick arm banded her waist and plucked her off her feet. Caught up against what felt like a warm wall, Maddy fought desperately to free herself.

How could this be happening? She'd stayed to protect the girls from human trafficking, yet here she was, about to disappear into the underworld, herself a victim!

"Listen," commanded a gruff voice, shocking her by speaking in English. "We're not going to hurt you. I just said we're U.S. Navy SEALs," he insisted, repeating the words she must have missed earlier, "and we're here to take you home."

Relief liquefied Maddy's bones. As she sagged against her captor, he removed his hand from her mouth freeing her to breathe again. But then the full meaning of his words registered, and resentment caused her to wrest free. She took two steps to the bed, stripped the sheet from it and wrapped it around her nakedness. *How could you, Daddy?* she seethed.

She should have guessed he'd veto her decision to stay here. But U.S. Navy SEALs? Her father apparently had more clout than she realized.

"Well, I'm sorry you've wasted your time," she said, smoothing the quaver in her voice, "because I'm not leaving."

"You have to come with us, ma'am. We have our orders."

Maddy kept her back to them. "I don't care about your orders. There are young women here who would be preyed upon in a matter of hours without someone to look after them."

"Well, that someone won't be you," the operative retorted in such an implacable voice that she whirled around to look at him.

His black hair and tanned complexion had made him appear Hispanic, which was why she'd assumed he was a local; only now, she could see that he was way too tall, his features distinctly Anglo.

A glance at the other man left an impression of light eyes and a crooked smile. What were the odds that she could outwit them both and get away? Probably one in a million, but she had to try.

"Fine," she conceded, thinking fast. "Just let me get dressed first. I need five minutes."

"I'll give you one," countered the dark brute. "Find some clothes," he ordered nodding at her bureau.

His high-handedness annoyed her; all the same Maddy pretended to obey. Feeling in the dark for a blouse, skirt, and sandals, she gathered them against her chest. "There's a bathroom in the hall." She backed toward the door. "I'll change in there and be right out."

The SEALs exchanged a knowing look.

"Negative," rapped the dark-haired one. "You'll change right here while we look the other way."

Her heart thumped with aggravation. She had to get into the hall in order to escape their clutches. "I will *not* get dressed in front of you," she said through her teeth.

"Then you'll leave town in the sheet you're wearing," he replied, eliciting a sound from his companion that ended in a cough.

Maddy bit her lower lip. What other escape was there besides the hallway? Just the windows, one of which could only be reached by running between the SEALs. That left the window beside her bed. She pictured the one-story drop to the grassy yard below. Could she even survive a fall like that? Possibly, if she rolled when she landed. And with enough of a lead on them, she could conceal herself where they'd never find her.

Thinking of the girls who counted on her for protection, she determined that she really had no choice. "Turn your back," she heard herself say.

When they both turned around, Maddy dropped the sheet. She burrowed into her blouse, stepped into her skirt, and jammed her feet into her sandals. Without a hint of warning, she swiveled toward the window, popped open the shutters, and heaved herself onto the sill, prepared to throw herself into the void.

Heavy hands banded her waist, dragging her down and back into the room. "Let me go!" she ordered, kicking and squirming.

The big SEAL tossed her onto the bed, where she promptly attempted to get up again. He tackled her into the mattress, subduing her struggles by pinning her with his weight.

"Stop it!" Maddy railed. The only thing she could move was her head, so she brought it up hard. *Crunch!*

"Shit!" He reared back, clutching his nose with one

hand. "Damn it, woman! Are you crazy jumping out of a window like that?"

"I told you, I won't leave."

"The hell you won't. Bronco, hit her with a dose of Lorazepam."

Bronco hovered uncertainly. "Are you sure, sir?"

"You want to deal with a squirming lunatic all the way to the exfil?"

Maddy gasped in outrage. "I am not a lunatic. I'm a United States citizen and I demand my right to self-determination!"

"Overruled. Bronco, stick her *now.*"

With a move that Maddy hadn't anticipated, the SEAL rolled, pulling her with him and exposing her bottom to his companion. In the next instant, the tip of a needle pricked her right buttock. She lurched, tightening her muscles to ward off the intrusion, but the effect of the drug hit her almost instantly.

Weakness swamped her, causing her to sprawl atop her captor, spread-eagle. Her head slumped to his shoulder where she inhaled his distinctly male but not unpleasant scent. *I've been beat,* she acknowledged. Her father wanted her out of Mexico. She had known all along that it would happen, didn't she?

Out of the corner of her still-open eyes, she saw the SEAL named Bronco tab a button on a cord strung across his chest. "Target recovered." He sounded subdued. "We're coming out."

So now she'd been reduced to a target instead of a human being taking a stand against corruption. Terrific. *Thanks, Dad.*

If she didn't understand why her father was so damn protective, she might actually never forgive him. Maybe one of these days he'd let her do what she'd been called to do and stop playing God, just because he could.

Haiku and Bullfrog had cleared the area around the school and called for their DEA contact to come and collect them. Sam knew via their ongoing communication that they'd 'tagged and gagged' two drunken civilians wandering up the alley behind the school dormitory. *Don't worry,* Haiku had assured him. *They'll never remember what happened to them.*

Scanning the street for any other potential witnesses, Sam squeezed out of the gated schoolyard with the recovery target lying limply in his arms. Bronco locked the gate from the inside, keeping the sleeping occupants secure for now. The girls inside might resist capture for a few more days, anyway.

*Not my problem*, Sam reminded himself.

Hefting his burden higher, he waited for Bronco to scale the wall and join him. His throbbing nose reminded him of Madison Scott's ferocious struggle. As feisty as she was, she had to know that she was no match for the scum who ruled the streets here. Or was she so foolishly naïve that she thought her reckless behavior wouldn't result in ugly consequences? Like an innocent kid going to jail?

Hearing Bronco drop from the wall beside him, he focused on their exfil, keying his mike. "Do you have a visual?"

"Roger that," Haiku replied. "All clear."

"Moving now. Keep us covered," he requested.

"Copy. Proceed."

With Bullfrog and Haiku poised to fire at anything that threatened them, Sam and Bronco dashed through puddles to the waiting taxi and jumped in. The other two joined them within seconds, and the taxi squealed away. Operation Dumb Broad had gone off with just one hitch.

Sam suspected his nose was broken.

As they sped through a maze of streets, headed for the exfil site several miles out of town, the DEA officer at the wheel looked at the woman in Sam's arms and nearly plowed into an oncoming vehicle.

"Keep your eyes on the road," Sam growled, though he was having difficulty leading by example.

Miss Scott's white blouse had gone transparent in the rain, making it obvious that she wasn't wearing a bra. With every lurch of the taxi, her breasts, so vivid in his memory, swayed enticingly. Sam could just make out the shadow of her naval at the center of her lean waist, the flare of her hips beneath the flimsy skirt she wore. Wasn't she just asking for trouble sleeping in the nude?

Feeling his body respond, he jerked his attention back to the maze of streets through which they raced, spraying water left and right, careening around corners. *Focus on the op, damn it.*

Gathering up her long damp hair, he drew it over her chest like a sash. Out of sight, out of mind.

Except the scent of her shampoo, feminine and flowery, only increased his awareness of her softly curving bottom nestled right between his thighs. It rubbed his package every time the car hit a bump in the road, which was pretty much constantly. The pleasant friction sure took his mind off his throbbing nose. Chagrined and praying she wouldn't wake up, he tried to adjust the way he held her. This was goddamn unprofessional of him.

Not my fault, he insisted. *She* was the one who'd lacked the sense to leave while the leaving was good. Waking up to a boner jabbing at her sweet ass was nothing compared to what might have happened to her if she'd stuck around.

He had to give her credit, though, for fighting like a tiger. This woman had guts and maybe a screw or two loose. When she woke up and realized she was long gone from Mexico, he had a hunch she'd be stomping mad, too.

Well, too damn bad. At least she was alive and in good hands, which she wouldn't be for very long if she stayed in this hell hole.

The sweeping light of a passing truck illumined her face briefly, and a shaft of alarm pierced Sam at the sight of a golf-ball sized lump swelling on her forehead.

*Oh, crap.* No one would look at that lump and believe that it was self-inflicted. He gulped against a suddenly dry mouth—least of all Maddy's father who'd promised to collect her on the aircraft carrier to which they were headed.

"*Demonio*," he swore in his grandmother's tongue. It was happening all over again.

Maddy awoke to a throbbing head and the thunder of helicopter rotors chopping the air with a deafening *whuppa, whuppa, whuppa.*

She lay flat on her back, strapped to some kind of a gurney. Too lethargic to open her eyes, she felt herself being lifted, jostled, then lowered into a gale-force wind that whipped her hair into her face. Light flickered beyond her weighty eyelids.

Then the wind and thunder faded abruptly, replaced by the cadence of heavy footsteps resonating with a metallic clang. The air felt still and close, now. The walls that she sensed on either side of her emitted a low, throbbing hum.

*What's going on? Where am I?*

The gurney made a sharp, right turn, delivering her into a chilly space redolent with the odor of rubbing alcohol. Several pairs of hands went to work unstrapping her, then lifting and lowering her onto a mattress. Someone tossed a blanket over her shivering frame and stuffed a pillow under her head.

"Why is she comatose?" clipped a female in accents of authority. "And why is your nose bleeding, Lieutenant?"

"She, uh, resisted us, ma'am. We had to tranquilize her."

The deep male voice raised the downy hairs on Maddy's body, but for the life of her, she couldn't identify the speaker any more than she could recall what had happened to bring her here. The last thing she remembered was falling asleep in her bed at *El Santuario.*

"Just how much tranquilizer and what kind did you administer?"

"Two milligrams of Lorazepam," said another male voice.

"Then she ought to wake soon," said the woman, "only I expect she'll have trouble remembering."

*Remember what?* Maddy's nerves jangled. What had happened to her? How had she come to be like this? And where in heaven's name *was* she? Cool, deft fingers lifted her eyelids, one then the other. Blinding light pierced each pupil.

"You hit her on the head?" the woman demanded.

"Oh, no ma'am. That was self-inflicted."

A tense silence filled the humming space.

"Her father's helicopter is fifteen minutes out," the woman announced. "If you're lucky, the swelling will go down before he sees her. She's coming out of it now," she added. "Stay with her while I fetch two icepacks." The tramp of her footsteps receded.

Maddy tried to swallow. Her throat felt raw, her mouth as if it had been swabbed with cotton. She ran her tongue over her dry lips.

"She's waking up," noticed one of the men.

"I'll get her some water," rasped the other. For some reason, that gruff baritone voice made Maddy shiver. The sound of running water preceded the feel of a large hand sliding under the back of her head, cradling it as he helped her to lift her shoulders. A paper cup touched her lips. "Here, take a sip, ma'am. It'll help."

The respectful term made her think of the military. As she swallowed a soothing draught, Maddy cracked her eyes and assessed her Good Samaritan through her lashes.

Definitely military, she confirmed. He was darkly handsome, thirtyish. Dried blood crusted the underside of his swollen nose. Dark green eyes regarded her with brooding intensity.

"Who are you?" she croaked, as he lowered her head and untangled his fingers from her hair.

"Lieutenant Sam Sasseville," he introduced himself. "This is Bronco, my chief," he added gesturing to the second man who wore a baseball cap over his burnished locks. Blue eyes shone out of an unnaturally bronzed face.

"Pleasure," said Bronco with a familiar chuckle.

Those blue eyes. That laugh. She'd met these men before. A wave of alarm rolled belatedly through her. "Where am I?" she demanded, coming up on her elbows to assess the small, sterile space. Even that small movement made her want to lie back down and close her eyes, but she didn't. "How did I get here?"

"You're aboard the *Harry S. Truman,* currently in the Gulf of Mexico," the lieutenant said, in a tentative manner. "We're SEALs. We were tasked to recover you from Matamoros. Your father must have friends in high places," he tacked on unnecessarily.

A muted roar filled Maddy's ears. She started to sit up all the way, kicking off her blanket in order to stand, but the lieutenant laid a heavy hand on her shoulder, pushing her shoulder toward the pillow.

Another memory stirred. Something violent and frightening.

"You shouldn't move," he said.

"Don't touch me!"

He snatched his hand back as she sorted through the rush of emotions.

Ignoring his cautionary statement, Maggie sat up carefully. The room went into a slow spin and then subsided. "So my father is the reason I'm here," she deduced, putting the pieces together.

"Yes," both men said simultaneously.

*Damn it, Daddy.* "And you—you what?—you slipped into the school while I slept and you grabbed me?" Surely her father would not have condoned such underhanded measures.

"Affirmative," said the lieutenant, but his inscrutable expression suggested there was more.

"Why can't I remember?"

"We, uh, we had to subdue you," he stiffly confessed.

The blue-eyed chief looked down at the floor, his lips crimped.

He was trying not to laugh, Maddy realized, outraged. The faces of Imelda, Graciela, Mercedes, and the other dozen girls at *El Santuario* flashed before her eyes. If they hadn't realized she was gone yet, they soon would. Her stomach cramped in anguish as she envisioned their confusion, followed by their terror when they realized how Maddy's desertion would impact them.

"What have you done?" she cried, directing her dismay at her father foremost, then glaring at the two men standing near her. "What have you done?" she repeated. "Those girls aren't safe without me!"

Lt. Sasseville's mouth firmed with what might have

been remorse. His companion—what was his name? Bronco?—clapped him on the shoulder.

"It's all you, sir," he stated with confidence. Then he nodded in her direction. "Feel better soon, ma'am." He backed swiftly out of the hatch, leaving Maddy to direct her fury at just one man.

In a matter of days—maybe a week if they were lucky—every girl in the school would be preyed upon by a man, her innocence forcibly taken from her. The knowledge lodged in Maddy's throat like a pill, too big and bitter to swallow.

Dropping her face in her hands, she hid her devastation. A tide of degradation was overtaking Mexico, and she was no longer there to deflect it.

"Go away," she begged wanting desperately to be alone, to sulk, and to reconsider her options.

But the SEAL didn't move, not even when the pain in her chest doubled. "Why are you still here?" she raged, lifting her face from her hands. She couldn't grieve with him here in the room.

At first, his only answer was silence. But then he broke it, speaking in a condescending tone that made her eyes widen. "You realize you would've ended up raped or murdered if you'd stayed around much longer," he pointed out.

She glared at him. "How does that concern you?"

"Concern me?" He gave a purely Hispanic shrug. "It doesn't. I don't give a damn what might have happened to you." Except that his irate, protective tone said otherwise.

Stung by his antagonism, all she could do was gape at him.

He took a step toward her, planting his hands on the edge of the bed and leaning down until his dark green eyes looked straight into her gray-blue ones, and his scent stole over her. "I *should* be halfway around the world right now, hunting down high-value targets, not wasting my time protecting the daughter of an oil tycoon." His tone made his resentment obvious.

Memories bombarded Maddy, flickering through her mind so quickly she could scarcely get a read on them. Silhouettes emerged out of the darkness.

"You attacked me," she recalled, seeing a vision of him hauling back her mosquito netting.

He straightened like she'd slapped him in the face. "No way." He pointed a long finger at her. "I told you exactly who we were, and you resisted us, remember?"

All she remembered was him grabbing her out of the window and throwing her atop her bed. "You mauled me on my mattress," she added, remembering how she'd fought back.

"No," he exclaimed, shaking his head vehemently.

But a touch to the knot swelling just above her eyebrows confirmed the accuracy of her statement. She sent him an accusing glare. "Yes, you did."

"No. *You* tried escaping out the window," he insisted, his expression growing sterner by the moment. "And then you went crazy. Look what you did to my nose!"

She eyed his swollen nose ridge with a smidgen of satisfaction. Without the flaw, the man was simply too handsome. "Serves you right for scaring me half to death," she said, dismayed by her behavior. But his was worse.

His chest expanded and his hands clenched. "What the hell were you thinking ignoring a mandatory evacuation?"

Maddy bristled. "I was thinking that I was protecting innocent lives. What was I supposed to do? Just abandon those girls? How dare you lecture me for doing what you do every day, you overbearing hypocrite!"

The epithet sent his eyebrows winging toward his hairline. A disbelieving laugh escaped him and he unclenched his hands. "You couldn't begin to do what I do, Miss Scott," he countered, propping them on his hips and sending her a confident smirk.

Maddy narrowed her eyes. Fury pounded through her. No man had ever put her back up in so short a time. "I never said I can do *exactly* what you do, Lieutenant. But I will risk my life for a cause that I believe in. In that sense, we're exactly alike."

His smile faded abruptly. "We are nothing alike," he insisted, his gaze sliding over her.

She sat up straighter, angling her chin at him. "Oh, I see. SEALs don't protect the weak and combat corruption?"

She thought she had him bested when he paused for the barest second. "No," he finally countered. "We kill the enemy, Miss Scott. That's the difference between us." He tapped his broad chest. "I'm not a potential victim." He pointed at her. "*You* are."

She had to admit, her situation had been getting tenuous what with all the teachers running off, even the local ones. She'd prayed night and day for help to come in some form or another. Perhaps her mother's spirit, her guardian angel, had guided Lt. Sasseville to Matamoros just in the nick of time.

Her rancor trickled away, leaving bottomless regret in its wake. "There's no one left to protect them," she reflected, her voice barely above a whisper. Empathy for the girls brought tears to her eyes. Feeling sick to her stomach, she blinked them back.

Sam Sasseville frowned and looked away.

Weariness swamped Maddy without warning. With a sigh of defeat, she fell back against the pillow and wallowed in grief. Why was it taking the female officer so long to find ice packs?

"I'm sorry," the SEAL startled her by apologizing. His gruff tone suggested that he did actually feel sorry for the hapless victims they had left behind. But then his next words ruined his apology. "You can't save the world, you know."

She turned her head in his direction. "Why not?" she demanded.

He rolled his eyes as if the question wasn't worth answering. "Well, for one thing, your father doesn't like it."

She frowned. How could he know that, or was he just assuming? "He's on his way here, isn't he?" she asked, remembering what she'd overheard earlier.

The lieutenant glanced at his watch. "He's about five minutes out. I expect you'll take a helo to Miami from here, and then he'll fly you home on his private jet." His tone dripped with disdain for such decadent jet-setting.

Maddy plucked at a thread sticking out of the blanket. The mansion in McLean wasn't her home. The world was.

Out the corner of her eye she watched Lt. Sasseville open a canister of gauze, wet a couple of squares with water and wipe off the dried blood under his nose.

"Did I break it?" she asked him.

"Probably."

"Sorry."

"Sure you are." He dropped the soiled gauze into a receptacle marked HAZARDOUS WASTE. "You know what I think?"

She heaved an inward sigh as he rounded on her again, his lecture clearly not over. "What?"

"I think you should work within the borders of the United States and leave third-world countries to men equipped to handle the danger."

What little goodwill Maddy harbored toward the SEAL evaporated.

"I read your file, Miss Scott," he volunteered, raking her huddled form with exasperation. "Your mother was Melinda Scott, the famous environmentalist whose plane crashed into the Amazon ten years ago. You're obviously trying to follow in her footsteps."

Maddy flinched. The tragedy, still so fresh in her mind, had shaped her into who she was today.

"You majored in Global and Environmental Studies, and you've participated in every disaster relief effort since the Great Tsunami. You've been to Bosnia, Thailand, Haiti, Afghanistan, the Philippines, and Mexico." He ticked the locales off his fingers. "Enough already," he declared. "It's obvious that you're an intelligent woman, but you don't belong in any of those places."

She sucked a breath into her tight chest. "Oh, really?"

"Really. No one wants to hear that you got killed in some shithole country where there's been infighting for four hundred years and where your death makes no difference. Just go back to the life you came from and enjoy the privileges you were born to."

The tears that had started to flow earlier threatened an immediate reappearance. He sounded exactly like her father, though Lyle Scott had never put it that bluntly. And like her father, he was obviously used to telling people what to do. Well, too damn bad. Maddy only ever answered to her conscience and the whispered pleas of her dead mother's spirit.

Angling her chin into the air, she checked the verbal arguments pressuring her tongue and asked, "Do you have a creed, Lieutenant?"

His face tightened with suspicion. He shrugged his massive shoulders. "Of course. I'm a SEAL. I live by my creed."

"Well, I have one, too," she explained, speaking over the lump in her throat. "And my work is every bit as meaningful to me as yours is to you. You don't have to be a trained killer to make the world a better place. Physical superiority isn't always the answer."

"Oh." He crossed his arms and nodded, pretending to consider her opinion. "What's the answer then?" His tone mocked her assertion.

"Respect for other cultures, communication, education, and empowerment. There are myriad solutions that don't entail using force."

For a moment, he appeared to give her words consideration. But then he said, "I see why your father has his hands full with you."

Her jaw dropped at his close-minded obstinacy. "Why, you insufferable ass!" she cried.

He briefly ducked his chin, closed his eyes, and fingered the swollen bridge of his nose. "That didn't come out right," he admitted. Looking up, he sent her a pleading look. "Just...promise me you'll go home and stay there."

"Is that what you're going to do?" she tossed back.

"Yes, actually. I was supposed to be in South-East Asia hunting down an arm's dealer, but instead I'm here with you. And right now we're talking about your safety."

The worry brewing in his dark eyes tempered Maddy's resentment. Maybe he wasn't an ass, just an overly protective, interfering, know-it-all.

She considered placating him then changed her mind. "Sorry, but that's not going to happen," she informed him steadily.

Frustration and fury stained the SEAL's cheekbones. She could understand his reaction, in part. He'd evidently given up a critical mission in order to pluck her out of Matamoros, and here she was, threatening to stray right back into danger. His gaze blazed a trail from her mouth to her breasts, now covered by the blanket, and she just knew he was remembering how she'd looked standing naked in front of him; the memory had clearly made an impact.

The *stomp, stomp, stomp* of approaching footsteps cut through the thickening tension. Maddy glanced toward the door expecting to see the female officer returning with the ice packs. Only she'd brought Maddy's father with her, as well, which explained what had taken her so long.

"Maddy!" Lyle Scott, a tall broad Texan, rushed to her bedside and engulfed her in a fierce embrace. His brown eyes widened as they took note of the lump on her forehead and the flushed, exasperated look on her face. His gaze swung promptly toward the source of her irritation, and he straightened to introduce himself. "You must be Lieutenant Sasseville."

"Yes, sir," the SEAL affirmed, still holding Maddy's baleful glare.

Her father divided a thoughtful look between them. "Well, thank you for bringing Maddy to safety," he said, extending a hand of gratitude.

For a split second, it looked like the SEAL might ignore the gesture. Then, gritting his teeth, he accepted the handshake and muttered, "You're welcome."

"My daughter means everything in the world to me, Lieutenant," Lyle Scott tacked on with a Texas drawl for which he was well known.

"Then you should keep her at home where she belongs," Lt. Sasseville had the gall to suggest. Maddy's blood boiled. Her father's silver eyebrows shot up.

The female officer broke the tension. "Lieutenant,

you're expected in the Joint Information Center, stat. Here's an icepack." She thrust one into Sam's hand then handed the other to Maddy.

"What happened, sweetheart?" her father inquired as she laid it against her swollen forehead.

On his way to the hatch with the icepack plastered to his nose, Sam Sasseville drew up short. His head turned, and he visibly braced himself for what Maddy would allege.

"I broke the SEAL's nose," she stated, in lieu of placing the blame at the Sam's feet.

"Oh," said her father, looking nonplussed.

The SEAL in question had the grace to blush.

"Lieutenant, they're waiting," the female officer reminded him.

"Yes, ma'am." He pointed a finger at Maddy. "Stay out of the hot spots," he commanded.

"I'll see you around, Lieutenant," she retorted sweetly.

The glare he sent her made her want to stick her tongue out at him, only her father was watching their exchange with interest, and she didn't want to put on more of a show than they already were.

The SEAL threw himself through the hatch like he didn't trust himself another second in her presence, and Maddy's pulse thrummed with the satisfaction at having had the last word.

Obviously, seeing her around was the dead last thing he wanted to do.

# CHAPTER 2

Sam straightened out of his Dodge Charger and stretched his 6'2" frame with a groan.

The three-hour drive from Virginia Beach to Northern Virginia had taken a god-awful six hours, no thanks to the late-summer thunderstorms that had broken over the I-95 corridor, triggering a number of fender-benders. The sun was setting by the time he'd finally arrived at Lyle Scott's home in McLean. Rumor had it the oil tycoon also had a home in Austin, Texas, from which he hailed. Sam was hungry, irritable, and more than a little wary as to why he'd been invited to an evening soiree here in the first place.

It had been weeks since he'd plucked the daughter of Scott Oil's CEO out of Matamoros, but that didn't mean Miss Scott hadn't altered her story about how she got that lump on her head. Maybe she'd decided to blame Sam, after all.

Surely an invitation from Lyle Scott meant the oil tycoon was simply grateful. But why had Sam been the only SEAL invited? He'd wanted to decline the invitation, but since that smacked of cowardice, he'd felt obliged to show up.

Not that he was at all motivated to see Madison Scott again, in the flesh—as opposed to in his dreams.

Taking stock of his environment, Sam took note of the Audis, BMWs, Mercedes, and Lexuses making his Dodge Charger look like a cheap piece of machinery parked amidst their presence. Rich people loved to flaunt their wealth. He doubted any one of the party's guests had started off life the way he had, with absolutely nothing.

Tugging the wrinkles from his dress white uniform, he headed up the flagstone path toward the opulent Georgian-style mansion basking in the late summer sunset. Inviting lights shone from every window highlighting the green, manicured lawn. Why would Madison ever want to leave a place like this? She'd made it plain that she lived to make the world a better place; still, he couldn't fathom her reasons for wanting to give up all this to do so.

The strains of Frank Sinatra grew louder as Sam neared the double front doors under the watchful eye of a security guard. "Evening, Lieutenant," that man said, reading his rank correctly. With a flourish, he pulled open the door.

"Thanks." Sam stepped into a vaulted foyer, his eyes sliding up the double-wide staircase to the crystal chandelier overhead.

Maybe opulent wasn't the word to describe the Scott residence; decadent seemed a more apt description.

Leaving his white billed cap hanging on an empty hat rack, he passed a dining room filled with glittering guests and a table groaning under trays of delicacies. Sounds of lively conversation beckoned him toward the open room at the back of the house where fifty or more impeccably dressed guests milled about holding cocktails. He didn't know a single goddamn soul.

*I'd rather freefall into enemy territory than join this party*, Sam thought. However, with a reminder of what he'd overcome—personal hardships followed by the most rigorous military training program in the world—he thrust aside his apprehension and stepped into the room with his head held high.

"You're late," said a husky voice that raised the hair on his nape.

He swung around to see Madison Scott pushing off the wall, a half-empty martini glass in hand. She wore a silk crimson cocktail dress that hugged her fabulous figure and imbued her honey-blond hair with tawny highlights. All he could think about as she stepped up to him was whether she wore underwear beneath that figure-hugging dress.

That punch-in-the-gut reaction he'd had the first time he'd clapped eyes on her—that had nothing to do with the environment, apparently. Back in Mexico, she'd reminded him of an exotic flower growing in a concrete jungle. Tonight she resembled a red hibiscus, right up to the decorative comb that kept her long hair coiled in a knot at the back of her head. Her equally thorough appraisal of him through blue-gray eyes left him feeling off-kilter.

"Madison," he said, managing to find his voice.

"Maddy," she corrected, thrusting her free hand at him. He took it automatically, registering just how slim and soft it felt in contrast to her firm grip. He hadn't held her hand the last time. Nor had she seemed so petite when he'd been wrestling with her on the mattress.

"Sam Sasseville," he reminded her.

Her lips quirked in that insubordinate smile he'd carried in his head for weeks now. "Yes, I remember," she drawled. Taking a leisurely sip of her martini, she eyed him over the rim of her glass. The slightly glazed quality of her lagoon-like eyes informed him that this was not her first drink.

"Sorry for my tardiness." It wasn't like him to be anything but exactly on-time. "Traffic was bad. Lots of thunderstorms."

"I figured you'd just chickened out," she needled with an innocent smile. "Can I get you a drink? There's an open bar at the end of the room."

"No, I'm fine. I have to drive back tonight."

She shrugged, drained her glass, and set it down on the nearest table. "Let's tell Daddy that you're here, then." With a familiarity that made him gulp, Maddy Scott looped her arm through his and drew him into the crowd.

Oh, yes, let's tell Daddy, who might well have invited him here to publically denounce him for mauling his daughter. The cotton T-shirt under Sam's uniform stuck to his suddenly sweaty back. Conversations dimmed as heads turned in their direction. He wished suddenly that he'd worn a tuxedo like everyone else.

Lyle Scott's tuxedo emphasized his broad shoulders and barrel chest. Standing at Sam's height, the CEO of Scott Oil struck Sam as larger than life as he kept a small crowd of people enthralled with whatever he was saying. His brown gaze shifted and brightened with recognition. He cut himself off, casting a smile at Sam that lit up the entire room.

"Lieutenant Sasseville," he declared, commanding the attention of everyone in the vicinity. He spread his arms wide then extended a hand in welcome. "We meet again."

A portion of Sam's tension eased as the tycoon pumped his hand with seeming pleasure and not a trace of a grudge. "Thank you for the invitation," Sam murmured.

"Well, of course. I could hardly overlook the man who saved my daughter's life. May I have your attention, everyone." Lyle Scott turned to address their growing audience. "I'd like to introduce our guest of honor. This is Lt. Sam Sasseville, a U.S. Navy SEAL."

*Guest of honor?* Sam shot Maddy a startled look. Her sugary sweet smile assured him that this was her doing. What the hell kind of game was she playing with him?

"A toast," Lyle Scott continued, holding his scotch tumbler aloft, "to the man who saved my daughter from certain peril."

The crowd echoed his toast with "Hear, hear!"

Finding a champagne glass in his hand, Sam took a quick, bracing sip. *Shit, I never should have come here.*

Guests swarmed him, offering words of gratitude. He managed to keep one eye on Maddy as she retreated into the background. He fended off admirers while simmering inwardly. This party had to be her conception, too—a passive aggressive way of avenging him for his part in removing her from Matamoros. He got his back pounded and his hand wrung countless times.

An effusive, perfumed woman in her fifties kissed him lingeringly on the cheek. "We are *so* very grateful to you, Lieutenant," she professed, her eyes suggesting he should take advantage of her gratitude.

Men asked him questions that he wasn't supposed to answer. More than once, he heard himself offer the standard glib reply, "I could tell you, sir, but then I'd have to kill you."

He should have tossed the invitation in the trash the day he'd received it. But then he wouldn't have the vision of Maddy poured into a crimson gown to add to the X-rated images he caught himself enjoying whenever he let his guard down.

"Would you like to see the gardens?"

Suddenly, she was there at his elbow, intervening before the next guest could assault him. She threaded her slender arm through his and drew him out one of the French doors that opened out onto a broad veranda. Inclining his nose toward her neck, Sam caught a refreshing whiff of her light, flowery fragrance, and his resentment moved to the back burner.

With the storms safely gone, an orchestra had set up their stands and chairs outside. As they applied themselves to tuning their instruments, Maddy drew Sam down a set of stairs into a damp yard. Intermittent gas lamps threw puddles of light onto the lush, wet lawn and the elaborate flowerbeds. But for the most part, the yard stood dark and blessedly uninhabited.

"Sorry about that," she apologized, removing her hand from the crux of his arm as she started down a flagstone path ahead of him. The laughter in her voice assured him she was anything but sorry.

Sam stopped dead in his tracks, forcing her to turn back. She eyed him inquiringly, the light from the house making her eyes appear translucent. "That was your idea, wasn't it," he demanded, "to name me the guest of honor?"

Her mouth wobbled as she fought to keep a grin in check. "Actually, my father was the first to suggest it. Personally, I never wanted to lay eyes on you again." She propped a hand on one hip and sent him a sassy smile. "But then I pictured your discomfort, and I realized it might be fun watching you squirm. I bet there aren't many situations that make you this uncomfortable, are there, Lieutenant?"

He didn't know whether to be amused by her candidness or offended by it. He only knew he'd like to kiss that smirk off her pretty little face.

"You seemed to take it all in stride," she added, easing his annoyance. "I'm impressed."

"What comes next?" he demanded. "Are you going to accuse me of manhandling you?"

She arched one slender eyebrow over the other. "You think I'd really do that? Go crying to daddy because the big bad SEAL drugged me against my will?"

"Technically, Bronco drugged you," he hedged, not liking how she'd worded her question. "I just ordered him to do it."

"But you did the grappling," she pointed out.

*Here it comes.* "You didn't give me much choice."

"No, I guess I didn't," she relented, taking the wind out of his sails. "How's your nose, by the way?"

Christ, he never knew what she'd say next. "It'll never be the same."

She sent him a hard smile, clearly cheered by that news. "Neither will the girls I left at that school," she reminded him. Turning her back on him, she stalked away.

"So, we're even then," he called, chasing after her even as his gaze slid helplessly to the sway of her curvy hips. He couldn't make out any panty lines beneath the smooth silk.

"Not by a long shot," she retorted.

Her reply kept him wary. Just when he thought Maddy wasn't as dangerous as she'd seemed, she said something to put him on his guard again. Plus, the alcohol she'd imbibed seemed to have made her feistier than he remembered.

"So, are you done avenging me, or is there more to your evil plan?" he demanded, wanting to know her intentions.

She cast him a droll look. "It's not evil," she assured him. "Come on. I want to show you something."

Trailing her to the end of the flagstone path, Sam found himself being drawn into the tree line. Anywhere else in the world, he would have balked at the possibility of wading into an ambush. The lamplight failed to extend this far, but the woods appeared tame with hardly any brush for cover.

Perhaps fearing he might stumble, Maddy grabbed his hand, causing his pulse to leap. Over the thudding of his heart and the strains of a violin playing back at the house, he detected the sound of trickling water.

What the hell was she up to, luring him out here? He hadn't pegged Maddy for the type to throw herself at a man, even if he was a Navy SEAL.

"I come out here all the time," she said in a conversational tone with no hint of seduction in it. "See the bridge?"

Through the tree trunks ahead, he could just make out a Japanese-style garden bridge arching over a shallow ravine. The water he'd thought he'd heard earlier had to be a brook wending its way through the expansive property.

"Nice," he said, still wary of a trap.

She started up across the bridge, drawing Sam behind her. At the top, she released his hand and clasped the railing, drawing a deep cleansing breath. Sam cautiously mirrored her movements, inhaling the scent of freshly cut grass and mature leaves.

"Whenever I stand right here," she said reflectively, "I like to close my eyes and imagine that I'm the water, racing to the Potomac and then to the Chesapeake Bay, flowing all the way to the ocean. It's the only way I can escape sometimes."

Her reflective comment drew a curious sidelong

look from him. Why would she want to escape from a paradise like this? But her eyes remained closed, indicating this was not the time to ask.

"Try it," she invited in a coaxing voice.

Sam shut his eyes, but all he could focus on was the heat of Maddy's arm where it brushed his.

"What do you picture?" she asked him.

With a frown of concentration, he cleared his thoughts until an image formed in his mind. "I see a village springing up at the edge of a river in Nigeria." He'd been there recently on an op that had left some key insurgents extremely dead.

"Where there's water, there's life," she agreed, oblivious to his gory memories. She turned toward him causing his eyes to spring open and his pulse to leap. "Without food, clean water, sustainable crops, and access to health care, life is little more than a struggle for survival."

Sam hadn't envisioned their conversation taking this turn. Once again, she'd managed to surprise him, her words disturbingly portentous.

"Tell me you are not going overseas again," he exhorted.

"Actually, my father just got me a job with The Global Environment Facility. GEF is an international group that addresses environmental issues in developing countries. I'll be testing the impact of oil wells on the environment."

"Overseas?" he queried. The part about developing countries had tipped him off.

"Of course."

"You know, there are plenty of environmental issues right here in the United States," he pointed out. "You don't need to head overseas to make a difference."

She tossed her head. "That's like saying we have

home-grown terrorists, so there's no need to chase after Al Qaeda," she countered sweetly.

Sam gripped the wooden railing until his knuckles ached. "Why do we argue every time we talk?" he wondered out loud. He would rather be finding out if she was wearing any underwear.

"I have no idea. Maybe it's because you think you have a right to tell me how to live my life."

His temples throbbed. She had to be goading him. "Obviously, you don't realize how small and defenseless you are," he concluded.

She tossed her head and glared at him. "Is that a threat?"

"What if it is?" One minute he was gripping the railing; the next, he was pulling her forcibly against him, crushing her breasts to his chest where his heart pounded with desire and frustration mixed. He didn't feel a bra.

"You don't scare me." The barest quaver in her voice undermined her taunt.

He'd never in his life forced himself on a woman. But in the culture in which he was raised, it was men who faced down danger. Women were meant to be sheltered from natural predators—mainly, other males. "You should be scared," he declared, overcoming her feeble efforts to free herself by holding her more tightly. "You think being an American gives you inalienable rights outside of this country?"

"I've traveled extensively. Of course I know that's not the case."

"Then you've been lucky. What happens when your luck runs out, and some man decides to abduct you and lock you up, sell you into the black market, or keep you for himself for as long as you bring him pleasure?" With every word, he inclined his head closer until his lips hovered threateningly over hers.

He could feel her trembling. Her eyes, luminous pools, resembled the blue gray waters surrounding Miami.

"Is that what you'd like to do?" she whispered.

Her words sobered Sam immediately. *What am I doing?* Realizing his grip on her arms was bound to leave marks, he abruptly released her.


Without Sam's arms to hold her upright, Maddy staggered backward only to be caught a second time and set her on her feet. His hands slid away, making her yearn again for contact.

Silence followed, charged with an undercurrent of excitement, desire, and frustration. Maybe she'd misjudged Sam Sasseville. She had thought for certain that if she explained her motives to him in just the right way, emphasizing how much they had in common, then he would understand. For reasons she didn't fully grasp, his approval meant a lot to her.

Except he didn't understand or approve. Instead, he'd tried to terrorize her into changing her plans. Maybe he wasn't the man she thought he was.

"Look, I'm sorry." His subdued tone kept her opinion of him from sinking too far. "I have a hot temper; I'll be the first person to admit it." He heaved a sigh. "If your work means that much to you that you're compelled to travel to unstable countries, then there's obviously nothing I can do about it," he grated. "But don't say I didn't warn you."

"It's not a compulsion," she insisted, still craving his blessing. "It's a calling. You of all people should *know* what a calling is."

For a long minute, he studied her in the dark, giving her hope that understanding had dawned. "We should go back," he said and started to turn away.

"Sam." She reached for him, tugging him back around.

Without questioning her actions, Maddy looped both arms around his sturdy neck, rolled up on her toes, and crushed her lips to his, taking for herself the kiss she'd hoped he would unleash on her seconds earlier.

A split-second's hesitation gave way to hungry participation. Palming her head in one hand, he angled her lips to better receive him, swept his tongue between her parting lips, and explored her mouth with a languorous, single-minded foray that stole her breath and made her head spin. With his other hand, he traced the contour of her hip, her narrow waist, and the delicate cage of her ribs, his palm sliding toward her left breast.

Pleasure engulfed Maddy. Behind closed eyelids, her world tipped off center. Had she known on some primal level that he would kiss like this? Her intent to convince him of their commonalities took a back seat to the passion flaring between them. Thankfully it didn't require conversation, which tended to get them into trouble.

Sliding her fingers into crisp hair at his nape, she let a whimper of want escape her lips as he slid his mouth to her cheek, her jaw, her neck, blazing a trail of pleasure as he went.

"Christ, you smell so good," he muttered thickly. "What is that perfume?"

"I don't wear perfume," she replied in a breathless voice.

"No?" He lifted his head, raking her dazed expression with a predatory look before capturing her mouth again and searing her with a deep, blistering kiss.

Maddy's toes curled inside of her high-heeled

shoes. She clutched Sam's broad shoulders praying this moment would never end. "Don't stop," she begged, and he kissed her again, long and leisurely. His hand closed warmly over her breast and gently squeezed.

He tore his lips from hers. "Don't you ever wear a bra?" he asked incredulously.

"When it's appropriate."

With a growl, he kissed her again, thumbing her stiff nipple and sparking shocks of pleasure at the juncture of her thighs. Sliding a hand down her spine, he grasped her bottom and pulled her hips to his, rocking her subtly against his glaring arousal.

*Dear God.* She'd never been swept away like this by any man.

He sucked her lower lip, releasing it reluctantly. "You're too much, you know that?"

"What do you mean?"

"I mean you're so fucking hot it's just dangerous."

"Me, dangerous?" She'd never been called that before.

"Are you wearing any panties?"

She loosed an incredulous laugh. "Is that what you've been wondering all evening?"

"Just answer the question."

"Why don't you find out for yourself?" The brazen invitation astonished her. Clearly, the two martinis she'd imbibed had robbed her of her inhibitions. On pins and needles, she waited to see if he would take her up on the offer, half-hoping, half-afraid that he would.

His glittering gaze raked her face then focused on the breast he was cupping. He circled the stiff peak, leaving her breathless as she anticipated his next move.

"You sure you want to go there?" he asked, his

other palm sliding up under the hem of her dress toward the curve of her derriere.

She wet her upper lip with the tip of her tongue by way of an answer. Expectancy alone had summoned moisture between her legs. Slowly, he slid the hem of her dress higher. Her breath came in shallow gasps. Cool air touched her steamy heat. He would touch her *there* at any moment. She closed her eyes and tipped her head back as his lightly callused fingers inched ever closer.

But then, not too far away, Maddy heard a twig snap and then another. Sam stiffened and his hand slid away. *Damn.* Her expectations took a nose dive as he straightened and turned his head.

"Someone's out here," he whispered.

"It's probably just another guest."

He hushed her. "Let me listen."

Maddy hung her head. It didn't matter if the interloper turned out to be a deer. The moment was shattered. She would take off for Paraguay a week from today and probably never see Sam Sasseville again. She hadn't exactly obtained his blessing, but at least he'd realized he couldn't stop her from answering her calling—no more than she could stop him from being a SEAL.

If only she could thrust him from her thoughts completely. That was going to be the hardest part— forgetting the desire that blazed inside of her whenever he was near.

It took Sam's dulled senses several seconds to categorize the data he was taking in. They were definitely *not* alone. Someone was prowling through the woods at the edge of Lyle Scott's lawn. Probably one of the security guards.

"Don't move," he breathed in Maddy's ear. At the

same time, he cursed the approaching guard's competence. He might never get to feel up under Maddy's dress or bring her to climax the way he'd been anticipating moments earlier.

In spite of his mistrust regarding her motives, he now felt distinctly cheated. Considering the way she kissed, she would probably go wild on him, and he loved wild women. The perfume of her arousal had done a number on him. And now this damn security guard was going to ruin his night, the son of a bitch.

Annoyed and frustrated, Sam peeked around a tree that blocked the man from view. The lamplight in Lyle Scott's yard emitted just enough of a glow for him to spot the man's silhouette, facing the veranda, oddly—not him and Maddy. And why was he so furtive? Sam tightened his grip on Maddy as she started to pull away.

"Hold still," he urged.

She craned her neck to peer up at him questioningly.

The intruder, who—now that Sam could just make him out—wasn't wearing a security guard uniform, stopped moving. As Sam continued to watch him, he put his shoulder to the trunk of a large tree and raised his weapon.

The silhouette of an Mk-11 sniper rifle sent a shaft of alarm up Sam's spine. The bulge of a suppressor on the end of the barrel congealed his blood. Only snipers out to assassinate people carried suppressors on their rifles. Whoever that man was, he sure as hell wasn't a security guard.

# CHAPTER 3

Adrenaline flooded Sam's bloodstream, counteracting his arousal. At the back of the house, the sultry strains of a viola played descant to the sounds of voices and laughter. The party had clearly moved outside onto the veranda. And one of the guests was about to be shot and killed if Sam didn't take immediate action.

He clapped a hand over Maddy's mouth and dragged her down to crouch with him. Her wide, perplexed eyes reflected the faint moon glow.

"Someone's aiming a rifle at the house," he informed her on a whisper, "and it's not a security guard. You promise to keep quiet?"

At her nod, he withdrew his hand, pulled his cell phone from his pocket, thumbed his security code, and pushed it into her palm. "Call 911. I'm going after the shooter."

"Go." She gave him a not so gentle push.

Sam didn't need any incentive. In full SEAL mode, he crawled into the dark, unfamiliar forest, wishing he hadn't left his Desert Eagle semi-automatic pistol in the glove compartment of his car, but where could he have concealed it? And without night vision capabilities, all he could do was feel his way toward his target, avoiding the occasional undergrowth and branches that snagged at his uniform. He had to get close enough to tackle the man. Scaring him might goad him into firing randomly.

A glance back at Maddy showed her holding her position. The display on his phone lit up briefly as she called 911. Fifty yards away, oblivious to their presence, the sniper adjusted his aim. Sam strained to follow the man's line of sight. Without the telltale dot of an infrared scope, he could only guess that the silver head of Lyle Scott milling amidst his guests was the likeliest target. *Oh, hell, no.*

The strains of Barbara Steisand's *The Way We Were* created a poignant backdrop to the unfolding drama. The assassin settled in, ready to fire, but Sam was still several yards away. He couldn't afford to wait. He abruptly charged the man without any attempt at keeping quiet.

But he was still too late. With a pop and a hiss of the suppressor, the hypersonic zing of the bullet cut the air. Glass shattered and people screamed as Sam tackled the shooter, bearing them both to the ground. The rifle bucked a second time as it fell from the shooter's grasp. The bullet struck a branch overhead, showering Sam and his opponent with bits of wood as they grappled for the upper hand.

Sam gained the leverage required to plow his fist into the man's face, only to grunt in surprise when his knuckles cracked against a granite jaw. The man jackknifed, utilizing a wrestling move that Sam had only experienced once before during close quarter combat skills training. Finding himself flat on his back, he jerked up a knee just in time to deflect an elbow to the gut. He seized the man's head and tried to gouge out his eyes, but the man had already gone for his throat.

A savage grin glinted in the darkness as the assailant squeezed Sam's windpipe. The power in the man's grip might have dismayed Sam if he didn't immediately free himself with a counter-move. He lunged upward, hooking an arm around the giant's neck as he sprang on top of him. But again his opponent dodged his efforts with another wrestling move that heightened Sam's concern. He was a trained fighter, half again his size.

Spinning in the opposite direction that Sam had anticipated, the man pulled back a hand to punch Sam's face. A glint of light was Sam's only warning that the man wore a ring. Precious metal, a gaudy gemstone, and four knuckles plowed into Sam's cheek. He turned his head hoping to diminish the blow, but pain radiated through his skull, and a ringing filled his ears.

Just then a high powered beam strafed the tree trunks and caught his assailant full in the face. The man blocked the light with his arm, and Sam used the distraction to send him sprawling onto his side. The shooter rolled, managing to snatch up his fallen rifle and come to his feet in one athletic move. Ignoring the guard's shouted command to freeze, he bolted into the dark, and the guard crashed through the woods after him.

Sam pushed to his knees, his cheek throbbing mercilessly. He tried to get up on his feet and go after him, but the snout of a pistol gouged his spine, arresting his tentative ascent.

"Don't move," grated a voice over him. Apparently, the first guard had come with a partner.

Pain encapsulated Sam's whole head. He wasn't certain he could move in any case.

"Who are you?" the security guard demanded

shining a penlight in Sam's eyes.

"He's the guest of honor, Ken," Maddy called, announcing her approach as she moved toward them.

The guard eyed her in surprise. "Looks like the perp was the other guy," he concluded, removing his pistol from between Sam's shoulder blades.

"You'd better help catch him," Sam advised, deciding it was both safe and feasible now to rise.

The guard split a considering look between them then took off after his partner. Sam deliberated whether he should join them in their hunt. He was still unarmed and not altogether certain he could run in a straight line. Maddy's gentle touch kept him where he was.

"Are you okay?" she queried, turning him toward the light. "Oh, your face!" she cried, cupping his jaw lightly.

"I'm fine." Fingering the welt on his left cheekbone, he winced. He had leaves in his hair and dirt on his uniform but if he'd saved Lyle Scott's life, it was worth it. "He was shooting at your father," he added, curtailing the fierce hug she threw around his chest.

"What? Daddy!"

As she spun away from him, he shot out a hand to catch her back. "Not so fast. There could be a second shooter," he warned. Tugging her behind him, he ignored his aching face and led her across the seemingly deserted lawn, using his body to shield her.

The scene awaiting them made Maddy gasp and pull free. He roped her in a second time as they approached the chillingly deserted veranda.

The guests had clearly fled into the house. The sniper's bullet had shattered one of the large French doors, and glass littered the surface of the veranda. It crackled under their shoes as they passed the toppled orchestra stands and scattered musical scores to enter the house. At least there wasn't any blood that Sam could see.

They came upon the guests huddling in the interior hallway, the only place in the house where there weren't any windows.

"Daddy!" Maddy caught sight of her father first and ran toward him.

Pacing protectively before his guests, his expression taut with concern, Lyle Scott whirled at the sound of Maddy's voice. He opened his arms in time to catch her as she hurled herself at him. "Maddy!" His eyes closed briefly in visible relief.

"I'm okay," she assured him. "How are you?" She pulled back to look at him. "Was anyone hurt?"

"No one." His gaze traveled over the top of her head and focused on Sam's swelling cheekbone. "My God, what happened?"

Maddy answered before he got the chance. "Sam saved your life, Daddy. I was showing him the stream out back when we heard someone in the woods."

The guests reacted with chorused dismay.

A fiery light entered Lyle Scott's eyes. "You saw the shooter?"

"We didn't just see him," Maddy replied. "Sam fought with him, and the man ran off!"

Astonishment gave way to wonder as Lyle Scott contemplated the guest of honor. "So now you've saved my life as well as my daughter's," he exclaimed. Setting Maddy aside, he laid his large hands on Sam's shoulders and stared deeply into his eyes. "Thank God you were here with us tonight," he added, giving Sam's shoulders a squeeze. "I don't know how I'll ever repay you."

"Just doing what I'm trained to do," Sam muttered self-consciously.

"What happened to the shooter?" Lyle asked,

dropping his hands.

Chagrin heated Sam's face. "I'm afraid he got away. Your security guards are chasing him now."

Lyle Scott paled and nodded. "I see."

The wail of several sirens penetrated the house's thick walls. Maddy ignored it, tugging on her father's sleeve until she had his attention.

"Who would want to shoot you, Daddy?" she demanded. "What's this about?"

Lyle Scott patted her hand. "Don't worry, honey. I guess it goes with the territory. Not everyone's keen on having an oil man as their next Texas senator."

"My father's running for political office," Maddy explained, glimpsing Sam's confusion.

He'd heard a rumor along those lines, and didn't it figure since only the wealthy could afford to run for public office these days?

Lyle Scott shrugged. "Thought I'd give back to the country that's given me so much," he explained.

Sam blinked at the unselfish remark. Perhaps the man wasn't as self-absorbed as Sam had assumed. "You might want to heighten your security, then, at least while you're running for office."

There came a pounding at the door and a cry of "Police!"

"I'll get that," Sam offered.

Two hours later, the search for Lyle Scott's shooter had garnered national media attention. A pair of dogs had been loosed to track the suspect, but they hadn't found him yet. Media choppers and law enforcement helicopters vied for airspace and shattered the suburban quiet, thundering late into the night. Still, no arrest was made. The shooter seemed to have evaporated into thin air, leaving first the security guards, then the local police, and then the FBI, who arrived last, all scratching their heads.

They canvassed the guests, hunting for witnesses. Sam and the first security guard proved to be the only ones who'd glimpsed the shooter's face, so they kept Sam from leaving, even after the last guest had departed. Maddy trailed him and the special agents into the back yard where he detailed his struggles with the suspect in the exact spot where he'd taken the man down. She eavesdropped unashamedly, curious to hear what Sam had to say.

"He clearly had some training in H2H," he admitted, shaking his head with confusion.

"H2H?"

"Hand to hand combat. Not many guys can get the best of me in a fight. I thought I had him, but then he used a wrestling move I'd never seen before. Plus he outweighed me by at least fifty pounds, so once he had me on my back, I had trouble getting up. When he punched my face, the ring on his right hand clocked me pretty hard."

"Are you sure you didn't let him get away?" asked the more suspicious agent.

*Silence.* "Excuse me?" The cold note in Sam's voice eliminated the possibility of a conspiracy. The man had the grace to look down at the iPad he was putting his notes into.

After wringing every possible detail out of Sam, the FBI returned to the house to corner Lyle Scott in his living room. Maddy cast a worried eye at her father as he paced the Persian carpet, murmuring replies with a perplexed look on his face. No one to Maddy's memory had ever disliked her warmhearted father. It had to have shaken him deeply to find himself hated to a point where someone actually wanted him dead.

Would this attempt on his life deter him from running for the Senate? She hoped not. Given his wealth and stature, security had always been a concern, but the stakes were higher now. Surely he would just hire more security guards and stay in the race; after all, he ran in honor of his late wife, who had always encouraged his political aspirations.

Sam touched her shoulder, reclaiming her attention. "Hey, the FBI says I can leave now. You going to be all right?"

Maddy's heart fell at the prospect of his departure. The night had gone from thrilling to horrifying in the blink of an eye. What would they have done if Sam hadn't been here to scare off the shooter? She could not begin to imagine her father dead right now.

"I'll be fine," she answered automatically, "but are you sure you have to leave?" She didn't want to see the last of him, not just yet. "Why don't you stay here?" she added, taking in his bruised and swollen cheek. Exhaustion weighted his red-rimmed eyelids. "You can drive back in the morning after a good night's rest."

The long look he sent her struck her as suspicious. What had she said that could be taken the wrong way? "It's the least we can do," she added on a firmer note, "since you saved my father's life."

Hearing a lull in the conversation behind her, she called to her father, "You don't mind if Sam stays the night, do you, Daddy?"

Lyle Scott brightened visibly at the suggestion. "Of course not. He must stay. Consider yourself family, Sam" he declared.

An odd-sounding laugh rasped in Sam's throat.

"There. You heard him," she said, leaving Sam with no way to decline. "Let's get you something to eat first."

She led him to the kitchen where he wolfed down several slabs of roast beef and emptied a bottle of cold beer. Maddy popped a cheese square into her mouth as she carried trays to the sink. The cleaning staff had been sent home after the shooting and would not be back until early the next day.

"All set?" she asked when Sam put down his empty beer bottle. "Right this way," she said, leading him toward the front hall and the stairs. "I'll find you a room where you can shower and *sleep.*"

She emphasized the word with a pinch of indignation. Hadn't he had his hand up her skirt and his tongue in her mouth a mere two hours earlier? Besides, too much had happened tonight for them to possibly pick up where they'd left off.

The tingling of her extremities as she led him to the second level belied her own rationalizing. Her desire for him had not waned one bit in the intervening time. If anything, he had made himself even more appealing by acting as a hero.

Casting open the door of the room next to hers, she snapped on the lights. "How's this room look?"

The queen canopy bed and marble topped armoire sent his black eyebrows winging. "This is a guest room?"

"It's one of them." She'd advised her father to purchase a modest second home as an outward sign of his commitment to the middle-class, but Lyle Scott's taste had been more extravagant than hers. "I'll find you something to sleep in," she offered, leaving the room to go raid her father's wardrobe.

Returning with an Argyle shirt and a pair of gym shorts, she found Sam standing in the center of the guest room, looking uncomfortable. "Here you go." She set the spare clothes on the bed. "There are towels in the bathroom, and there are always new toothbrushes under the sink. If there's anything else you need, just give me a holler. My room's right next door."

His wary gaze jumped to hers.

*Now, why did I say that?*

Backing out of the guest room, she pretended that his conjecturing stare didn't make her blood race. "Good night." Face flushed, she shut the door and retreated to her room.

Had she meant for her words to be an invitation?

*Yes.* No! Her attraction for him might have been augmented by the frightening turn of events, but magic could not be recaptured so easily. Still, she left her door intentionally cracked just in case he decided to seek her out. She took a quick shower, lathered herself in body lotion, and gargled with mouthwash. Then she slipped between the sheets naked, as was her custom, and waited on pins and needles in the hopes that he would join her.

Minutes passed, then half an hour. Reality stared her in the face. She punched up her pillow. He wasn't coming.

Fine. Good. She'd be leaving for Paraguay in less than a week, with or without Sam's blessing. If he wanted to remain at odds with her, refusing to acknowledge their commonalities, that was his prerogative. Maybe the passionate words he'd uttered about her desirability were just empty words, and the passion she'd felt flowing between them was all just in her head.

*Forget him,* she advised herself. She was under no obligation to make him happy by ignoring her calling, not when her mother's spirit urged her to continue her work. Even her father had proven surprisingly cooperative by finding her a job that met with his approval. Life went on, with or without Sam Sasseville's blessing.

\* \* \*

The C-17 Globemaster III descended on the empty runway in Mariscal Estigarribia like a fat mallard, smoothly hitting the tarmac before it braked with unnecessary urgency. The Air Force pilot obviously wished to convey that he could land a Tomcat on an aircraft carrier in a hurricane, if need be. Good for him.

The transport plane screeched to a shuddering halt, flinging all thirty five SEALs sideways in their bench seats. Sam saw Master Chief Kuzinsky roll his eyes at the pilot's antics.

"All right, everybody listen up." The task unit commander, Max MacDougal, shook off his harness and stood up. Built like a double-wide refrigerator with a bristling brown mustache and small, slate-colored eyes, Mad Max reminded Sam of a bull walrus, one you didn't ever want to tangle with.

"The less attention we draw to ourselves the better. So grab your gear, head to the bus that's taking us to camp, and get onboard. No messing around."

The locals weren't supposed to know that the military men were SEALs on a mission dubbed Operation Anaconda. Under the guise of training the Paraguayan Special Forces stationed in this area, they had come to defend the American-owned oil wells from terrorists training in the region. Sam hadn't asked which oil company *owned* the wells. He was afraid he'd find out that Scott Oil Corporation truly had the U.S. Navy at its beck and call.

Not that Lyle Scott was Scott Oil's CEO anymore, he remembered. In order to run for the Senate, he'd relinquished control to the company's vice-president to avoid any conflict of interest. As a senator, he would probably have more influence than ever, but it wasn't Sam's job to question the ways of politics. His job was to stop terrorists from using South America as a staging platform—period, the end.

With that reminder, he thrust thoughts of Maddy and her father out of his head for the umpteenth time that day.

Mad Max swiveled toward his second-in-command. "Anything to add, Master Chief?"

Rusty Kuzinsky had seen more combat than any active-duty SEAL of Sam's acquaintance. His dark auburn head barely cleared the CO's chin, but his reputation made him a giant in the Teams.

Dark brown, nearly black eyes raked the faces of the younger men. "We'll be staying in an old Army installation where you'll be surrounded by civilians, not one of whom needs to know of our agenda. So watch what you say and who's around you when you say it. Am I clear on that?"

"Hooyah, Master Chief," the two platoons roared.

"Move out," Mad Max ordered.

Sam headed up Echo Platoon, but with two experienced petty officers, Bronco and Bullfrog, all it took was a nod at them to get all sixteen of his men moving. Between Echo and Charlie Platoons, thirty-two SEALs comprised the task unit, commanded by an HQ element of three seasoned leaders: Mad Max, Master Chief Kuzinsky, and Lt. Luther Lindstrom, the ops officer.

With leadership like theirs, Operation Anaconda posed a formidable threat to terrorists plotting to undermine American interests.

Walking out the back of the plane onto a sizzling tarmac, Sam scanned the arid terrain of El Chaco Boreal, Paraguay. The desert-like breeze wafting through the light canvas of his desert BDUs made him think of the soft exhalation of Maddy's breath.

*Christ, would you forget about her already?* But regret wrung his heart at not giving her a proper good-bye. The next morning after the party, he had sneaked out of her home before either she or her father had risen from their beds, mostly because he'd had no earthly idea what to say to her.

He thought her amazing, but crazy. Frankly, she scared the pants off him.

Bottom line was he didn't trust her father *or her* not to have ulterior motives. He couldn't shake the suspicion that Lyle Scott had deliberately thrown him and Maddy together by inviting Sam to his party and naming him the guest of honor.

Might the future senator be angling to have a SEAL for a son-in-law?

It hardly mattered now. Sam had washed his hands of the Scotts the morning that he'd left McLean. If only he could banish Maddy from his thoughts as easily, he'd be in great shape.

Snagging his duffle bag out of the pile being tossed from the plane, he waited for his men to find their rucksacks before leading them to the waiting bus.

It wasn't until all thirty-five SEALs were jammed inside and lumbering down the airfield that Sam's nape prickled. Whose idea was it to pack them into one vehicle, anyway? If the terrorists had any advance knowledge of their arrival, a single rocket propelled grenade could take them all out in one fell swoop. Obviously, the Paraguayan attaché who'd organized their transport hadn't counted on word of their arrival getting out.

Crowded with bodies, the temperature in the bus immediately rose.

"Open the windows," Mad Max ordered as they swung onto a road in use by several cars.

The modest city of Mariscal Estigarribia sprang into view about two miles up the road. Home to a mere fifteen hundred people, it was little more than a hodgepodge of cinderblock structures all clustered around the walls of an old military facility. The color scheme of the simple buildings reminded Sam of South Florida—the walls were pastel pinks and blues, the roofs topped with red ceramic tiles.

He was lowering the window next to him when the sound of a vehicle gaining on the bus summoned his defensive instincts. Several other SEALs heard it, too, swiveling their heads to ascertain whether the speeding car might be a threat. An olive-colored Jeep barreled up the lane next to theirs, determined to pass on the wrong side. Through the lowered driver's window, Sam caught sight of honey colored hair streaming out of the window. A slender arm and a familiar profile came into view next.

It couldn't be.

He would never in a thousand years have envisioned running into Maddy Scott in the wilds of South America. A wave of disbelief accompanied by an equally powerful wave of attraction washed over him as she leaned forward to punch on her radio. Sam's clear view of her face corroborated his sighting. Ignoring the busload of men straining their necks to stare at her, she sped past. Bronco went from whistling his appreciation to gaping in astonishment.

"What the hell?" He craned his neck to look at Sam. "Sir! Was that who I think it was?" he shouted.

Sam flinched and flicked a wary glance at Kuzinsky's auburn head. The master chief just emphasized the secret nature of their operation. He wouldn't appreciate Sam knowing someone in the area who might blow their anonymity if she caught sight of him.

Christ, what were the odds that she and the SEALs would both be working in the same remote region called El Chaco Boreal, one of the last untainted grasslands left in the world?

Luckily for Sam, Bullfrog and Haiku, who were sitting on the other side of the bus, hadn't seen her. "Negative," Sam growled, shooting Bronco a quelling look.

He prayed Kuzinsky hadn't overheard Bronco's question. But then nothing escaped the Master Chief's attention—nothing. Not that Kuzinsky had anything to worry about. Sam wasn't going anywhere close to Maddy—oh, hell, no. Seeing her here only solidified his mental image of Lyle Scott as a grand puppet master. If her father had found her this job then he must have somehow known where the SEALs were headed next, and he'd intended to throw them together.

The SEALs' destination was supposed to be a closely guarded secret. So, not only did the former oil magnate have connections way up the food chain, but he also likely had an agenda known only to him. Or was Maddy in on it, too?

Sam scowled. *Doesn't matter either way. I'm not going anywhere near her.*

Maddy averted her gaze from the bus crammed with American servicemen. Men in uniform made her think of Sam, and she was determined to forget about him. But how could she, when the memory of his kiss still seared her senses like the hot breeze wafting through the window?

Resentment over his unexplained departure from McLean helped to temper her unrequited longing. What had she done or said to make him leave her home early the next morning without so much as a good-bye note? She'd thought they'd forged a connection of some kind. Apparently, not. The sooner she accepted his rejection and moved on, the more she might enjoy her new job in Paraguay.

She had her work cut out for her today. Recalling the challenge ahead of her, Maddy swallowed hard. In the short time she'd been here, she had yet to perform her duties for GEF on her own. It was her colleague Ricardo who drove the Jeep on the treacherous roads to the areas where they collected soil and water samples. Ricardo also carried a pistol on his hip and he knew how to use it, as evidenced by the day he'd shot and killed a poisonous snake about to spring at Maddy's calf. With Ricardo at her side, she'd felt no qualms about striking out into the semi-arid wilderness.

Without him? Not so much.

But today Ricardo's wife was having a baby. Insisting that he remain at the hospital to witness the birth, Maddy volunteered to do the day's work by herself. He'd tried to talk her out of it, but she'd reminded him of the report due on Friday. With a heavy sigh, he'd handed her the keys to the Jeep and begged her to be careful.

It wasn't until Maddy started driving to the lab that doubts began to percolate. Negotiating the near-impassable and unmarked roads to the remote locations where they gathered samples could be baffling, even with GPS. El Chaco Boreal was the dead last place a young blonde female ought to venture on her own, which was why she donned a grass cowboy hat whenever she worked in the field. The porous border area between Paraguay, Bolivia, and Argentina offered a haven to drug-traffickers, smugglers, and counterfeiters. There were even rumors of Hezbollah extremists training in the area.

*Stay out of the hotspots.* The memory of Sam's warning made Maddy cringe. It also inspired that same perverse impulse to defy him. Tightening her grip on the steering wheel, she roared up the *Ruta Transchaco,* raising the volume on her radio and letting her long hair whip in the wind.

Her mother would have applauded Maddy's work with GEF. Her father stood behind her efforts, for once. Nothing bad was going to happen.

# CHAPTER 4

The 1930's era military installation turned out to be an impressive collection of all-brick buildings encircled by a high wall and boasting large rooms with flaking paint on the walls and unreliable plumbing.

After the SEALs were freed to settle into their barracks, Sam divided his platoon into groups of four, selecting the same three men who'd accompanied him to Matamoros as his roommates. He then picked out the largest room at the head of a long corridor where he claimed the bottom bunk on the right for himself. Testing the hard mattress, he stretched out and tried to ignore Bronco's pointed stare.

"I know that was her, sir," Bronco finally insisted, tossing his rucksack on the bunk over Sam's head. "I'd recognize her anywhere."

The statement wrested Haiku and Bullfrog from a game of rock/paper/scissors as they contended over the lower bunk. "Who's he talking about?" Haiku asked Bullfrog who merely shrugged.

"Madison Scott," Bronco explained, and Sam immediately hushed him.

Bullfrog clearly recognized the name. His intelligent

features reflected skepticism. "No way. What would she be doing here?"

"I don't know, but she passed our bus in a Jeep," Bronco insisted. He turned back to Sam. "I'm telling you, that was her, sir."

Sam groaned and briefly closed his eyes. "Shut the door," he requested.

Haiku, a Japanese American, kicked it shut with his heel, muffling the sound of the task unit settling into their new digs.

"Listen." Sam leveled a stern look at his closest colleagues—Chief Brantley Adams, who was called Bronco for his ability to stay atop a wild horse; Petty Officer First Class Jeremiah Winters, also known as Bullfrog for his ability to swim; and First Class Chuck Suzuki, nicknamed Haiku for his depth and brevity. "You heard Master Chief remind us not to rub elbows with the civilians here. So, even if that *was* Madison Scott—and I'm not saying that it was—I'm not going to reach out to her. She knows what I do, and rumors would start to circulate."

He offered the kind of logic they would understand, though his own reasons for avoiding her were far murkier and had more to do with mistrust than national security.

Bronco folded muscular arms across his lean but powerful chest. Suspicion flattened the customary quirk that rode the corner of his mouth. "What the hell is she even doing here?" he demanded.

Sam shrugged. *Good question.* "Her father got her a job with an environmental company. She's probably testing the impact of the oil wells on the environment."

"Like she was testing the water in Mexico when the drug lords got the upper hand," Bronco recalled.

"Exactly."

"Why would her father want her working in the vicinity of terrorists?" Bullfrog asked.

Sam sighed. "I don't know. It doesn't make much sense," he admitted, recalling how protective Lyle Scott was of his only daughter.

"Maybe he owns the oil wells," Haiku suggested, his slanted eyes narrowing. "Aren't they owned by Scott Oil Corporation?"

Sam couldn't remember. "Are they?"

Haiku nodded. "I'm pretty sure I read that in a report."

Sam brooded. "Still doesn't make sense. Her father's not even the CEO anymore. He had to abdicate control in order to run for the Senate." The suspicion that Lyle Scott wanted to throw him and Maddy together again stitched through his thoughts a second time. "Forget it," he said, rolling abruptly to his feet. "We're not here to socialize anyway. Let's just keep the hell away from her and stick to the mission."

Bronco sent him a slow grin. "You tryin' to convince yourself or us?" he needled.

Sam's thunderous scowl sent most men scuttling away from him. Chief Brantley Adams merely issued his signature evil chuckle and turned away. Glaring at the chief's sun-streaked head, Sam realized Bronco was right. He was trying very hard to convince himself.

GEF's chemical lab was a cinderblock building topped by a tin roof and surrounded by a chain-link fence. Erected in a desolate area between the town Mariscal Estigarribia and the wilds of El Chaco, it took Maddy twenty minutes to arrive at the guard house.

She leaned out of the driver's side window with a

smile. "Hey, Enrique," she sang out.

The fulltime security guard set aside the comic book he was reading and frowned to see her all alone. "Where is Señor Ricardo?" he demanded.

In fluent Spanish, Maddy explained Ricardo's happy circumstances, adding that she'd be collecting samples on her own today and not to worry. Enrique unlocked the gate and swung it open, locking it again as Maddy parked the Jeep inside.

Pressing the four-number code into the combination lock on the lab's only door, she admitted herself. Kept at a cool sixty-six degrees by the generator that ran nonstop outside, the interior offered blessed relief from the heat. She flipped on the lights and dropped into the chair at the computer where she logged in and printed out the list of the supplies she would need that day.

Carrying the list down the aisles, she collected kits to test alkalinity and Ph along with baggies and vials in which to store the samples for the titrometric, eletrometric, and colorimetric tests she would run that afternoon when she got back.

She had just returned to the desk with her supplies when a loud *pop!* sounded over the grinding generator. Maddy dumped the supplies on the desk and hurried to the door to peer through the inset window.

A vision of four swarthy men dressed in military-style uniforms, brandishing pistols, and standing over Enrique's prone figure brought a cry of horror to her lips.

Whirling, she headed straight to the landline phone and snatched up the receiver. The dead silence that greeted her had her pushing buttons to no effect. As she slowly hung up, her gaze went regretfully to the door. Her state-of-the-art satellite phone, a gift from her father, was sitting uselessly in the cup holder out in the Jeep. *Now what?* The only thing left to her was to hide.

Heart pounding, she ducked behind a shelving unit and waited.

Would the locked lab door keep the intruders out? As the seconds ticked by, curiosity got the better of her. Just as she peered around the corner a man peeked through the inset window. She snatched her head back. But it was too late. He'd caught sight of her. Pounding at the door, he demanded entrance.

*Oh, God, what do I do?* There was no immediate way out of her predicament, no second exit, no way to call for help.

A series of shots volleyed at the lock brought a whimper to her lips. Sweat filmed Maddy's skin as the door yawned abruptly open, admitting a wedge of sunlight. She backed up, but with a wall at her back and shelves on either side, there was no escape. With furtive footfalls, the four intruders rounded the shelves with their pistols pointed directly at her.

Maddy swallowed hard. Their bearded faces and bone structure identified them as Middle Easterners, not locals. She'd traveled enough to tell the difference. The murderous intent in their tanned faces gave way to astonishment as they beheld the lone white woman staring back at them.

Into the awful silence, Maddy whispered, "*As-salam alaykum*," greeting them in Arabic. Communication, as she'd once told Sam, was the key to negotiating peace.

One of the men, a young handsome soldier with a trimmed beard and startling turquoise eyes, stepped closer. He cocked his head, running a thorough gaze over her conservative blouse and light-weight capris. Vulnerability left her feeling as naked as the night

Sam and Bronco had surprised her in Matamoros.

Orbiting like a raptor circling its prey, he stretched out a hand, caught a tendril of her bright hair and slid it through his fingers. She held her breath, determined not to flinch or show fear.

Why, oh, why hadn't she listened to Ricardo? These men had to be the terrorists she'd heard rumors about, and they'd just shot Enrique. Surely they would shoot her, too—or rape her first and then kill her.

The leader seemed to recollect himself, releasing her hair. "You're North American?" he demanded, speaking flawless British English.

"Yes," Maddy admitted reluctantly. Being American wouldn't endear her to these men, but she couldn't bring herself to betray her country and lie.

"We are looking for nitric acid," the leader told her unexpectedly. "You must have some here."

Maddy's brain responded sluggishly. Her heart thudded with the hope that they'd let her live if she gave them what they sought. "I think we have several liters."

"Show me," he invited with an eloquent sweep of his hand.

On knees that jittered, she stepped between them, leading them back toward the front of the room toward a unit of shelves near the desk. There the brown glass bottles of nitric acid, used to determine trace metals in fresh water, lined the lower shelf. She counted six in all. "Help yourself," she offered, praying they had no nefarious plans in mind for the nitric acid.

As the leader holstered his weapon, an older soldier, heavily bearded, with black-eyes and an ugly scar on his cheek, kept his pistol trained on her. The leader bent over, selected the bottles one at a time, and passed them off to the other two soldiers until the shelf stood bare. Returning his attention to Maddy, he then murmured something in his native tongue to his companions. While completely unintelligible, the words could only mean one thing.

*This is it.* Maddy swayed on her feet, rocked by the force of her thundering heart. *Now they're going to kill me.*

A harsh protest to the leader's words issued from the scar-faced soldier. Clearly, he objected to whatever his leader had just said. He gestured rudely at Maddy. Hatred radiated from his dark eyes and his lips twisted into an ugly sneer. It couldn't be more obvious that he wanted her dead.

Maddy felt the blood drain from her cheeks.

The handsome leader sent her a contemplative look. Then, in a quiet voice nonetheless redolent with authority, he gestured toward the exit, clearly exhorting the others to leave. Two of the three soldiers exchanged suspicious looks, but the youngest, who bore a resemblance to the leader, turned unquestioningly to the door, and the others grudgingly followed. The door clanged shut, and Maddy found herself alone with their superior.

The supplies she had dumped on the desk earlier caught his eye. Her heart beat an irregular tattoo as he stepped closer to them. He picked up the sheet she'd printed out and scanned it.

"Madison Scott?" he asked.

The sound of her name on his lips bewildered her, but then she realized he'd just read it off the printout.

He looked up at her sharply, thoughts flowing behind his jewel-like eyes. "Is that your name?"

"Yes," she admitted, seeing no point in lying. No one knew who her father was here in Paraguay so what difference did it make?

"Hmm." He folded the printout three times and slid

it into his breast pocket. Then, to her horror, he drew his pistol from the holster at his hip, flicked the safety with his thumb and pointed it at her.

"Please don't." Maddy's voice came out on a whisper. How could he be so handsome and so ruthless at the same time? But then, Sam was, too. A wave of regret rolled through her. She would never get to see Sam again.

"Turn around," the terrorist ordered.

Tears rushed into her eyes as she struggled to accept her helplessness. No amount of talking or pleading could help her now. He was set on killing her. Dread-filled, she slowly turned her back on him.

*Bang!* A bullet cracked through the air, and Maddy's legs buckled, her knees striking the cement floor.

# CHAPTER 5

*I'm dead.* The shocking realization slammed through Maddy. But she could still feel her heart pounding, hear the blood roaring in her ears. And the floor under her hands and knees felt cool to the touch, which meant she couldn't be dead.

With a gasp, she glanced up and craned her neck too look back at the shooter. Maybe he'd missed? Evidently, he hadn't. He stood with his pistol aimed up at the ceiling where a pinpoint of light now shone through the tin roof overhead. He'd fired at the ceiling, sparing her life.

Looking almost angry with himself, he stalked toward her and crouched until his face was even with her own. "Say nothing of this to anyone," he hissed. "You came here and you found the guard dead, the place broken into. Do not mention me or my friends, and I will let you live. If not," He nudged her chin with the tip of his pistol, his warm breath fanning her cheek, "I will find you, and I will kill you. Am I clear?"

His perfect English screamed of an Oxford education. Maddy sought her voice. "Yes," she wheezed.

"Good." His blue-green gaze centered on her lips and, for a dreadful moment, Maddy feared that he would take advantage of her subjugation to force a kiss on her. But then he straightened, and air whooshed out of her lungs.

Without a backward glance, he stalked on his booted feet to the exit. The door opened and closed firmly behind him. She heard him issue instructions to his companions. Their boots tramped across the yard, moving away from the building. Then, in the distance, an engine purred, tires spun up gravel, then all went quiet.

Maddy didn't move. Scarcely daring to breathe, she waited to see if the terrorists would come back. But then she remembered Enrique, and she clambered shakily to her feet.

The sunlight blinded her as she staggered out the door and across the yard to the guard lying face-down in the dust. Maddy dropped down beside him only to stifle a cry of horror. There was nothing she could do for the man whose brain was partly gone.

The leader's warning replayed itself in her mind. It dawned on her that by firing that one shot he'd led his companions to believe she was dead, also. For some unknown reason—human decency?—he had let her live. But there was nothing decent about the way Enrique had been killed.

Rising, she weaved a moment, overcome by shock and the oppressive heat. Then she tottered toward the Jeep, where she reached for her satphone sitting undisturbed in the cup holder. With hands that shook, she dialed GEF headquarters. When the operator answered, she heard herself tell him exactly what the soldier had told her to say.

Being the only blond American woman within a hundred mile radius, it wouldn't be hard for him to hunt her down. Leaving Paraguay was not an option, either—not when she had barely just arrived and was still so eager to accomplish something meaningful.

And so she stuck to the story.

Hanging up a minute later, she sat in numb disbelief until the distant wail of a siren grew louder, pulling her from her trance. GEF headquarters had called the authorities for her. She wouldn't tell them a word about what had actually happened.

Only the top brass within the task unit got to meet with their CIA contact. As one of the two platoon leaders, Sam found himself included, along with his chief, Bronco. Charlie Platoon's leader and chief were there, as well, plus the three men in charge: Mad Max, Master Chief Kuzinsky, and Lt. Lindstrom. If the CIA case officer, Ricardo Villabuena, felt intimidated in the presence of such experienced warriors, he didn't show it. To Sam's astute eyes, he looked perfectly at ease, even a little tired.

"You'll have to forgive me if I fail to make much sense tonight," he said, taking his seat at the long table in their make-shift Operations Center. Ornate chandeliers, remnants of an earlier era, hung over the heavy table casting shadows of Ricardo's long eyelashes onto his cheekbones. "My wife just gave birth to our first child three hours ago. It was a long labor, but they're both doing well."

Commander MacDougal's bushy eyebrows shot up. "Good for you!" he exclaimed as the other SEALs chimed in with words of congratulation. "Boy or girl?"

"Baby girl," Ricardo answered, heaving a weighty sigh.

Given the man's line of work, Sam marveled that his family actually traveled with him.

"My wife is Paraguayan," the operative added, clarifying Sam's confusion. "I met her here just a year ago."

"I see," said Mad Max. "You didn't waste any time starting a family."

"I don't believe in wasting time," Ricardo agreed, sitting forward and segueing smoothly into the reason for their meeting, "so I won't waste yours." In subtly accented English that suggested he was Puerto Rican by birth, the case officer, whose intelligence on the terrorists was the reason they were here, explained that Lebanese males wearing military-style uniforms had first been spotted shopping in the market in Mariscal Estigarribia.

Since Ricardo had first arrived to study them, they had grown into an Army of seventy-two soldiers. Calling themselves the National Liberation Army, they trained weekly in a camp located in the wilds of El Chaco. They owned three armored trucks, along with an unknown arsenal of military supplies flown into Mariscal Estigarribia from the Middle East.

"There are plenty of Lebanese in Paraguay, so most of the soldiers are Paraguayan by birth. However, the weapons they carry and the uniforms they wear come straight from Hezbollah. Here's where their camp is situated."

Leaning over the table, Ricardo helped himself to the laptop that displayed a map of the region. He first zoomed in on Mariscal Estigarribia, then toggled north and west to Paraguay's border with Bolivia. "It's ninety-three kilometers from town and only eight kilometers from the nearest oil well."

"Owned by Scott Oil Corporation," Mad Max finished.

"Exactly."

Sam's pulse spiked to hear his suspicions

corroborated. He exchanged a knowing look with Bronco. So, the wells were, in fact, owned by Scott Oil, but Lyle Scott no longer ran the company. What did that mean? Had he influenced the Joint Special Operations Taskforce to get the SEALs to protect the oil wells, or not?

Ricardo sat back to regard every man in the room. "Having only one Special Forces battalion and no air power to speak of, Paraguay relies on the U.S. to defend what are essentially our own interests— twenty-eight oil wells, spread out across the region." He nodded at the papers he had handed out. "In your packet, you'll find a copy of my surveillance notes. Turn to page three."

Sam flipped through the stapled pages to a crude drawing of the terrorists' base camp. "That should give you a comprehensive picture of their facility. It took me several months to gather this much information. My cover job keeps me busy doing other things."

"What's your cover job?" the operations officer inquired.

"I work for an environmental company, the Global Environmental Facility," Ricardo offered.

A humming filled Sam's ears. The realization that Ricardo Villabuena probably knew Maddy Scott, maybe even worked with her, made his heart pump irregularly.

"What do you do for them?" Lindstrom asked.

"We perform water and soil samples around El Chaco, measuring the impact of the oil wells on the environment. As a matter of fact, something happened today at the lab where I work that makes me suspect that the terrorists were involved."

The offhand statement garnered Sam's full attention. "What happened?" he was the first to ask.

"My colleague found our security guard shot in the head. The lock on the warehouse door had been compromised and six bottles of nitric acid were stolen. As you probably know, nitric acid is a base ingredient in most high-velocity explosives. It looks to me like these terrorist are preparing to blow up a target. Scott Oil is aware of the threat and upping security of their wells and processing plants."

"What makes you so sure terrorists broke into the lab?" Commander MacDougal asked. "It could have been anyone."

"The gun used to kill the guard was Russian, probably a Makarov, given the bullet found in his skull."

"Well, it's a good thing your colleague wasn't there," Mad Max observed.

Ricardo nodded his agreement. "A *very* good thing," he agreed, "especially since she's a young woman. Who knows what they might have done to her?"

Sam must have made some kind of choking sound because every set of eyes in the room, including Kuzinsky's, flicked in his direction. He cleared his throat and looked down at his hands in order to mask his consternation. Only Bronco could have guessed the reason for it. Ricardo's colleague had to be Maddy Scott. What other young female would be skirting disaster?

The rest of the meeting passed in a blur. He heard Ricardo insinuate that Hezbollah had realized they could strike at the heart of the Great Satan by attacking U.S. interests in South America versus attacking the U.S.A outright. It was up to the SEALs to stop them.

After taking a few questions, Ricardo glanced at his watch and said that he had to be going.

Mad Max appeared a bit nonplussed that the case

officer was wrapping up the meeting prematurely, but in deference to the man's exhaustion and to his status as a new father, Max agreed that they could pick up the conversation at their next meeting. The CO stood up and the others followed suit, their height and breadth making the CIA contact look slight by comparison.

Compelled to share a private word with Ricardo, Sam arrived first at the door, but then protocol demanded that he hold it open while everyone filed out ahead of him—all except for Bronco, who trailed him down the flag-stone corridor.

"I can't believe she's here," he said out of the corner of his mouth.

Sam ignored him, keeping his gaze fixed on Ricardo's dark head. When the man excused himself and slipped out of a side door, Sam gestured for Bronco to proceed with the others. He waited for all the SEALs to turn a corner before ducking out of the door and giving chase.

Pushing outside, he allowed his eyes a split second to adjust to the dark. He'd emerged in the grassy area between the administration building and the outer wall of the installation. As a gate clanked shut before him, he chased Ricardo's shadow through it and, seconds later, stepped out onto the main road. The headlights of an approaching car illuminated a lone figure crossing the street. Sam checked the urge to call Ricardo's name as he couldn't risk being overheard.

Dodging the oncoming car, he pursued the operative. By the time he reached the other side, the man was gone. Sam searched the stoops of the squat buildings to the left and right. Spying an alley between two buildings, he waded into it.

"Ricardo," he called softly.

A scuffling sound was his only warning before he

found himself flung face-first against the wall of a house. The rough adobe surface scraped his cheek.

"Why are you following me?" a silky voice inquired.

While he marveled at Ricardo's stealth, the man was no match for him. Still, Sam submitted to having his arm twisted behind his back. "I'm not," he said. "I just have a question for you."

The case officer released him. "And you couldn't ask me this question earlier?" He glanced toward an open window as a light came on, and they both moved away from it into the shadows. "What is it?"

"Your colleague," Sam began, "the woman who works in the lab with you. It's Madison Scott, isn't it?"

Ricardo's dark eyes flashed with surprise. "How do you know Maddy?"

Sam didn't care for the sound of her nickname on another man's lips. "I'm a friend of her father's." Not technically a lie since he'd saved Lyle Scott's life. "Sam Sasseville." He stuck out a hand and Ricardo shook it.

"Oh, yes, she mentioned you once." Ricardo's gaze flickered over him, appraising him. "You're the Navy SEAL who took her out of Matamoros. She'll never forgive you for that."

Initial satisfaction that she'd mentioned him gave way to disquiet upon hearing that she still held a grudge. "Is she okay," he asked, "after what happened at the lab?"

Ricardo's gaze flickered toward the lit window where a silhouette moved behind the curtain. "Why don't you ask her yourself?" he suggested, gesturing toward it. "This is her condo. Mine is attached on the other side." Turning, he started to walk away.

Sam ripped his gaze from the window. "Wait! No, I

can't talk to her," he protested, but Ricardo had managed to vaporize into the night. The silhouette behind the curtain disappeared.

*Maddy.* Sam's blood thrummed at the realization that she was just on the other side of that glass. He'd told his men that they weren't to have any contact with her, and yet here he was, practically on her doorstep and, for the life of him, he lacked the willpower to simply walk away.

As he took the few steps to her front door, casting guilty glances at the barracks across the street, he told himself he would only check to see how she fared at having come upon a murdered guard that day. Not that he owed Lyle Scott any sort of allegiance, but any father would appreciate a friend checking on his daughter's emotional state following a scare. Making up his mind, he approached her door.

The downy hair on Maddy's forearms prickled. Someone outside her window had been watching her. She had sensed a presence when she went to ascertain that the window was locked. Hauling the flimsy curtain across the glass, she tucked herself in the corner of the room and hugged herself in fear.

Were the terrorists watching already, waiting for her to slip up?

She hadn't told a soul about the threat to her life—not even Ricardo. With the advent of darkness, her fears overwhelmed her suddenly. Had the leader with the blue-green eyes regretted his impulse to let her live? Would he find her as he'd threatened and finish her off?

Glimpsing the night sky through her kitchen window, Maddy darted across the room to draw the curtain over her sink. Feeling slightly safer, she turned and eyed her small refrigerator. She had yet to eat but she had no appetite to speak of, not with the vision of Enrique's fissured skull still so fresh in her memory. Perhaps a stiff drink would calm her jitters.

In the cabinet, she located the bottle of native rum she had bought at the market and tipped the bottle to her lips, swallowing a gulp. The sweet, scalding liquid made her eyes water. She went to take another sip only to freeze with the bottle halfway to her mouth when a knock reverberated through her half-furnished condo.

*Good God!* She set down the bottle before she dropped it. Her heart threw itself against her breastbone as she envisioned the Middle Eastern leader on her doorstep. Perhaps he'd decided she would betray him and his men, after all? She would open the door and he would shoot her on the spot.

She edged toward the hallway, intending to hide under her bed or, better yet, crawl out of her bedroom window and run to Ricardo, who could protect her with his gun.

She had just fled into her dark room when the knock came again. "Maddy," called a distinctly American voice. "It's me, Sam."

She whirled and stared at the door in stupefaction. *Sam?* How could Sam be here? Her gaze darted to the rum still sitting on the counter. She had to be hallucinating.

"Open up. I want to know if you're okay."

That had to be Sam. No one else was so infernally bossy. She retraced her steps to unlock the door with uncertain hands. The light from her condominium fell on Sam's rugged beauty—crooked nose and all—his broad shoulders and long legs. Without thinking, she launched herself at him, hugging him with a whimper of relief.

"Whoa, hey, hello to you, too," he exclaimed,

clearly not expecting such a warm welcome. With a glance over his shoulder, he maneuvered them both inside of the building and shut the door with his heel, all without releasing her.

Maddy held tight, absorbing reassurance from the breadth of his chest and mustering the strength to stop digging her fingers into his camouflage jacket. She couldn't afford to look weak in front of him. Collecting her composure, she released him and stepped back. "What are you doing here?" she demanded.

He didn't answer right away. Jungle green eyes raked her pale face, sliding down her rigid torso to the fingers she was curling into fists. "What's going on?" he countered.

"What do you mean?" A sudden suspicion had her clapping a hand to her forehead. "My father sent you here again?" she railed, anger driving back her fear.

"No."

His immediate assurance only confused her more. "Then he sent you here to spy on me," she concluded, still bristling.

"Wrong again. I just met your colleague, Ricardo."

"Ricardo?" What did Ricardo have to do with any of this?

"He mentioned what happened at the lab today."

An image of Enrique flashed before her eyes.

"Are you okay?" Sam continued. "You seem...," he angled his head with suspicion, "you don't seem like yourself."

She tore her gaze from his all-seeing eyes and fixed it on the bottle sitting on the kitchen counter. "I think I'm drunk," she said, seizing the first excuse she could think of.

He glanced over at the bottle. "The bottle's still full. You sure you're not just scared?"

Maddy lifted her chin a notch. "Of course not." She ruined that assertion by all but jumping out of her skin as Sam laid a hand squarely over her thumping heart.

"Tell me what happened today," he exhorted.

Maybe she was dreaming him. That was all she seemed to do lately. She couldn't wrap her mind around the fact that he was here in the flesh, in a place where she'd never expected him to be, regarding her with concern. Part of her longed to share her terrifying experience, but she couldn't. Sam would have her packing and on a plane headed for home by sunrise tomorrow.

"Nothing," she said with a shrug.

"You found the body of the guard at the lab," he stated.

"Right. But nothing else happened." She winced the instant the words passed through her lips because they so obviously sounded like a lie.

He cocked his head a second time, suspicion brightening his eyes. "You saw the men who killed him," he immediately guessed.

Maddy shook her head. "No." She forced the denial past her tongue.

He stepped closer, using his height and breadth to impose his will on her. "Were they foreign soldiers?" he interrogated, ignoring her denial. "Lebanese, maybe?"

Surely he could see the pulse galloping at the base of her throat. "I don't know. I never saw them," she insisted.

"Then why are you so terrified right now?"

"I'm fine." She cast a longing glance at the bottle of rum. Maybe another shot or two or three would convince her of that.

"Maddy." Sam's large hands rose without warning to capture her face between his large, warm palms. A frisson of awareness arced clear to her toes. "Those men have been identified as terrorists. If you know anything about them, anything at all, we could use that information."

"That's why you're here," she realized, putting two and two together. He hadn't chased her to the Southern Hemisphere just to be close to her again. Of course, not. Why would she even think that when he'd left her home in McLean without so much as a fare-thee-well?

He released her with a grimace of annoyance. "I can't talk about that," he told her flatly. "Our presence here is top secret. No one is supposed to know, not even you. Promise me." He held up a warning finger.

Maddy glared at it. She hated when he pointed his finger at her. "I know how to keep secrets," she averred, flinching inwardly as she realized she was keeping one from him now.

Doubt reared its grizzly head. If the Lebanese soldiers were terrorists, then shouldn't she tell Sam everything she knew? But then she would have to admit that her life had been threatened, and Sam would insist that she leave the country.

Besides, what could she tell him that might possibly be useful?

He flipped his wrist over to glance at his watch. "I have to be going," he said. Looking back at her, his gaze centered on her mouth.

Craving a kiss, Maddy touched her tongue to her parched lips. "I can't believe you're here," she marveled. "It's almost like you're following me," she added, laughing self-consciously at her wishful thinking.

"Pretty amazing coincidence," he agreed. Cynicism curled the edges of his upper lip. "I'm not supposed to have contact with any civilians in the area," he added, putting a damper on her expectations.

"Oh." Her giddiness evaporated. "I see." He would leave without another backward glance, just like the last time.

But he didn't. Instead, he stood there taking her in with such brooding intensity that it dawned on her that he didn't really want to leave. The pleasure that bloomed from that realization emboldened her. Seizing the front of his BDU jacket, she jerked him closer and stole the kiss she'd been craving.

The feel of Sam's supple lips made her groan in remembered pleasure. He responded with initial restraint, his body tense with self-control. But then his control crumbled suddenly, dissolving into an avalanche of desire as he palmed her head, cupped the curve of her bottom and plundered her mouth like a man starved for the taste of her.

Behind closed eyelids, Maddy's world tipped off its axis. A shimmering heat spread to her extremities. She could feel Sam's heart thudding beneath her palm, his sex swelling against her hip. Would he stop? Did she even want him to?

Then, with a frustrated growl, he raised his head and gazed at her from beneath hooded eyes. Breathing harshly, he brushed her cheek with the pad of his thumb and reluctantly released her.

"Stay out of trouble," he ordered, turning to the door. He flicked off the light before stepping through it—to keep anyone outside from seeing him, she realized—and shut the door firmly behind him.

Maddy released a whimper as her expectations drained abruptly away, leaving her feeling deprived. She drifted to the door, locked and bolted it, and then went to peek through her kitchen window, hoping to catch another glimpse of Sam, but he had disappeared. There was nothing to see except the sandy front yard, a scraggly cactus plant, and an empty street. Would he even come back? she wondered, or would he keep away like he said he had to?

She reached for the bottle of rum and tossed back one more swig. One thing she was grateful for, she wasn't so terrified anymore. By some miracle, Sam Sasseville, her unlikely guardian angel, had followed her to Paraguay. And oddly enough, his assignment was to get those men who'd almost killed her today— the men who had murdered Enrique and terrorized her.

Once they were dealt with, Maddy wouldn't have to worry that the leader might change his mind and come looking for her. God, she hoped Sam and his SEALs dispatched those men quickly!

Putting the bottle away, she retreated to her bathroom to prepare for bed. As she laid her head on her pillow minutes later, she prayed she would dream of Sam and not the Lebanese leader with the blue-green eyes.

# CHAPTER 6

Maddy cast Ricardo a puzzled glance as he drove them from the Guaraní village back toward the lab. "How do you even know Sam?" she asked him.

Dark eyes flickered her way. "Who?"

"Lieutenant Sasseville. He's a friend of mine. How do you know him?"

"Oh, him." Ricardo shrugged his shoulders, staring straight ahead. "You mentioned once that he saved your father's life."

The wind whistling through the Jeep's lowered window sent her hair into her eyes. "He said he spoke to you last night," she relayed.

"Hmm. We must have run into each other at the Cantina. I stopped by for a drink."

"Oh." The bar Ricardo referred to was the only place for drinks in Mariscal Estigarribia. She supposed Sam might have run into Ricardo there, but his kiss hadn't tasted of beer or liquor. If he'd gone there at all, he hadn't had a drink. Maddy surrendered the mystery with a shrug and changed subjects. "Do you think that cow died from toxins in the river?" she queried.

The dead cow had been the topic of conversation

among the indigenous villagers who relied on the Pilcomayo River for their drinking water as well as to water their livestock. Her gaze traveled past Ricardo's profile to the red and white striped oil well raking the blue sky. "That oil well there can't be more than two miles from the village."

Ricardo didn't take his eyes off the rutted dirt road. "No way," he replied. "The alkalinity and the pH are both within normal range, and we haven't come across any significant hydrocarbons."

Maddy's gaze remained fixed on the spire of the closest oil well. There were two dozen more in El Gran Chaco that she couldn't see. "So you don't think the wells contaminate the environment," she concluded. "And there's no link between the dead cow and the locals complaining of gastro-intestinal trouble and dizziness?" Half the older population at the Guaraní village had mentioned similar symptoms in the last month.

"From the tests we've performed, that doesn't appear to be the case," Ricardo answered smoothly. "The river water is clean."

So the tests suggested, but Maddy remained skeptical. The wells had to be impacting the environment somehow; it was merely a matter of determining where and how.

"What about the water in the Poseidon ponds?" she demanded, referring to the enormous reservoirs dug throughout the region. Water, siphoned from the ponds, was mixed with sand and chemicals and injected under pressure into the shale deep beneath the ground to break it apart, releasing the oil and gas trapped beneath the earth. It was then then collected, refined, and shipped off to market. "Where does it come from?" she demanded.

Just then an 18-wheeler rumbled toward them,

kicking up dust as it beat the worn road. "They truck it in," Ricardo said, pointing to the approaching tanker truck.

"You sure about that?" Maddy asked, studying the approaching vehicle. "It takes four hundred tanker trucks to supply one well with what it needs. You saw how low the Pilcomayo River is running."

Ricardo flicked her wry glance. "What are you saying?" He had to shout to be heard over the truck as it barreled past. "Scott Oil upholds the highest standards. I thought that was the reason you work for GEF—to prove to the world that your father's company is harmless."

Maddy snatched the hair out of her eyes. "You know who my father is?" she asked in astonishment.

He shrugged. "It's hardly a secret. You share the same last name. Plus, I saw his photo on the company website. You have the same stubborn chin."

Irritation fizzed in Maddy's veins. Would she never get out from under her father's shadow? "It's not his company anymore," she bit out. "My father stepped down as CEO so he can run for the Senate."

"Ah," said Ricardo with a dubious nod.

Maddy frowned at him. "And I am *not* here to make Scott Oil Corporation look good. My mother opposed these wells from the moment my father started prospecting in this part of the world. She would never have tolerated contaminants leaking from the waste barrels and containment walls and getting into the river, and neither will I, if I find out that's what's happening."

Ricardo's lips twitched as if he were fighting the urge to smile. "And what are you going to do about it if your father's not the CEO?" he demanded. "All GEF can do is publish reports and make recommendations."

"I'll tell my father to pass stricter laws," she shot back.

"American law has no authority in Paraguay," Ricardo pointed out.

Maddy crossed her arms under her breasts and scowled. Ricardo's assertions were accurate, unfortunately. Had her father secured her this job with GEF because he wanted her to make Scott Oil look good? Why, if he wasn't the CEO anymore?

"Look," Ricardo said, extending her an olive branch, "the way I see it, Scott Oil improves the economy more than it harms the environment. Have we seen radioactive material in the river? No, but the economy is thriving, people needing jobs are finding them, and industries are burning cleaner energy. It's all good," he asserted with a shrug.

Maddy cut him a suspicious look. "You don't talk like an environmentalist," she accused.

He chuckled, unoffended by her words. "That's because I'm a realist first," he replied. His smile of amusement slowly faded. "What's this?" he muttered, applying the brakes abruptly and jerking Maddy's attention to the cargo truck cutting them off as it swung onto the road in front of them.

The dreaded sight of men in olive-colored uniforms sent Maddy's heart jumping up her throat. Beards darkened the lower halves of a dozen faces peering out of the back of the truck. Resentful eyes stared back at Ricardo and Maddy as the cargo truck gained speed and pulled away.

Ricardo brought their Jeep to a standstill while Maddy fought her shock at coming across the terrorists so unexpectedly. She thought she'd recognized a face or two amidst the men piled into the back. Relieved by their departure, she turned her head to find her colleague eyeing the grove of *quebracho* trees out of which the truck had emerged. A rutted road disappeared between the tall trunks.

Wordlessly, Ricardo turned the Jeep off the main road onto the rutted track.

"Where are we going?" Maddy asked, fearful of coming across more terrorists.

"I want to see what they were doing."

The trees thinned, and they found themselves looking at a half-constructed oil well. Its unfinished tower rose some thirty feet into the air where a jagged spire seemed to tear at the blue canvas of the sky. Ricardo slid the gear shift into park and killed the engine. Maddy swallowed nervously.

"Stay here," he said, taking off his seatbelt. He leaned across her knees to pull his pistol out of the glove compartment.

"What do you need that for?" Her voice came out an octave higher.

He sent her one of his mocking looks. "Don't worry," he said. "You saw them leave. I just want to know what they were up to."

*That's not your job*, she longed to point out, but her throat was too dry. She watched Ricardo step out of the Jeep and wend his way cautiously through the spiny shrubs that carpeted the sandy soil. A hush seemed to have fallen over the area. Not a single bird arced across the sky. No more 18-wheelers roared by to deliver water to the Poseidon ponds.

Maddy lost sight of Ricardo's dark head as the land dipped then spied him again as he neared the well, peering up at it, shielding his eyes from the sun with a raised hand.

Suddenly, a ring of light flickered at the base of the tower. In the next instant, the light flared like an exploding star, blasting Ricardo off his feet.

A deafening repercussion shook the ground and a

scream filled Maddy's ears—her own, she realized. With her hand clapped to her mouth, she watched the tower list, tipping toward the spot where Ricardo had fallen and emitting a terrible groan as it crashed to the ground. A cloud of dust billowed upward.

"No!" Maddy found herself out of the vehicle and sprinting toward Ricardo. Grains of sand floated in the air, obscuring her vision and irritating her eyes as she dodged brush and cactuses to get to him. The fear of finding him crushed beneath the tower turned her limbs to lead.

"Ricardo!" she cried, coughing up the fine powder and searching around the fallen monstrosity that lay in her path.

Through the tangle of red and white bars, she caught sight of him at last—not under the tower as she'd feared but just off to one side, his face speckled with blood.

"Oh, God!" As she rounded the mound of mangled metal, an image of Enrique's shattered skull flashed before her eyes. She hit her knees beside her colleague. "Ricardo!"

His long eyelashes fluttered. The blood, she could see, was a result of myriad bits of shrapnel imbedded in one side of his face. She searched his body for further injuries. Finding none, she gave him a gentle shake. "Ricardo, wake up. Please!"

To her great relief, his dark eyes opened. "Maddy," he said, sounding disoriented. "What happened?"

"It exploded. The tower blew up and then it almost landed on you! Can you move? Are you hurt?"

He raised a hand to his battered cheek and hissed in a breath of pain. "I think I'm okay. What about you?"

"I'm fine. Let me help you back to the Jeep."

"I just need a moment," he begged adjusting his legs with a grimace.

She ran another worried gaze over him. "What's wrong?"

He didn't immediately answer. "I think I broke something," he finally said. "My back."

She eyed him helplessly then racked her brain for a solution. A glance over at their four-wheel-drive Jeep made up her mind. "Stay right here," she said. "I'll come and get you."

Ricardo mumbled a feeble protest, but Maddy was already sprinting back to their vehicle. The shrubs were thorny, yes, but not prohibitive. She could drive right over them if she had to.

Minutes later, she parked the Jeep alongside Ricardo's prone figure. At his instruction, she hefted him beneath his armpits and dragged him toward the passenger seat. He seemed incapable of using his legs for anything more than holding up his weight. By the time she'd stowed him in the Jeep with his seat tipped way back—the only position he found tolerable—he'd turned a sickly shade of gray. Sweat glistened on his brow and upper lip.

"I'll get you to the hospital," Maddy promised.

"I'd rather you went slowly and avoided bumps." His tortured expression plucked at her heartstrings.

She slipped into the driver's seat, eased the car into drive, and drove as gingerly as possible back to the main road, where she accelerated until the land on either side turned into a streaming blur in her peripheral vision. She focused all her attention on the rutted track in front of her, doing her best to avoid the potholes. Flicking her attention now and then to the GPS mounted to the dashboard, she confirmed that she was headed in the right direction. Her thoughts went back to the terrorists. The same men who'd shot Enrique had nearly killed Ricardo.

"They made that well explode didn't they?" she

finally asked, curiosity getting the better of her. My God, had they used the nitric acid she'd given them to make the bomb?

Ricardo had closed his eyes. "Yes," he admitted.

"Why would they do that?" she raged, but the answer was obvious. The men were terrorists. They hated Americans so, of course, it suited their agenda to destroy a well owned by Scott Oil. Did that mean all of the wells were in danger of being targeted, even the ones manned by oil workers? Sam and his SEALs wouldn't let that happen, she assured herself. Nonetheless, guilt over having aided the terrorists burned in her belly like the acid itself.

It seemed like hours but was probably more like twenty minutes before Maddy swerved onto the paved *Ruta Transcheco*. Ricardo gave a groan as the Jeep bounced onto the pavement and accelerated toward the small hospital in the heart of town. When the red tiled roofs of civilization came into view, she allowed the tension in her shoulders to ease.

At last, she pulled up before the doors of the modest facility, laying a hand on the horn until the orderly taking a break outside tossed aside his cigarette and called for a stretcher. Within minutes, Ricardo was being wheeled into the building.

"Maddy." He groped for her hand and caught it. "I need you to tell Sam what happened."

He'd only just met Sam last night, supposedly. "Okay," she agreed, confused but in total agreement.

"Tell him to come and see me."

"I will." She trailed the stretcher into the hospital only to be banned from the examination room. Ricardo would have to be X-rayed, the shrapnel removed from his skin. Shaken by the close call—he could so easily have ended up dead—Maddy whirled and walked out.

When she got back in the Jeep, she took a moment to compose herself before traveling the four blocks to the military facility. She had no idea how best to find Sam to convey the awful news. The terrorists who'd sworn her into secrecy had just made an unforgivable move.

"Come on, sir, just one more. Don't let him win."

Bullfrog stood on one side of the chin up bar cheering Sam on, while Bronco stood on the other, determined to undermine Sam's confidence.

"He ain't gonna win," drawled the native Montanan in his big-sky-country dialect. Bright blue eyes mocked Sam's trembling arms as he continued his uncertain ascent. Just one more complete chin up, and Sam would beat Bronco's record of forty in one minute.

"You've got all the time in the world," Bullfrog countered, glancing at his wrist watch, "and plenty of power left."

Sam wasn't so sure of that. His biceps were about to explode. His knuckles ached from grasping the bar too hard, and a callus on the palm of his right hand had broken open and was stinging like a sonofabitch. Plus the sweat that dampened his hairline was starting to slide into his eyes.

"You're all washed up, Sam," Bronco predicted, addressing his platoon leader by his first name, not just because they were friends first, but to rub his nose in the fact that he was about to lose. Sam longed to point out that he had three inches and twenty pounds more bulk than Bronco to heave around, so he could quit his gloating, only he couldn't talk with his teeth clenched.

"You got this, sir," Bullfrog insisted. Taller than Bronco with dark hair and an intelligent face,

Jeremiah Winters had endured his share of harassment over the years for being empathic. He felt other people's pain. The hard ass instructors at BUDs and SEAL Qualification Training had done their best to harden him, but Jeremiah's empathy was what Sam liked best about him, especially in times like this, when he needed all the positive input he could get.

"Shit!" he raged through his molars. The bar hovered six inches over his head, and it wasn't getting any closer.

Suddenly, the door to the workout facility burst open, admitting the youngest SEAL in Sam's platoon and breaking his concentration. He gave up, letting his arms go slack, then dropping to the floor in defeat, ignoring Bronco's evil chuckle though it grated on him like fingernails over a chalkboard.

"Anyone seen Lieutenant Sasseville?" huffed the newcomer. Raking his eyes over the fifteen bare-chested men, he spotted Sam and hurried over. "Sir!"

Dubbed Bamm-Bamm for his blond hair and willingness to club anyone he thought deserved it, Petty Officer Third Class Austin Collins had developed a case of hero worship for his platoon leader. As the lowest ranking SEAL, he'd been given the job of developing rapport with the Paraguayan Special Forces whom they were supposedly here to train.

"What's up?" Sam asked, wiping the sweat from his brow.

Bamm-Bamm's gray eyes were as big as quarters. "Sir, there's a woman at the gate asking for you. She's covered in blood and talking about an explosion!"

The announcement hit Sam squarely in the solar plexus as the weight room went suddenly quiet. *Maddy?* Jesus, what had happened to her now?

Snatching his T-shirt off the weight rack, he

burrowed into it. "Chief and First Class, you come with me," he said to Bronco and Bullfrog. "Everyone else stays here," he ordered, engendering looks of disappointment as all of his platoon members prepared to pour out of the door at once.

As the three men chased Bamm-Bamm down a maze of hallways, anxiety twisted Sam's intestines. "You said she was covered in blood. Is she hurt?" he asked the young SEAL.

"Uh, I don't think it's her blood, sir."

*Thank God.* Finally, they exited the building from a door that put them near the vehicle entry. Sam spied Maddy on the other side of a closed gate. She wore practical cargo pants, a stained yellow blouse, and sturdy shoes, and she still looked sexy. The Paraguayan soldiers had lined up on the other side of the gate, professing concern as they visibly drooled over her.

"Maddy," Sam called. Relief registered on her blood-flecked face as she turned her head to catch sight of him.

"Sam!" she cried.

"Let her in," Sam requested of the Paraguayan soldiers.

They took one look at his stern expression and unlocked the gate.

Sam drew Maddy inside, squelching the urge to throw an arm around her. Gripping her elbow, he could feel a slight tremor in her frame. "What happened?" he demanded, with Bronco, Bullfrog, and Bamm-Bamm all standing close enough to overhear.

"It's my colleague," she said. With words flooding out of her mouth, she told him a story involving the terrorists, an oil well, and an explosion. "The whole thing collapsed practically on top of him," she relayed in a shaken voice. "I managed to get him in the Jeep and drive him to the hospital."

"Who's she talking about?" Bullfrog asked, looking confused.

"Someone she works with," Sam said, sharing a knowing look with Bronco, who'd attended the meeting with Ricardo just the other night. "How badly hurt is he?"

Maddy wrung her hands together. "He has cuts to his face and maybe a broken back. He can't walk," she added, biting her lower lip to keep from breaking down.

He squeezed her shoulders, proud of the way she was holding herself together. "You did the right thing coming to me." But the realization of how close Maddy had come to a personal encounter with the terrorists made him shudder.

He glanced at his colleagues. "Bullfrog, go get Master Chief. Bronco, you fetch the CO. Ask them to meet me in the TOC, stat. Bamm-Bamm, give us some privacy."

All three men disappeared with a "Yes, sir," and Sam looked back at Maddy, unable to mask his concern for her. "Are you sure you're okay?" Raising a hand to wipe a speck of blood off her cheek, he was glad to discover it wasn't her own. "Do I need to call your father?"

She knocked his hand away, her eyes flashing fire. "I'm fine," she insisted.

"Okay." He had to respect her determination. "I'm just concerned about you. Did you see any of the terrorists up close? Could you identify them?"

She blinked as if caught off guard by the request. "Well, they wore olive uniforms with pistols on their belts and rifles across their chests. They did appear to be Lebanese," she confirmed. "And their leader has blue-green eyes," she blurted then bit her lip.

The unexpected detail rocked him back on his heels. "You were close enough to see his eyes?" he demanded, horrified.

"No. Yes." She looked abruptly away from him. "I have good vision."

Her flustered response confused him, but he didn't have time to analyze it. At the moment, there were bigger fish to fry. If Hezbollah had targeted one well already, chances were they would go after others. They'd probably used some of the stolen nitric acid to make the accelerant that fueled the bomb.

"Who else have you told about this?" he wanted to know.

She shook her head. "No one."

"What about the people at the hospital?"

"I don't know what Ricardo's telling them. He just asked me to tell you. His wife doesn't even know yet."

"The fewer people who know, the better," Sam agreed. "You can go tell his wife now. I've got to go talk to my superiors, but I'll get back to you later," he promised, guiding her back to the gate. "Will you be all right?"

She nodded, avoiding eye contact. "Yes."

"Okay. I'll see you soon," he said, reluctant to let her go. "Thanks for coming to me."

Sam waited for Maddy to climb into her Jeep. Her expression struck him as pensive as she turned the vehicle around, pointing it toward her condo.

"Austin, come here," Sam said, catching sight of Bamm-Bamm and waving him back over.

"Sir?"

"I've got a special assignment for you," he said. He nodded toward the retreating Jeep. "The woman you just met is the daughter of a future senator." That was assuming Lyle Scott won a Senate seat, which Sam was pretty sure he would.

"Whoa."

"And that's where she lives," he added as Maddy swung into the alley by her house. "I want you to keep an eye on her. Don't let anyone near her without me hearing about it right away."

"Yes, sir," Bamm-Bamm agreed with enthusiasm, his gaze glued to Maddy as she walked from the Jeep to her door.

Wishing he were in Bamm-Bamm's shoes and not about to face Mad Max and Master Chief, who would want to know, as he had, why Madison Scott, whom they'd recovered out of Mexico, was now here in Paraguay, Sam swiveled on the balls of his tennis shoes and headed toward the Tactical Operations Center in his workout clothes. It wasn't until he was bearing down on the TOC that a belated suspicion skewered him, causing his stride to break.

Ricardo would never have brought Maddy in such close proximity to terrorists that she could make out the color of their leader's eyes. And yet she'd seemed so certain of that detail; he knew she wasn't making it up. The only alternative made him break into a cold sweat: She'd lied about the incident at the lab. She *had* seen the men who'd broken into the facility and stolen the nitric acid. In fact, she'd probably come face-to-face with them and had somehow lived to tell about it.


Maddy paced the floor of Ricardo's condominium with a tiny bundle in the crook of one arm. After an hour of fussing, baby Isabella had finally ceased to fret, lapsing into a peaceful sleep. If only Maddy's churning thoughts would also subside.

She worried about Ricardo and his prognosis. What if his injuries kept him from returning to work? She'd just gotten to know him and rely on him. She couldn't possibly get the land and water samples required for the lab on her own. Why, oh why, had he wanted to know what the soldiers were up to in the first place?

Perhaps Lucía would have some answers when she returned, which ought to be any minute now. Maddy had been watching the baby for several hours already.

Carrying Isabella to the bassinette beside her parents' bed, Maddy lowered her gingerly into it, and paused to tuck a small, soft blanket around her. Isabella, still so tiny, so vulnerable, slept on.

Resting her hands on her thighs, Maddy studied the baby's perfection with no small amount of wonder. Isabella had inherited her father's long eyelashes. In her sleep, they feathered her plump cheeks. A dark wedge of hair topped her round head. Her chin sported a tiny cleft. Her tiny hands were a masterpiece of craftsmanship, right down to the perfect little fingernails.

A seedling of maternal feelings rooted into Maddy's heart, catching her off guard. For the first time in her life, she wondered what her own child might look like and how she would raise it.

*Not here*, she assured herself, suppressing a protective shudder. *Her* daughter wouldn't grow up anywhere close to danger. Her lips twisted at the irony that she now understood her father's reluctance to let her leave the safety of the United States.

The sound of a key jiggling in the lock pulled Maddy's attention from the baby. Lucía was home at last. Easing out of the bedroom, she found Ricardo's wife closing the door behind her, looking careworn and more than a little frazzled at having left her baby for so long.

"How was she?" Lucia asked, depositing a bag on the sofa and peering past Maddy toward the bedroom.

"She was an angel," Maddy assured her in Spanish. "She fell asleep after I changed her diaper and fed her the formula you left me."

"Oh, good. Thank you so much."

Noting the lines of worry etched into the young woman's face, Maddy asked how Ricardo fared.

Lucía grimaced. "His tail bone was shattered from his sudden fall," she relayed. "They'll perform surgery tomorrow to remove the chipped pieces. After that, he should heal quickly. His face will be scarred but still handsome." Her voice wavered and she forced a smile.

Maddy laid a hand on the shorter woman's shoulder. "I'm so sorry this happened to him, Lucía."

"It's not your fault. He's been through worse. It's a small thing."

But one that shouldn't have happened in the first place. "I don't understand why he got out of the Jeep at all. It's not his job to protect those oil wells."

Lucía's expression became impossible to read. "Ricardo is too curious for his own good," she said, dismissing the subject with a wave of her hand.

"I guess he is," Maddy relented. "Well, I'll leave you to rest now."

"Thank you again for watching the baby."

"Any time." With a swift hug for Lucía, she headed to the door. "Good night. I'll check on you in the morning." She would also be calling GEF headquarters to see whether they expected her to carry on her work alone.

As she slipped into the balmy night air, Maddy's gaze went straight to the lights of the military installation across the street. A yearning to see Sam stitched through her. He'd been so concerned and tender toward her this afternoon. She thought about her slip of the tongue when she'd mentioned the color of the terrorist leader's eyes. The explosion had obviously addled her wits, causing her to say too much. Or did she feel guilty for perhaps contributing to Ricardo's injury by giving the terrorists the nitric acid without questioning what they intended to use it for?

Either way, she wanted desperately for Sam and his SEALs to halt the terrorists' evil intent.

With her emotions in a tumult, she turned toward her own front door, a mere ten steps away. Uncertainty assailed her as she mounted the stoop and reached for the door knob.

What if the terrorist leader had glimpsed her in the Jeep today the same way she'd thought she'd recognized a couple of the men? Even from a distance, her light hair and fair skin would have given her away. He would only assume upon seeing her so soon that she'd broken her promise not to tell a soul about the incident at the lab. That being the case, what would stop him from hunting her down and killing her as he'd threatened?

With Ricardo's Jeep parked right off the main road, advertising her location, it would be so easy for him to find out where she lived. Except she wasn't the only person living in this duplex, which meant that Lucía and her baby were in danger, as well.

Stricken by that terrifying thought, Maddy fumbled to unlock her door. As she edged into her dark house, flicking on the lights, the vision of a man sprawled across her couch brought a cry to her lips. He jerked awake at the frightened sound, sitting up and planting his feet on the floor in less than a second.

# CHAPTER 7

"Sam!" Maddy's runaway heart slowed to a more acceptable tempo. As she sagged against the door, Sam swiped the sleep from his eyes then lowered his hand to study her intently, taking note of the relief she couldn't hide.

"You were expecting someone else?" he mildly guessed.

Did nothing escape his notice? "No," she refuted, shutting and locking the door behind her and assuming a more assured demeanor. "You caught me by surprise, is all. How'd you get in?"

He ignored the question completely. "Where have you been?" he asked.

What was this about? She gestured next door. "I was babysitting so Lucía could visit her husband."

"Ah."

She got the impression that he already knew that.

"How's he doing?"

"He has to have surgery tomorrow to remove the broken pieces of his tailbone. He should be fine after that."

Sam nodded. "That's good," he said.

"Why are you here?" If he stuck around for long she

was afraid she'd throw herself in his arms and blurt the truth about the lab incident.

"I want to ask you something." He pushed abruptly to his feet and approached her.

Maddy had to lock her knees to keep from backing up. Sam's jaw, darkened by stubble, made him look doubly appealing. Since the night he'd extracted her from Matamoros, his hair had grown significantly. The glossy waves curled around his ears and at the back of his neck, making her itch to run her fingers through it. Recalling the blistering kiss they'd shared the other night, her pulse ticked upward, accompanied by a rise in her internal temperature.

"Ask me what?" she asked in a huskier voice. He stood within six inches of her, so close that she could smell his alluring, purely masculine scent.

He held her gaze captive. "What really happened the other day at GEF's lab?"

A muted roar filled her ears. So, he had noticed her slip of the tongue earlier—of course he had. And now he wanted an honest answer. Unfortunately, she had no ready lie available. "I can't tell you," she whispered.

He would tell her father who would insist she leave the country, and she wasn't ready to go. Not yet—not when the effects of the oil wells were just beginning to crop up. Not before she could prove their effect on the environment.

Sam's eyes narrowed accusingly. "You came face-to-face with the men who killed the security guard didn't you?"

The awful memory stormed her thoughts. She could feel the blood draining from her face, leaving the top of her head suddenly cold.

"What happened?" Sam's voice roughened. His caught her upper arms in hands that were like manacles and lightly shook her as if that would loosen her lips.

Maddy shook her head. "I can't tell you" she insisted, her voice rising with distress.

His dark green eyes flashed. "Your partner Ricardo almost got killed today, and you can't tell me what you know about the men who did it?"

His quick temper made her own temper rise, but she thought about Lucía and the baby, potential targets to terrorists looking for Maddy, and she shook her head. "No."

With a scowl of frustration, Sam dropped his hands from her shoulders and whirled away. He stalked to the nearest window and stood there peering outside for a moment. Maddy held her breath wondering at his next move.

Suddenly, he yanked the curtains shut so that no one outside could see in. Maddy's heart thudded uncertainly. He swiveled on the balls of his feet, pulling a folded piece of paper out of his back pocket as he approached again.

"Fine," he said, extending a printout of headshots of what she assumed were high-profile terrorists. "Don't tell me anything. Just point with your finger if you recognize any of these men."

In dread, Maddy eyed the swarthy, bearded faces in the photographs before her, fully expecting to recognize her nemesis. When she came to the last picture, she started again at the top, certain she had overlooked him. On her second pass, she stifled a gasp as the scarred face of a heavily bearded soldier snared her attention. The man in the next photo also looked familiar.

"Point," Sam urged, watching her reaction closely.

Maddy raised a reluctant finger and pointed to the man who'd wanted the leader to kill her. "Him," she said. "And him," she added, deciding that the second man had also been present in the lab that day.

"Only two?" Sam persisted. "There were at least four intruders."

Maddy skimmed the printout one more time. "The other two aren't here."

"What about the one with the blue-green eyes?"

She looked again. "Not here." She would have recognized his picture anywhere.

"But these two were?"

"Yes." She wondered what terrible event she had just set into motion by breaking her word. "He said he would kill me if I told anyone," she added, suddenly afraid.

Sam gave a blistering curse. "No one's going to kill you," he vowed. Lifting her chin with his fingertips, he forced her to look him in the eye. "Do you hear me? These terrorists aren't going to get anywhere near you."

She nodded, wanting very badly to believe him.

Curling a hand around her elbow, he drew her toward the couch. "Have a seat," he offered. "I need you to tell me everything."

By the time Maddy had concluded her story, Sam's temples throbbed. Hearing her describe how she'd stood toe-to-toe with Hezbollah terrorists and lived to tell about it made him want to throw her over his shoulder and run for the airfield, where her father would be waiting in his private jet to take her home.

Maddy's sharp fingernails dug into his forearm. "Don't you dare think you can drag me out of here the way you did in Matamoros," she warned.

He exhaled forcefully, a harsh punctuation of sound that betrayed his frustration. "If anything happens to you," he averred, "your father will ruin my career."

"He would never do that. Besides, nothing's going to happen." She sounded far more certain of that now than she had just minutes ago. "You just said yourself that you were going after these men, regardless of my description, and you expect to catch them soon," she added with a hopeful expression.

He had just told her that. Finding his hand on her shoulder, he lifted it to stroke her silky hair while considering her profile. The fact that the terrorists had let her live in the first place was a good sign. "I'm not going to let anyone hurt you," he said, meaning that he wouldn't hesitate to remove her from the country at the least indication of danger.

But her small smile of gratitude, accompanied by a pretty flush, told him that she'd taken his words to mean that he would protect her. That purely feminine response summoned an overwhelming desire to do just that—to stand between her and whatever harm might come her way.

He grew suddenly conscious of her thigh touching his. His gaze slid lower, snagging on the neckline if her thin cotton blouse, the one she'd substituted for the bloodstained top she'd worn earlier. He could just make out the curve of her breasts, lifted by the bra she was wearing. Even through the added fabric, her nipples played peek-a-boo, making it hard for him to keep his thoughts pure.

"I should go," he heard himself say. It was late. And in three hours, his platoon would pile into several Humvees and drive toward the Hezbollah camp to relieve Charlie Platoon's reconnaissance. He could certainly use the sleep between now and then to keep his senses sharp.

Maddy's face fell. Her gold-tipped lashes swept downward, covering stormy eyes that betrayed want and worry.

*Oh, what the hell.* Stifling the doubts in his head, Sam tipped her chin up and crushed his mouth to hers. Her groan of relief sealed his decision to stick around a little longer. He hadn't intended for this to happen, but she was just so damned vulnerable and—damn it—he was only human.

The brush of Maddy's breasts against his chest proved irresistible. Gathering her closer, he filled his hands with her alluring curves until the blood stormed his veins and his senses demanded release.

Without a word, he swept her off the couch, carrying her in his arms to the dark bedroom. Keeping the lights out, he shouldered his way through the door and kicked it shut behind him. A platinum moon peeked through the curtains revealing an unmade double bed. The room smelled like the intoxicating perfume that was uniquely Maddy's. It doubled his temptation to stay. He lowered her onto the rumpled sheets where the moonlight found reflection in her eyes.

"Last chance," he warned, hovering over her.

By way of an answer, she pulled his mouth to hers, parting her lips, and kissing him with an open invitation to take it all the way.

Christ, he loved how sweet she tasted, how responsively she kissed, with a single-mindedness that made him wonder for a moment if she didn't have an agenda at hand other than just forgetting the events of that day.

But then he felt her working to part the buttons on her blouse, and none of that seemed to matter as he helped to expose her breasts. They were everything he remembered and more—soft and plump and tipped with perky, pink nipples. He lowered his head with a groan to close his mouth over a velvety peak. The sweet soft texture inflamed him.

She squirmed beneath him, intent on shimmying out of her shorts. Distracted, he paused to help her. A glimpse of plain cotton panties set his mind at ease. "You're wearing underwear these days," he remarked.

"It was really hot in Matamoros."

"Feels pretty hot here too," he said, watching her toe off her sandals and push her panties over her hips. His mouth went dry as he helped her draw them down her long, shapely legs.

Fully naked, she settled back against the pillows and arched luxuriantly, seeming totally at ease with her body—then again, why wouldn't she be considering how good she looked?

"You're beautiful," he heard himself say. Beautiful and every bit as dangerous as she'd been the night of the party at her father's house. "You should go home, Maddy," he said without thinking. "You don't belong in this place."

His words turned her rigid, making him want to recall them right away. For an awful moment, he was certain she would thrust him off the bed while ordering him to go to hell. She lurched upward and he braced himself for the worst. Instead of pushing him away, however, she pulled him closer, groping lower to release the button of his fly.

She tackled his zipper with gusto, keeping all words locked in his throat as she freed his erection. Her cool fingers encircled him, stroking him so sweetly that he almost felt like weeping.

"You want me to leave right now?" she inquired in a husky voice.

Her unpredictability kept him mute. Desire shackled him with invisible, silken restraints. The realization that she could wield tremendous power over him had him pulling reluctantly from her touch.

He lowered his mouth again to her tempting nipples,

determined to discover what pleased her. With Maddy firmly on the receiving end, he would retain the upper hand, fully in charge.

Maddy yielded to the magic of the moment. *I can't believe this is happening.* After months of dreaming about Sam Sasseville, he was finally doing all those things she'd fantasized about, suckling her nipples into stiffness, blowing cooling air across the sensitive tips then drawing them intently into his hot mouth.

She sank her hands into his hair, reveling in its crisp, silky texture. He seemed in no hurry to join her in a naked state. Only when she arched her spine in silent invitation did he shift his weight lower. Raking his teeth over the curve of her ribs, he followed the sweep of his open hand across the plain of her abdomen toward her hips. Maddy lurched from his prickly jaw, unable to contain a shout of laughter.

His eyes glinted up at her. He neither laughed nor smiled but remained intently serious, sliding off the end of the bed to catch her feet in his hands.

She tried to snatch them from his grasp. "Oh, please, no."

He held her ankles fast, kissing the arch of each foot and making her gasp.

"Is this some kind of kinky Navy SEAL torture?"

He didn't answer. He was too busy pressing scalding, open mouthed kisses up her calves, toward the backs of her knees, and then to her inner thighs. She could scarcely breathe for the expectation filling her lungs.

"I'll tell you anything you want, just, please, have mercy."

And then he did, spearing his tongue into the swollen, feverish folds at the junction of her thighs. Maddy's hips came off the bed. She caught back another peal of laughter, one that ended in a moan as she threaded her fingers through his hair, riding the pleasure that his skilled mouth lavished on her. Gazing down, she was struck by the erotic vision of his dark head between her pale legs. *Dear God.*

He muttered something sensual and beautiful in Spanish, but all she caught was *querida*—darling. In mere seconds, Maddy was fisting the sheet beneath her, out of her mind with pleasure. Heat breached the surface of her skin. Sensations too sweet to be contained bubbled over in an upwelling of ecstasy. She came in a powerful rush, riding the crest of sweet surcease for what seemed a lifetime before her pleasure slowly ebbed.

The realization that Sam Sasseville had just rocked her world kept her silent as he crawled up the length of her body looking down at her. His broad shoulders blocked the moon's glow. His eyes glinted in the dark. Her body thrilled to receive his weight as he stretched over her, pressing her down against the mattress. At the same time a thread of concern wove through her heart.

If he could render her completely mindless with his mouth, imagine what he could do with the rest of his body. Once he laid claim to her, nothing would ever be the same again.

He still wore his clothing, his pants sagging at his hips. She could feel his sex, pressing like a velvet brand against her inner thigh. Any second now, he would stretch and storm her, and make her his without even intending to. He had that much power over her. She froze, caught between wanting to welcome him and asking him to stop.

She was saved from having to do either by a pounding at the door.

Sam heard it, too. Bounding off her bed in one

move, he pulled up his pants and fastened them, returning himself to a fully dressed state while she lay as naked and vulnerable as the day she was born.

"Stay here." As he left her room, pulling the door shut behind him, Maddy rolled off the bed, drawing the blanket with her. She wrapped it around her frame, aware that her knees felt spongy in the aftermath of that life-altering climax. Putting an ear to her door, she heard voices. Sam and another man exchanged terse, fact-filled words. Seconds later, the doorknob turned and Maddy scuttled backward. There was Sam, leaning through the opening, his gaze inscrutable and impersonal.

"Hey, sorry, but I have to go. That was my chief, Bronco. You remember him."

She could tell by his tone that he was chagrined his chief had come looking for him.

"All right." Disappointment vied with relief. On the one hand, her body still clamored for his possession. On the other, her heart and mind weren't ready to belong to anyone just yet. In her line of work, a woman had to be free and unencumbered. "I guess you'd better go, then."

He hovered for a moment, just looking at her, and she wondered what he was thinking. But then he turned away without another word, leaving the door cracked. She heard her front door open and close and, still, she didn't move.

Standing in a puddle of moonlight with the heat of their passion still radiating off the blanket enfolding her, Maddy didn't feel free at all. She felt abandoned.

As they left Maddy's condo, Sam shot Bronco a hopeful look. "When you say the CEO of Scott Oil is here, you don't mean Maddy's father, do you?"

"No," Bronco answered, disappointing him. "It's

the new CEO."

*Damn.* For a moment there, he'd dared to hope Maddy's father had shown up in his private jet ready to drag Maddy kicking and screaming out of the country and out of reach of the terrorists. Instead the new CEO, whoever he was, wanted to hold an emergency meeting in light of the attack on one of his oil wells. "Why the hell does he want to meet at this ungodly hour?" Sam groused.

A desert-like breeze, sharply colder by night than by day, cooled his overheated skin. His man-parts gave a throb of deprivation at the mental snapshot of Maddy's naked body, still so vivid in his mind.

"It's not just him," Bronco said as they hurried across the street headed for the TOC. "Some general from SOCOM is with him."

Sam paused at the mention of the Special Operations Command. "SOCOM doesn't have any authority over task units abroad," he objected.

"I know, but Kuzinsky said this general is friends with Maddy's father. That's why we were tasked with retrieving her from Matamoros."

Just as Sam suspected—Lyle Scott had friends in high places. But his thoughts seized on a more immediate concern. "Does Kuzinksy know where I've been?"

"I told him you couldn't sleep so you went out for a run."

Sam shot him a grateful look. "Thanks, Chief."

"Bamm-Bamm knows where you were, though. He's the one that told me."

"Right. " Bamm-Bamm had been keeping his word and watching Maddy's front door at all times, which was how Sam knew she'd been babysitting Ricardo's daughter earlier. He made a mental note to thank the young SEAL for his vigilance.

"After you." Bronco pushed the gate open and Sam slipped through it. Together they entered the administration building and hurried toward the TOC.

An immense stranger guarded the door with his arms locked around his massive chest and a brim of a baseball cap pulled low over his eyes. Sam sent him a curious glance and promptly did a double-take.

"Who's that?" he muttered out of the side of his mouth. Something about the man looked familiar.

"The CEO's bodyguard," Bronco whispered.

The bodyguard caught sight of them and wordlessly opened the door for them to enter. Sam was trying to determine if he knew him, but with seven sets of eyes now locked on his entrance, he relinquished the mystery and turned his attention to those in the room. Master Chief raked his rumpled attire with a suspicious once-over.

With a muttered apology, Sam took one of the two empty chairs while Bronco dropped into the other. Ricardo Villabuena wasn't in attendance, of course, as he was still in the hospital.

Commander MacDougal introduced him to their two guests. "Gentlemen, this is Lt. Sasseville. Sam, this is General DePuy, head of SOCOM."

"Sir." Sam nodded respectfully to the silver haired man at the head of the table, the friend of Lyle Scott.

"And this is the CEO of Scott Oil Corporation, Paul Van Slyke."

"Nice to meet you," Sam said with another nod.

Van Slyke was a once-handsome man in his fifties. Like Lyle Scott, he was tall and barrel-chested, but years of comfortable living had put bags under his eyes and left him with a paunch, whereas Maddy's father had kept fit. Blue-gray eyes, similar to Maddy's in hue, held a keen light as he returned Sam's greeting before addressing the group as a whole.

"I apologize for the lateness of the hour, but I think circumstances certainly call for it," he insisted with an air of natural command. No doubt he felt his wealth entitled him to it. "Not only has Well 23 been destroyed but now I fear for the fate of the other wells, not to mention my employees."

General DePuy chimed in his opinion of the bombing. "This is just the beginning," he insisted. The loose jowls around his face quivered with certainty. "The CIA has been cognizant of the threat for more than a year now. It's taken that long to get our Special Forces positioned to do something. Now this. I consider the attack today a blatant declaration of war."

Sam was sorry Ricardo wasn't here to defend his reconnoitering.

"Blatant," Van Slyke echoed. He set his hands with their neatly manicured, interlaced fingers on the table top and eyed Commander MacDougal expectantly. "The threat has got to be annihilated before any lives are lost."

Sam fully appreciated Kuzinsky's perplexed expression. Why was the CEO of a private corporation telling the SEALs what to do? Even General DePuy was also overstepping his bounds. It was the Joint Special Operations Task Force that made decisions in the field, not SOCOM. Who'd invited these gentlemen down here in the first place?

General DePuy cleared his throat in the ensuing silence. "I'm sure the SEALs are planning to take immediate action," he stated with confidence.

The scornful lift of Commander MacDougal's mustache negated DePuy's assertion "It's not our job to protect Scott Oil's employees. Until we're cleared by JSOTF to take preemptive measures, our hands are tied."

DePuy nodded his understanding. "Well, that's only

a matter of time, Commander," he insisted. "I can assure you that *all* of the Joint Chiefs of Staff are in full approval of taking immediate action."

The CO clearly could have cared less what the Joint Chiefs thought. "Our reconnaissance of the terrorist camp began twelve short hours ago. Thanks to the CIA, we have a rough headcount of the hostiles, but no knowledge of the extent of their arsenal. Before you can defeat the enemy, you must know them, General. You know that. Raw force begets more violence. If we attack Hezbollah here, you can bet your ass they'll retaliate elsewhere. We have diplomats and contractors in Lebanon who'll want advanced warning before they find themselves targeted. When I hear from JSOTF, that's when I'll take action."

"And, in the meantime, my wells remain vulnerable," Van Slyke objected with a tragic shake of his head.

"I'm sorry if you feel like you wasted a trip down here," MacDougal replied, his tone overly polite.

"Not at all." Scott Oil's new CEO waved aside the apology. "Actually, I own a house nearby, the one on top of the hill. Perhaps you've seen it?"

Sam pictured the monstrosity to which the man had to be referring. There wasn't any way to overlook it. Once home to Paraguay's top generals during the Chaco War, the stucco mansion lorded over Mariscal Estigarribia like an aging aristocrat.

Mad Max appeared less than thrilled to learn of Van Slyke's proximity. "What about you, sir?" he asked DePuy.

"Heading back to Tampa tomorrow. I'll convey your reservations to the Joint Chiefs. I'm sure you'll be hearing from JSOTF shortly," he added, pushing his chair back.

Keeping an eye on Van Slyke, Sam was the last to stand. He pondered Van Slyke's relationship with Lyle Scott. Was he a good friend, a relative?

At last, the man took note of his curious regard. "I'm sorry, but have we met?" he inquired, flashing a smile that showed bleached white, perfectly even teeth. "You look familiar."

Not unless Lyle had mentioned him. Sam broke eye contact. "I don't think so," he muttered, sensing Kuzinsky's watchful gaze.

"Hmm." Van Slyke considered him a moment longer, then turned to the door with a shrug.

Sam was glad to see him go. However polite, the man's insinuation that the SEALs should protect his oil wells reminded him of what he loathed most about the filthy rich. They simply assumed that those beneath them, even U.S. Navy SEALs, catered to their wishes.

As Van Slyke eased into the hall, Sam caught another glimpse of the CEO's bodyguard. Recognition shook the bars of his caged memory. Where the hell had he seen that man before?

"That's one big SOB," Bronco murmured, following his gaze.

"Sure is." Sam glanced at his watch and jumped in alarm. "Shit! We're supposed to relieve Charlie Platoon in half an hour," he hissed, lifting an alarmed gaze at Bronco then a wary glance in Kuzinsky's direction.

Bronco sent him a wry smile. "Vehicles are gassed up, and the men are waiting."

Sam could have hugged his chief for saving his hide yet again, but not with his superior officers still milling about. "Man, I owe you," he said, giving Bronco's shoulder a squeeze as they both headed for the door. Kuzinsky's voice stopped Sam in his tracks.

"Lieutenant, a word with you?" Kuzinsky had hung back as the room emptied.

"I'll meet you at the gate," Sam said, freeing his chief to go ahead while resigning himself to a subtle ass chewing.

The CO left, too, taking the last few SEALs with him. Rusty Kuzinsky didn't waste any time getting to the matter at hand. "I know you weren't out running earlier, so where were you really?" His nearly black eyes seemed to look straight through him.

Being an officer, Sam technically outranked the senior enlisted man. He could have told him to mind his own business. However, considering Kuzinsky's twenty five years of experience and the fact that he'd survived some of the worst firefights in SEAL history, it was no secret to Sam who was really in charge. The man deserved a decent explanation, even if it meant putting himself in the hot seat.

Dipping two fingers into his breast pocket, he pulled out the folded printout of the known Hezbollah extremists and handed it to Kuzinsky, who glanced at it quizzically.

"I went across the street," he admitted, "to ask the GEF employee if the men responsible for blowing up the oil well looked like any of these guys."

Kuzinsky shot him a sharp look. "You mean Villabuena's colleague? What makes you think she got a look at them?"

"She didn't—not today, anyway. But she was at the lab when they broke into it."

Master Chief's freckled forehead puckered. "That's not what Villabuena told us."

"That's because she kept the truth from him. Tonight, she admitted to me that she was in the lab when the terrorists shot the security guard and broke in. Their leader, a man with blue-green eyes, threatened to find her and kill her if she said a word about it."

"One of these men?" Kuzinsky frowned down at the printout.

"No. The only tangos she could identify were this guy and this guy." He tapped their photos with his finger. "Their leader isn't here."

"Ashraf Al-Sadr and Musa Hamade," Kuzinsky muttered, flicking Sam a grave look. "These are some bad motherfuckers, Sam. She's lucky she's alive."

Sam swallowed hard. Hearing Kuzinsky articulate just how lucky Maddy was made him suddenly queasy. By some miracle, the terrorists had let her live. He should probably get on the phone tonight and convince Lyle Scott to snatch Maddy out of the country, with or without her consent.

Kuzinsky's dark eyes skewered him again. "You made the right decision to question her, but next time you clear it with me, first." He paused then added, "I hope you're not getting friendly with this woman."

The memory of licking Maddy's heated skin jagged through Sam's thoughts like a bolt of lightning. *Little too late for that.*

"No, Master Chief," he muttered, feeling his face heat. "But you should know who she is."

"What do you mean, who she is?"

"She's Madison Scott, the woman we were tasked to recover from Matamoros."

Kuzinsky's eyebrows shot to his hairline. "And now she's here?" he asked, looking thunderstruck.

Sam shrugged. "Go figure." He inclined his head toward the shorter man's just in case the wall had ears. "Then along comes the new CEO of Scott Oil telling us to hurry up and eliminate these terrorists that are threatening his oil wells. Makes you wonder if General DePuy lives in Scott Oil's back pocket," he added. "I mean, are we protecting the oil company's interests or American interests?"

Kuzinsky's dark eyes studied Sam's cynical expression. "That's a pretty serious insinuation, Lieutenant."

Sam straightened. "Yeah, well, I'm a pretty serious guy, Master Chief."

The other man rubbed his jaw in a familiar, harried gesture. "We'd better keep these thoughts to ourselves for a while," he suggested. "In the meantime, I'd advise you to steer clear of the honey pot."

Another wave of heat climbed Sam's neck. "Roger that, Master Chief." All too conscious of the fact that Maddy's scent still clung to his upper lip, he averted his hot face and fled the room.

If his platoon was going to relieve their counterpart on time, they'd better get a move on.

As for Maddy, he'd found it impossible to keep his distance so far. How was he going to find the strength to stay away now that he'd almost caved into his attraction? All he could think about was how to reach heaven in her arms without disobeying a direct command or getting emotionally entangled with a woman who might not be leveling with him about her motives.

# CHAPTER 8

With a face caked in camouflage paint, Sam squirmed into position next to the dark form of Charlie Platoon's leader—Lt. Junior Grade Corey Cooper.

Sam didn't envy Cooper's impossible task of filling his predecessor's shoes. Tyler Rexall, the smartest most confident SEAL Sam had ever known was the previous leader for Charlie Platoon. Eight months ago, T-Rex had had his foot blown off when their task unit had operated in Malaysia on a mission to capture the notorious arms dealer, Haji Telemong. That effort had ended with Tyler's injury and the task unit's premature departure.

This past spring, Sam had missed out on the opportunity to avenge Tyler's fate when the task unit returned to Malaysia. Instead, he'd been tasked with snatching Maddy out of Mexico, along with Bronco, Haiku, and Bullfrog. Luckily, the rest of the task unit had completed the mission without them, locating and eliminating Haji Telemong for good. But the arms dealer's death couldn't give back T-Rex his foot or even the career he'd lost in their first failed attempt.

And now Cooper was having a tough time trying to

replace Tyler. The lanky SEAL had found a sheltered location on a sandy berm protected by a thicket of thorny bushes a hundred yards from the terrorist's training camp. He sent Sam a look that, even in the dark, conveyed frustration.

"Sit rep," Sam whispered, requesting a situational report. He could tell by the agitation thrumming in the high-strung Cooper that the situation wasn't what he wanted it to be.

"There is no situation," Cooper reported, not bothering to whisper. "As far as we can tell, no one's even here."

*Seriously?* Sam stole a peek over the top of the impenetrable vegetation. Circumscribed by tall coils of concertina wire, then a chain-link fence topped by more barbed wire, the terrorists' camp consisted of several crude wooden structures and a training yard complete with an obstacle course. Not a single light flickered in the buildings' few windows. There were no voices to be heard, no sign of movement whatsoever. A chilly desert breeze kicked up spumes of dust here and there contributing to the impression that the place lay utterly deserted.

Sam looked back down at Cooper. "I thought we had a confirmed sighting of unfriendlies earlier this evening."

"We did." Cooper came up on his knees next to him. "Four men arrived in that vehicle right there." He pointed to an old Range Rover, its doors dented and pocked by bullet holes. "They all got out and went into that building there." He pointed again. "And we haven't seen or heard from them since."

"Maybe they're sleeping," Sam suggested.

"Without posting anyone on watch?" Cooper's tone conveyed skepticism. "Honestly, it's been so quiet, I'm wondering if there isn't another way out, besides the only gate. I don't feel like anybody's here."

"You mean like an underground tunnel?"

"Yeah, maybe."

Sam considered the possibility. There had been rampant fighting in this area eighty years earlier. How likely was it that either side had dug tunnels into the sandy soil? Or maybe the terrorists themselves had shoveled out an escape route.

*Only one way to find out*, he thought to himself, but the CO wouldn't want to shake things up this early in the game. Standard operating procedure entailed a forty-eight hour reconnaissance before any kind of action was recommended, not to mention the fact that Mad Max insisted on waiting for JSOTF's direct orders. And just because the camp appeared empty, that didn't mean that they should search it. The whole goddamn place could be booby trapped.

"Well, we've got it from here," he said, relieving Cooper. Clapping the younger man on the shoulder, he wished him a good-night's sleep. What he wouldn't give to tuck into his own rack about now. Instead, he'd sacrificed his sleep for a stolen interlude with Maddy.

And what an experience that was! Cravings, doubly potent for having gone unsatisfied, left him hankering for fulfillment. He marveled at how recklessly close he'd come to burying himself in Maddy's welcoming heat. He'd had no intention of going all the way with her but, honestly, if Bronco hadn't interrupted them, that might have been exactly what happened. No woman had ever tested his resolve the way Maddy did.

If they'd gone all the way, he would truly be entangled now, irrevocably involved with a woman whose father he didn't trust. For that matter, he wasn't sure he even fully trusted Maddy not to be informing on the SEALs for her father, who perhaps wanted to know whether his oil wells were safe. He might not be the CEO anymore, at least not technically, but he had to be deeply interested in the fate of the corporation he had founded. For Maddy to be here in Paraguay, so close to the SEALs, it still struck Sam as utterly suspicious.

Adjusting his NVGs to better keep an eye on the enemy camp, he tabbed the mike on his radio, requesting a status report from each of his platoon members.

One by one, fourteen members of his sixteen-man platoon reported that they'd relieved their Charlie counterparts. Bronco had taken the place of two men since Bamm-Bamm had been left behind to keep an unofficial eye on Madison Scott. The leadership, Mad Max and Kuzinsky, had no idea Sam had assigned Bamm-Bamm that special detail, and so long as his men didn't rat on him, they would never find out. Sam had promised Maddy that he wouldn't let anything happen to her, and he meant what he'd said.

Doubt speared him briefly as he wondered whether one junior SEAL afforded her enough protection. Austin Collins didn't have much tactical experience but he was one hell of a scrapper, and being as green around women as a blade of grass, Sam didn't have to concern himself with whether he'd steal Maddy out from under his nose.

Not that he considered her in any way his exclusive property—but no other man with less-than-honorable intentions had better come near her.

Digging his elbows into the soil, he adjusted his position so that he could see over the vegetation without straining his neck. The terrorist camp lay beneath a gossamer-thin blanket of silvery moonlight. Aside from the wind, it lay as still and deserted as an old mining town. With a pulse tapping at his temples, he studied the dark windows and plumbed the shadows for the barest suggestion of occupation.

Could the terrorists have realized already that they were being watched—by no less than the Americans whom they loathed? Certainly it was not beyond possible that some enterprising villager had identified the American soldiers' uniforms and sent gossip spreading throughout the region, alerting the terrorists to their presence. What if they blamed Maddy for summoning the American forces?

The possibility made Sam's scalp prickle. If the terrorists weren't here at their camp, or if they'd sneaked out via some unseen tunnel, then where the hell were they?

"I saw the woman in the vehicle behind us as we drove away. She is alive," Ashraf Al-Sadr declared with wild-eyed accusation. The whites of his black eyes had turned red for lack of sleep. "You let her live!" he hissed, pointing an accusing finger at his leader. "And now the Americans hound us!"

Salim Ghazal heaved an inward sigh. He'd suspected when he'd spared the lab technician's life that he was going to regret his decision. Still, he would not have been justified in killing her. Her cooperation in locating the nitric acid amidst hundreds of vials of mysterious reagents had earned her a reprieve. Salim wasn't a cold-blooded murderer like Ashraf Al-Sadr, who'd shot the guard unnecessarily.

But reports of an American military presence had circulated almost immediately following their impromptu raid on GEF's lab. The rumors let him know that Madison Scott, despite her promise to keep their encounter secret, had betrayed him. He had not expected treachery from a woman so beautiful.

Meeting the furious gazes of his top soldiers, he paused to formulate his response to Ashraf's accusation. Their situation was already tenuous. Claiming a volunteer army of just seventy soldiers, they couldn't hope to drive out the Americans, who appeared to be about half that many in number but whose arsenal certainly surpassed their own and whose resources were endless.

Not even Ashraf and Musa's experience in warfare could tip the scales in their favor. Their only recourse was to disband. Salim had sent their volunteer soldiers back to Asunción from whence most of them hailed. Rigging their camp to explode when the Americans forced their way inside, the four leaders had then fled via a crumbling underground escape route that spat them out half a mile away.

It was now dawn, and the first suggestion of sunlight framed the shuttered window of the private home they occupied, situated on the edge of town. Paid for with Hezbollah funds, the safe house was where they gathered when they were not actively in training.

"Your suspicions are correct, Ashraf," Salim acknowledged, meeting that man's baleful gaze with a calculated mix of authority and humbleness. "I did not kill the woman as I led you to believe. Forgive my deception, but I conceived then, as I believe now, that she is of more use to us alive. Hear me out," he suggested when the man made to cut him off.

The room, one of six that comprised the large house, had been strewn with rugs. They sat cross-legged in a circle, a loaf of bread and an empty ewer between them. Their mugs of chai perfumed the small space with its pungent aroma. The single light fixture, a lamp in the corner, illumined each man's skeptical expression.

"As we know, the lab is owned by the Global Environmental Facility, a group comprised of esteemed scientists from all over the world. Imagine the pressure those scientists would put on Scott Oil should one of their employees be held hostage until Scott Oil sells a majority of its shares to Paraguayan investors or leaves the country altogether."

Interest lit the faces of his captive audience.

Ashraf Al-Sadr stroked his thick beard. "It would be simpler just to blow up the wells as we had planned."

Salim frowned. "The American force has eliminated that option. They have come here to annihilate us. We would not be able to escape their notice."

"So, that's it? We abandon our objective without a fight?" The scar on Ashraf's face stood out starkly as his anger mounted.

"Of course not," Salim soothingly replied. "Scott Oil has robbed Paraguay of her natural resources and robbed her of profits that are rightly hers. We cannot stand for that."

Ashraf, a mercenary, snorted. He could care less about Paraguay's citizens or even the National Liberation Army which he helped to train. His only goal and the goal of Hezbollah who sponsored him was to undermine U.S. interests so that Hezbollah could claim the area for themselves. Salim wasn't fooled into thinking their objectives were any more lofty than Scott Oil's, but for now, Hezbollah aided his personal agenda.

"We could seize the woman tomorrow," proposed Salim's younger brother, Nasrallah. "We will stop her on her way to the lab."

"She has not been to the lab since the incident," Salim informed them. "I've had her under surveillance. I know where she lives," he added.

His brother eyed him curiously. Salim knew more

than that. Prompted by his persistent visions of the blond beauty and intrigued that her last name was Scott, he had researched his prospective hostage thoroughly. What he'd found out about her made her a very desirable target, indeed, only he could not afford to let his colleagues know that Madison Scott wasn't just an environmentalist with GEF. She was the daughter of the founder of Scott Oil, himself.

How better to force Scott Oil Corporation to accede to his demands than to use Madison Scott to make his ultimatum?

But the Hezbollah warriors mustn't learn the truth for then they would use her to further their own objectives, none of which resembled the objectives of the NLA. Moreover, they wouldn't hesitate to abuse her, rape and defile her, regardless of her political value.

And Salim could not have that. Her beauty was not made to be destroyed but rather cherished. He would take her hostage—yes. But he would protect her as he leveraged her value for the sake of his adoptive country.

"It's settled then," he announced, appeasing Ashraf's rabid desire to attack the enemy the only way they could. "We will seize the environmentalist tomorrow night."

Maddy awoke late the next morning. Even with sunlight beaming around her tightly closed curtains and with Sam long gone from her bed, his essence still enveloped her. She reached for her phone, checking for messages. GEF had called while her phone was on 'silent' to say they had yet to find her a replacement partner—she had the day off.

Relieved not to have to scour the countryside alone, Maddy jumped out of bed and stripped her sheets.

Washing her linens ought to eradicate Sam's scent, which continued to fill her with continuous longing for more of the same. She gave a soft moan as a ghost of that exquisite experience haunted her. How could she not long for more?

She'd never come across a man she desired so desperately. And yet...she wasn't ready to belong to him. Knowing Sam, commitment to him would surely mean having to surrender her personal quest to improve the world and to follow in her mother's footsteps.

Feeling restless, she threw herself into cleaning her condo. At noon, she popped next door to check on Lucía and the baby, both of whom fared well. Lucía had heard that Ricardo's surgery was underway, and she asked Maddy if she would drive her to the hospital that afternoon to visit him. That way she could bring the baby for Ricardo to see. It would motivate him to heal faster.

With a couple of hours to waste, Maddy called her father; after all, he'd been kind enough to gift her a phone that made international calls so easy.

"Sweetheart!" he answered, clearly pleased to be hearing from her. Under normal circumstances, Maddy preferred to keep her calls to a minimum. For one thing, the long-distance calls could not be cheap and her father paid the bill. For another, the news she had to share invariably agitated him. "How's your work with GEF?" he asked. "Is Scott Oil defiling El Chaco like you expected?"

"Probably," she replied, eliciting a skeptical grunt. "But I can't prove it yet," she admitted.

"And you never will," he said with certainty. "Scott Oil does good things for the world."

"Is that the reason you got me this job?" Maddy demanded, recalling Ricardo's accusations the other day. "Are you counting on me to report to the press that I couldn't find any toxins leeching from Scott Oil wells or refineries?"

"Of course not, honey. I got you the job because I knew you'd love it the same way your mother would have loved it. Besides, Scott Oil's not my company, anymore. If anything, I'm counting on you to hold my successor accountable, even if he's family."

Maddy pictured the second most powerful man in the corporation. "You made Uncle Paul the CEO," she guessed. Of course he had. Her father and her mother's brother had been friends since high school. They'd started up the company together, using her father's money, and they'd been running it like a captain and his first mate ever since.

"He's holding the position for me until I'm free to take it again," her father explained.

"And you trust him to keep the same high standards?" Maddy stood up and started pacing. "I know he's your best friend, Daddy, but he's not like you." Uncle Paul was handsome and robust and charismatic, but he was essentially self-centered, something her father failed to see.

"He's family, Maddy. He would never intentionally harm me. But, you're right. He might cut corners in the way we handle waste. It wouldn't hurt for you to keep an eye on the job he's doing."

"Gotcha." It was just as she'd suspected, then. Her father had gotten her this job for a reason—to monitor Uncle Paul's handling of waste. She heaved a sigh of frustration at finding herself under his thumb, yet again. But at least his motives were pure and his first concern was for the environment, just as her mother would have wanted.

"Any news?" he asked, changing the subject before she could take him to task.

She thought about her run-in with the terrorists, but couldn't tell him about that without arousing his immediate concern. Her thoughts skipped to another subject, like Sam. "You'll never guess who I ran into down here," she began, hating the way her blood heated and her pulse raced at the mere thought of him.

"Who could that be?" her father asked.

His smug tone aroused Maddy's suspicions. *Wait just a darn minute.* It sounded like he already knew what she was going to say. In running for the Senate, her father had become privy to all sorts of top secret military information. Lyle Scott might not be the catalyst behind the SEALs' presence, but he might certainly have known that they'd be down here, addressing the growing terror threat.

"Lt. Sasseville," she said, her ears pricked to the slightest nuance that her father already knew.

"No kidding." He sounded more pleased than surprised, cementing Maddy's suspicions.

"You knew I'd run into him again," she accused.

A nervous chuckle sounded in her ear. "Now, why would you think that?"

"I don't know, Daddy. I just have this feeling that you're throwing us together. Is that true?" she demanded.

"Well, even if I were, I couldn't think of a better man to look out for you."

That confirmed it. Her father was trying to play matchmaker. The realization made her more determined than ever to remain her own woman, free to carve her own path. "I have to go check on a friend right now," she said, too annoyed to continue speaking with him.

"Sam?" her father asked.

"No, my colleague, Ricardo. He was injured in an explosion."

The sudden quiet on the other end made her realize that she'd said too much.

"Not the explosion at the future well site," Lyle Scott guessed.

"Yes, actually," she replied, not at all surprised that her father had heard about it. He might not be running Scott Oil, but he would always keep his finger on the pulse of the enterprise he had built from the ground up.

"What the hell was he doing snooping around the well?"

She'd asked herself that very question. "I have no idea."

"Honey, you be careful down there. I don't like those rumors of terrorists in the region."

*They're not rumors.*

"It's bad enough that they're targeting Scott Oil Corporation. I don't want them going after you."

A vision of the man with the blue-green eyes assailed her. "I'll be fine, Daddy." Sam had promised he would protect her—though how he intended to do so while chasing after terrorists remained a mystery. "I've got to go," she repeated.

"I love you, sweetheart. Be careful."

"I will. Love you, too." She put her phone away and flopped onto the bed with her mother's journal, a little bound booklet into which Melinda Scott had scribbled her philosophies about global and societal issues, opinions that Maddy had embraced as her own. The final entries in the journal discussed her mother's objections to her father's prospecting in El Chaco. Melinda made it clear she didn't want her husband sucking oil out of one of the last pristine wildernesses in the world.

It'll ruin the delicate ecosystem, she'd penned in her elegant scrawl. Toxic waste will spill into the waterways and leach into the flora. The livestock of the local ranchers will die off first. Eventually, the people living off their meat will develop various cancers and perish painfully.

Maddy thought of the dead cow and the symptoms the older natives were experiencing—God forbid that their illnesses would become long-term. She had hoped her work with GEF would corroborate her mother's assertions, but so far the tests she and Ricardo had run hadn't indicated at all that the environment was being adversely influenced.

*It's just a matter of time,* she assured herself. And when she finally substantiated her belief that the oil wells had to go, she would appeal to her father to dismantle them, just as her mother would have wanted. Out of love for her mother, Lyle Scott would reluctantly agree. Except, if he didn't run the corporation, he'd have to convince Uncle Paul to pull the plug.

An hour later, Maddy set the book aside. It was time to drive Lucía and the baby to the hospital. Leaving her condo locked, she crossed to the Jeep to start it as she waited for her neighbor to join her. The sun beat down on the Jeep's roof, encouraging her to lower all the windows. She turned the key in the ignition and a *click, click, click* greeted her ears. Puzzled, Maddy tried again to no avail. Either the starter had given out or the battery was dead.

Seeing Lucía step out of the adjacent condo, Maddy pushed out of the driver's seat to explain the situation. "We'll have to walk," she apologized with a grimace. "I'll help carry the baby."

Lucía peered off into the direction of the hospital. "It's not too far," she answered, patting the little bundle in the front pack. "I'm fine with her."

"You just had a baby," Maddy protested.

"Ricardo's waiting," Lucía replied and started walking.

Admiring the woman's spirit, Maddy hurried ahead to lead the way.

As they skirted storefronts and simple dwellings, the sun burned ever brighter, heating the top of her head and making her long for the straw cowboy hat she had thoughtlessly left in the Jeep. Her blond hair tended to drew unwanted attention from the male population. Giving them a show wasn't her intention.

Still, with her head exposed, she felt nearly as vulnerable as she had last night. She could feel several sets of eyes tracking her progress as she picked her way along the uneven sidewalk. Were they friendly and brown? Or were they hostile, blue-green eyes that calculated her every move to decide whether she should live or die?

# CHAPTER 9

Six hours of sleep was plenty to keep Sam's platoon alert during the briefing called by the CO. At fifteen hundred hours, he ordered Haiku to roust the men out of their bunks. They'd been sleeping ever since Charlie Platoon relieved them from their reconnaissance that morning.

No sooner had his platoon members thumped into their seats in the briefing room than Mad Max, Kuzinsky, and Lt. Lindstrom swept in, shutting the door behind them.

"At ease," Mad Max called out, keeping them from having to jump to their feet to salute. "Master Chief, give these men the latest sit rep," he ordered, folding his arms over his broad chest and letting Kuzinsky take over.

"Charlie Platoon has nothing to report," the master chief relayed. "The camp still appears deserted. Luckily, we just received JSOTF's blessing, which means we're cleared to insert tonight."

A wave of excitement rippled over the captive audience.

Lt. Lindstrom, whose six and a half feet of pure muscle made Kuzinsky look even shorter by comparison, toggled the laptop and brought up an aerial view of the terrorist training camp onto the flat screen TV.

"You'll join Charlie Platoon on site tonight at twenty hundred hours," he explained. "They'll provide backup while you men do the insertion." He briefly met Sam's gaze. "You've had more rest than they have," he said, defending that decision, "plus you've got the best breacher in this task unit." His gaze slid toward Petty Officer Carl Wolfe, a rangy SEAL with reddish brown hair and sunburnt skin. "And odds are high that this camp is laden with IEDs."

Humble to the point of being a martyr, Carl Wolfe's cool head around explosives had secured Sam's respect back in Afghanistan. His father, a New York City fireman, had perished in the World Trade Center on 9/11, a tragedy that had inspired Carl's desire to join in the fight against terror. He hadn't spoken more than a dozen sentences in Sam's presence the entire year that he'd been in Sam's platoon. All Sam knew about Carl was that he loved cats, he was quiet, and didn't make waves. The men trusted their very lives to him.

Lindstrom proceeded to illustrate their entry in timed segments. Like choreographed dancers, Echo Platoon would breach the outer perimeter while Charlie broke away from the camp in an expanding circle looking for squirters—enemy combatants fleeing the scene either above ground or via unidentified tunnels. At the same time, Echo Platoon, with Carl in the lead, would penetrate the camp. On the lookout for trip wires or pressure plates that could trigger ordinances to explode, they would home in on the large shelter into which the terrorists had disappeared.

With a trickle of foreboding, Sam acknowledged the possibility that he or one of his men might be maimed or even killed tonight, depending on how effectively the tangoes had built their bombs. Would Maddy even look at him twice if he lost a foot like T-Rex? Reassuringly, the answer wasn't an immediate *No*. Maddy was nothing if not compassionate. Her calling to help wherever she was needed was proof of that. Hell, she might even like him *better* if he couldn't walk.

With that only slightly reassuring thought, he focused on the details coming out of the Ops officer's mouth. Even though Lindstrom would remain a radio call away, platoon leaders were the highest ranking officers on site. The responsibility of ensuring that everything happened the way it was supposed to rested solely on his and Lt. Cooper's shoulders, while the leading petty officers, Bronco and Bullfrog included, ensured that everything went according to plan. They'd done this kind of thing a zillion times in training and a dozen times in real life. They could do it again.

Except that nothing ever went down the same way twice.

"We're looking for a backdoor," Lindstrom continued. "Old photographs and letters from the 19th century indicate that there were gold mines in the area, later used in the Chaco War to hide supplies and men. Our targets may have used a tunnel to escape the area unseen."

He bent way over to tap a key on his laptop, and the photograph of a wild-eyed, scar-faced terrorist superimposed itself on the screen. "One of the guys we're looking to capture is this Hezbollah extremist, Ashraf Al-Sadr." Sam recognized the man as one of the two Maddy had identified.

"This son of a bitch," Lindstrom said, using language he reserved exclusively for the most sadistic assholes on the planet, "is believed responsible for the rash of car bombings in Beirut earlier this year. He fled Lebanon sometime in March, before he could be arrested, and he apparently wound up out here. If you come across him, debilitate him if you must, but we want him alive. Any questions? Yes?"

As Haiku asked a question about radio frequencies, Sam looked past him and caught Bamm-Bamm eyeing him hopefully. The kid so obviously wanted to be included in the action tonight. No SEAL worth his salt would want to be left out, but it wasn't to be. With a subtle shake of his head, Sam let Austin Collins know that—no, he was needed right here at camp, keeping watch on Maddy's condo.

The kid actually had the audacity to roll his eyes in frustration. Sam's temper flared, but then he acknowledged that he'd reacted similarly when he'd been forced out of that op in Malaysia in order to snatch Maddy out of Matamoros. Now it was Bamm-Bamm's turn. Hopefully, they'd catch the terrorists tonight, and then he wouldn't be saddled with a job he felt was beneath his skills and training.

In the shadow of the military installation's outer wall, Bamm-Bamm smeared his face with dark-green camouflage paint. The stuff went on like mud. It was even harder to take off than it was to put on. He hadn't been told he *had* to use it, but he'd been spotted last night by Chief Adams who'd been looking for Lt. Sasseville, which meant he needed to step up his game tonight.

Feeling cheated for having been left out of a highlight event in Operation Anaconda, Bamm-Bamm reminded himself what an honor it was to protect the daughter of a future senator. And if the reason had something to do with that scar-faced terrorist Lt. Lindstrom had showed them during the briefing, then his protection detail might actually put him into confrontation with some nasty terrorists—not that he wanted them to target Miss Scott. But if they did, he'd be ready.

Pushing the tin of camo paint into his breast pocket, he checked that the clip on his MP-5 was fully loaded, pushed his helmet more securely onto his head, and nimbly swung his compact frame up into the *quebracho* tree behind him. The tree, one of dozens that had been planted inside the military installation, grew up close to the wall and well above it, affording him a bird's-eye view of Miss Scott's condo while keeping him within the perimeter of the camp.

Fifteen feet into the air, he lay back on the thick, forked branch that had been his perch last night when he'd watched Lt. Sasseville break into her door with a credit card. The lieutenant had stayed in there until he was joined an hour later by Miss Scott, who'd come out of the neighbor's house. The two might have spent the entire evening together if Chief Adams hadn't come huffing up to the tree asking Bamm-Bamm if he knew where the LT was.

Sure enough, he'd known. He'd even had a good idea of what Lt. Sasseville was doing at the time, and Master Chief Kuzinsky wouldn't like it, but Bamm-Bamm wasn't about to rat on his platoon leader for getting a piece of action when they weren't supposed to have anything to do with the civilian population.

Tonight, Miss Scott's condo looked dark and deserted. The sky had turned a deep indigo blue in anticipation of nighttime. Already, it was shot with the same stars that had prompted him last night to recollect the names of all the constellations. As a bright kid growing up in the hicks of Kentucky, he'd taught himself to identify them all. But tonight he would remain vigilant, so no stargazing. Miss Scott, he already knew, liked to keep the lights blazing. Her dark condo told him that, despite the vehicle parked out front, she wasn't home.

Flipping down his NVGs, he scanned the street, wondering where she might be and scoping out potential threats. His thoughtful gaze returned to a nondescript van parked a block up the road from her home. A man sat unmoving in the driver's seat. Squinting through his NVGs, Bamm-Bamm wondered if he was seeing a neon-green beard or if the man was wearing a fuzzy sweater. He swiveled his head in the opposite direction, and that was when he caught sight of two individuals hustling up the sidewalk from the heart of town.

The long hair and lithe curves of Miss Scott made her immediately identifiable as she hurried ahead of a shorter woman. That woman was her neighbor, Bamm-Bamm determined, spying a sling across her chest with the baby in it. The women walked as quickly as they could along the unlit and uneven sidewalk, looking antsy about the lateness of the hour.

Suddenly the lights on the van blinked on, catching them in its high beams as it pulled from the curb and rumbled toward them. Bamm-Bamm's pulse accelerated as he split his attention between the women and the approaching van. He willed it to rumble right past them. Miss Scott finally saw it, her stride faltering. He saw her step in front of her companion as if to protect her.

"Drive on by," Bamm-Bamm whispered, hefting his submachine gun just in case.

The angles were not at all in his favor. With a tell-tale screeching of brakes, the van slowed as it neared the women, blocking them from Bamm-Bamm's view. A misfired shot might go right over the top of the van or through a window and strike either one of them.

"Damn it!" he hissed, debating whether to jump out of the tree and get a better angle. But then the wall would briefly obstruct his view and he didn't dare take his eyes off Miss Scott.

Except that he couldn't even see her. The sound of a van door grating open greeted his ears, followed by the bark of a male voice. This wasn't good.

A woman screamed, prompting Bamm-Bamm to make a decision. Aiming at the tires, he depressed the trigger, deflating both passenger-side tires in an instant. The van listed. A door slammed shut and the van pulled forward, tires slapping the ground. Jiggling wildly, it nonetheless accelerated, pulling farther and farther away, leaving one woman cowering on the sidewalk where there had been two previously. Miss Scott had been taken.

"No!" Horrified, Bamm-Bamm shot at the retreating taillights. They exploded under the onslaught of his bullets, but the vehicle didn't stop.

With a wild leap out of the tree, he managed to land on his feet. Sprinting to the gate, he yanked it open and stepped out into the street, swinging his MP-5 up to shoot, just as the van turned out of sight at the next intersection.

*Too late.*

Stunned, Bamm-Bamm stared in consternation at the neighbor now screaming for help in front of her condo. Knowing there was little he could do for her, he lowered his weapon and crossed the street to see if she was injured. The necessity of telling his platoon leader what had happened made him cringe. He'd screwed up royally. Lt. Sasseville would never trust him again.

This isn't a dream.

The blue-green eyes that had haunted Maddy since the incident at the warehouse glinted within the shadowy interior of the vehicle, making it suddenly clear what was happening. One minute, she'd been anticipating the cool shower awaiting her inside her condo, the next she'd been staring into the barrel of the gun and realizing if she didn't cooperate, then baby Isabella and Lucía might be gunned down. Her nightmare had just morphed into reality.

To the accompaniment of gunfire—coming from where?—the besieged van had lurched forward, and her nemesis had caught her against his uniformed chest, keeping her from losing her seat. The sound of shattering plastic paired with the *thunk* of a bullet embedding itself in the van's bumper had given her to realize that *someone* endeavored to prevent her from abduction. Only, it was too late now. Though hampered by flat tires, the vehicle had nonetheless lumbered from the scene, and the sound of gunfire ceased.

Peering through the dark, her heart thundering, Maddy recognized the same men who'd forced their way into the lab last week. The cruel one with a scar bisecting his right cheek seized her wrists, cinching them together and binding them with a plastic zip-tie while the youngest glared up at her from the floor. Their leader, meanwhile kept a firm arm around her shoulders as the fourth man drove the van. Even with flat tires, it floundered on.

Steeped in shock, Maddy failed to respond to the spate of Lebanese being muttered in her ear. The sting of a brisk slap brought her sharply to reality. Not a dream at all.

"Enough," barked the leader, speaking in English for her sake, she realized. The scarred devil who'd slapped her backed off.

Taking heart from her nemesis's mercy, Maddy turned her head to regard his handsome profile. His jewel-like eyes returned her scrutiny. He'd spared her life the last time. She could only hope he would do the same now.

But the inscrutable lines of his face said otherwise as he returned her frightened gaze with a long stare. Dread chilled Maddy to the bone. She averted her eyes, her thoughts flying at once to Sam. He had failed to keep her safe. What made her think he could find and rescue her now that she'd been taken?

She was doomed—unless she admitted to these terrorists whose daughter she was. Would that guarantee her safety? Her father would pay any sum required to secure her freedom, but what if money wasn't their goal?

It probably wasn't. She shouldn't tell them anything.

Sam and his teammates would have to rescue her. But how would they know where to find her? *My satellite phone!* She could feel it burning a hole in her back pocket, broadcasting her location with its built-in GPS. Hope surged through her, driving away the paralyzing effect of shock. But if the terrorists found it, they would immediately seize it and destroy it. She had to keep it out of sight, perhaps even hide it before they found it.

With the wobbling van masking her movements and hampered by the cuff that bound her wrists, she managed to draw her phone from her back pocket. Silencing it with her thumbnail, she deliberated where to hide it. Here in the van or wait until they arrived at their final destination? The longer she held it, the more chance it would be seen and seized.

The seat on which she sat provided a solution. She could feel a crease right at her fingertips between the bench and the back of the seat, with just enough room in between to push the phone out of sight. With trembling fingers, she slid it into the aperture.

*Find me, Sam!* Tears of desperation swarmed into her eyes. *Find me and save me!*

*God, I hate spiders.*

"Sir, wait!"

Carl Wolfe's last-second admonition froze Sam in the act of reaching past the EOD expert to sweep aside the spider web that draped like a curtain from the tunnel's low ceiling. Directing his gaze downward, Sam saw what he'd completely overlooked in his quest to keep all spiders from dropping onto his helmet and scuttling down his back: the glint of a needle-thin filament bisecting the tunnel right in front of the foot he was about to lift.

The terrorists hadn't been content with wiring the shed to blow sky-high. They'd bobby-trapped their escape route, too, apparently.

A cold sweat breached Sam's pores in an instant. Lifting his right arm at an angle, he wordlessly communicated to Bronco, who followed some distance behind them, to halt.

"You might want to step back, sir," Carl suggested sounding as calm and unruffled as a still pool of water.

Swallowing hard, Sam slowly backed up. With his shirt sticking to his back and his mouth desert-dry, he watched the EOD expert crouch over the menacing filament and follow the path it took to a tin bucket standing inconspicuously off to one side.

The tunnel had been built just wide enough to allow

a wagon to be pulled through it. Littered with relics of two past eras—mining and war—it was filled with rusted trowels, buckets, and bottles, all vestiges of decades gone by. The bucket didn't look any more suspicious than the others Sam had seen. But Carl's low whistle conveyed that it was packed with enough gunpowder and hardware to shred a man's flesh.

As Carl went to work disarming the device, Sam sought to slow the tempo of his convulsing heart. His gaze flickered to the lumber and metal plates buttressing the crumbling walls. Over a hundred years old, the tunnel had obviously been put back into service by the terrorists, who'd used it to sneak past Charlie Platoon's reconnaissance because they sure as hell weren't in the camp anymore. They weren't down here, either, not with the place rigged to blow sky high.

Sam had never envisioned himself being buried alive. But that was the death that awaited him if Carl failed to disarm the IED. A rivulet of sweat trickled between his shoulder blades.

*I should have gone all the way with Maddy.*

Of all the regrets he might have entertained, that was the one that came to mind. He'd cheated himself out of a life-defining moment, and if he didn't survive this night, he'd never get another chance to make her his.

In an effort to distract himself, he keyed his mike. "Cougar, this is Eagle," he murmured, smoothing the tremor of uncertainty from his voice. "Any idea yet where this tunnel ends?" He and his men had been following it for half a mile or more. If he knew the end was near, maybe he could shake the sense of doom pressing down on his shoulders.

Lt. Cooper's chipper reply was a balm to his ears. "Roger that, Eagle. We've located your exit. Looks like it was trespassed a while back by our targets. You've got maybe two hundred yards to go. How's it going down there?"

"It's ugly," Sam reported, revealing his true feelings. His earpiece crackled as another voice broke into the conversation.

"Sir, this is Bullfrog. HQ reports a secondary situation."

Something in Jeremiah's voice suggested Sam wasn't going to like what he heard. "What is it?"

"Bamm-Bamm just informed Master Chief that Miss Scott was abducted. She was grabbed right off the street as she approached her house. Bamm-Bamm managed to compromise the vehicle—a white van—but it got away all the same."

The tunnel seemed to shrink in on Sam, boxing him in on every side. He stared desperately at Carl who was now bent over the IED wielding a pair of specialized clippers. *Come on, buddy. You can do it.*

"You need me to repeat, sir?" Bullfrog asked.

"No." Sam's thoughts raced, even as his muscles quivered with a frustrated need to respond. "We have to find her before they can..." He trailed off, unwilling to consider what would happen to her now. His thoughts went to finding her instead. "Wait, she carries a satellite phone everywhere she goes. If we're lucky, she's got it on her. Tell Master Chief to call her father. Get her number and use GPS to track her location. Call me back when you know more."

"Yes, sir. Over."

*Christ.* "How much *longer*, Carl?" he raged.

A soft *snick* preceded Carl's answer. "All done, sir." He rose fluidly to his feet. "You'll want to stay behind me," he chided gently as he slipped his tools back into his pockets.

Sam acknowledged the subtle admonition with a

nod. The spiders could have at him for all he cared. Still, considering Maddy's present terror—God, she had to be beside herself!—he chafed to sprint for the closest exit. But who knew how many more filaments lay in his path? An explosion of any size would bring the earthen ceiling crashing down on their heads. He licked the salty sweat off his upper lip and gestured for Carl to proceed.

*This is a nightmare.*

The terrorists, if they could see him now, would gloat at his predicament. Here he was, trapped in a tunnel laden with IEDs, looking for *them* when they were already long gone. More than that, they'd seized a prize that Sam had failed to sufficiently protect.

The walls of the snaking tunnel blurred as denial raged inside of him. An image of Maddy lying beneath him, her gaze unfocused and glazed with passion, swam before his eyes.

*My beautiful Maddy.* He should have done more to keep her safe. One junior SEAL pitted against a handful of experienced terrorists wasn't enough. Christ, if anything awful happened to her—and the odds were sickeningly high that something would—he would simply never forgive himself.

# CHAPTER 10

Maddy awoke with a crick in her neck that came from sleeping sitting up while propped against a wall. *Where am I?* For a panicked second, she failed to recognize her dark, cramped surroundings. But the scratchy blanket under her hip and the numb fire licking up her arms reminded her of her predicament.

Her thoughts went back to the moment when the terrorist had thrust her out of the van and hustled her into a dark house, surrounded at a distance by other buildings. The sound of the van pulling away, taking her satphone with it, had made her cry out in denial. Another stinging slap delivered by the scar-faced devil had shocked her into silence.

Overwrought by the fact that her only hope, her satellite phone had gone on without her, she'd scarcely registered that they'd stuck her in a closet on the home's second level and secured the door from the outside. Grateful to be left alone, she'd bewailed her circumstances and begged her mother's spirit to save her. At some point, she must have fallen asleep.

Wincing in discomfort, Maddy used her shoulders and her feet to brace herself as she pushed to a standing position. Faint light shone through the seam around the door, suggesting that it was morning. She had managed to sleep quite a while, then, but now her bladder needed relieving. "Hello," she cried out, loath to draw attention to herself but even more reluctant to pee in the closet. "I have to use the restroom!"

Putting an ear to the door, she heard footsteps on the stairs and drew back. Her heart galloped as one of her captives paused before her closet. The knob gave a click, and the door swept open, revealing the youngest of the three, a youth she hadn't paid much attention to back at the lab except to note his resemblance to the leader. This morning, he clutched a deadly-looking knife that earned her full attention. He regarded her mistrustfully, his hazel eyes wide and wary.

Keeping his dagger trained on her heart, he crooked a finger at her, gesturing for her to step out. She did so fearing the worst, and he roughly turned her. Maddy gasped as the knife sliced between her wrists and snapped the plastic cuffs in half. Her arms fell to her sides and she shook them out, stunned and grateful.

"Walk," he ordered in English, giving her a shove.

On quaking knees, she preceded him into a sparse bedroom. Given the two beds, a uniform folded neatly on the dresser top and the smell of man—not unpleasant but distinctly masculine—she surmised the room belonged to this youth and his older brother, the leader. Her captor extended her a folded garment then pointed out the adjoining bathroom. "You may wash," he instructed, his English not as fluent as his brother's.

Wordlessly Maddy accepted the gray robe and equally drab scarf and backed into the bathroom, shutting the door and quickly locking it. The flimsy lock wouldn't keep anyone out for long. Turning, she assessed the possibility of escape with a hopeful heart. However, the only window, high and narrow, was comprised of thick, cube-shaped glass, impossible to break or even to see through, and her hopes plummeted.

Perhaps she might find a weapon that she could conceal and use later?

But after peering into the cabinet under the sink and sifting through modest supplies, she realized why her captors didn't own even a single razor—because they all wore full beards. There was only soap and toilet paper and a few thin towels for drying off. She had better make use of those amenities while she could.

Minutes later, shivering from a cold shower, her damp hair wetting the coarse *chapan* she had tunneled into, Maddy eyed herself in the mirror. A pale frightened face stared back at her. *I won't be here long*, she assured her reflection. But now that her phone was gone, driven off to God-knew-where, how would the SEALs ever track her down?

A knock at the door startled her. "Madison Scott," said a voice that thinned her blood, "Step out."

The leader had sworn that he would kill her for betraying him. Maddy scooped up her balled clothing, raised the drab scarf over her head, and pulled the door open, gripping her bundle tightly. The impact of her captor's stare drove the air back into her lungs.

"I never told anyone," she blurted, although technically that was a lie. She'd told Sam about the incident two nights ago.

A cynical smile made his soft-looking beard twitch. "Indeed. Well, it makes no difference now. The Americans are here, aren't they? My name is Salim," he added, surprising her by making introductions. He rendered a slight bow.

"Your English is excellent," she observed, since they were exchanging niceties.

"It should be. I studied at Oxford for six years—

politics and environmentalism," he added with a knowing look.

Similar to what she'd studied. "What do you intend with me, Salim?" she dared to ask him.

His thinning lips conveyed disapproval. "A typical American," he observed, "so forthright, so rude," he chided, not unkindly. "Please, have a seat. Let us get to know each other while you eat."

She saw that he'd provided a plate of bread and goat cheese, along with a cup of orange juice.

Obviously, he didn't mean to kill her right away. Thoughts of a lengthy captivity kept her from celebrating. Sinking into the chair he'd indicated, she put the plate in her lap and began to nibble at it as he sat across from her on one of the two beds. The springs creaked.

Highly conscious of his watchful gaze, she chewed a bit of cheese without tasting. When he kept silent, she did the same with a portion of the bread. If communication was the key to world peace, as she'd told Sam, she needed to bring up a neutral topic to ease the tension between them.

"The younger man, is he your brother?" she finally asked.

A hint of a smile hovered over Salim's mouth. "His name is Nasrallah," he said by way of an answer. "It means Victory of God."

"That's lovely. I wish I'd had a brother, but I'm an only child."

"Sounds lonely."

"It was," she admitted, letting him glimpse her regret. "What about the others," she continued. "Who are they?"

All hint of pleasure fled his face. "Their names you need not know," he said in a harsh voice.

"You don't like them," she surmised.

"I do not. They are Lebanese, and I am Paraguayan. My family left Beirut in 1982, before I was born. This is my native country."

"Why do they work for you then?" she asked, referring to the other soldiers, not his family.

"They were sent to me by Hezbollah to help me address the exploitation of my country by the American oil company."

The sun in the window rose higher drawing a shadow over the upper half of Salim's face. "How is it exploiting you?" she asked, intrigued by his assertion.

"The United States of America has no business sucking the wealth from Paraguay," he stated with suppressed outrage. "I have requested that Scott Oil sell half its shares to my countrymen—that would make it equitable, don't you think?"

"Yes," she said, completely honest in her reply.

"But the company refuses. Therefore I must keep you here as my unwilling guest until they change their mind."

*Unwilling guest.* The words chilled her. "What makes you think they care anything about me?" she asked, but deep down, she already knew that he knew.

He loosed a soft chuckle. "Well, I could say that your being an employee of GEF, I would rely on the international scientific community to put pressure on Scott Oil. But the truth is, I don't have to, do I?"

She searched his exotic eyes. He most certainly knew.

"I know who you are, Miss Scott," he added quietly, corroborating her guess.

She didn't bother pretending not to understand. That would only anger him and insult his intelligence. She merely inclined her head. Then she said, "But my father is no longer in control."

His expression hardened. "I know that. But now

your uncle is the new CEO. And your father may be even more powerful soon. Isn't that right?" He glanced out the window and then back at her. "I'm counting on your *family* to choose your life over the profits they earn from pillaging my country's resources."

Her life! The implication that he would kill her if his demands were not met sent the blood draining from her head. "Eighty percent of Scott Oil's proceeds remain here in Paraguay," Maddy quoted. "That was stipulated in the trade agreement."

Salim *tsked* his tongue and shook his head. "If only the new CEO abided by the agreement," he lamented.

She bristled in defense of her uncle's integrity. "How do you know he doesn't?"

"My family are all in politics. Trust me—when I say that he keeps all the profits for himself, I am not lying. It's no secret that Scott Oil has violated its promises."

*Really?* Her father would be stunned to hear that her uncle had altered the company's policies and violated previous agreements.

"But the economy is thriving, right?" In desperation, she pointed out the good that Scott Oil had done for this country, citing Ricardo's arguments. "For the first time in history, Paraguay exports oil without having to rely on Argentina's imports."

"Perhaps," Salim conceded. "That doesn't alter the fact that Scott Oil is profiting from resources that should be ours alone."

Maddy kept her mouth closed. It wasn't difficult at all for her to empathize with Salim's viewpoint. "I actually agree," she finally conceded. She'd had that opinion all along. Looking up, she caught a glint of approval in his eyes.

"I will send a ransom note to GEF," he explained, switching topics and causing what little food she'd eaten to turn to rocks in her belly. "I will count on them to inform your uncle and your father of our demands. If Scott Oil opens their doors to Paraguayan investors so that fifty percent or more become shareholders, then I will release you," he said, kindly.

She searched his expression for any hint of deception. "But that could take weeks," she protested. Tears of frustration and fear rushed into her eyes, brimming over her lower lashes.

Salim took note of her fragility. "You have nothing to fear," he said encouragingly. "Not from me nor from my brother. And we will protect you from the others."

The memory of the stinging slap she'd received had her touching her cheek. Intuition whispered that this man and his younger brother were the only entities standing between her and the radical terrorists whom the SEALs were hunting. Nausea threatened to upend her stomach. She set her plate abruptly aside and took a quick sip of the watery juice.

"I must film you in captivity," Salim said, producing a cell phone from his breast pocket and accessing its camera feature.

Maddy regarded the Motorola with faint hope. If he sent his film of her via wireless cellular transmission, it might be possible for the authorities to trace the way it had been routed and triangulate her location.

"You will identify yourself when I tell you to," Salim instructed, "and answer my questions succinctly. And if you must cry again, now would be the time to do it."

Sam paced the perimeter of the table in the TOC, unaware that he was circling his colleagues like a satellite orbiting the earth. Commander MacDougal flicked him a censorial look. "Have a seat, Sam.

You're making us dizzy."

He dropped into the nearest chair. Dragging fingers through his crisp hair, he glared at the monitor. "How much longer?"

"Almost there," Kuzinksy promised as he worked to open several image files.

It'd been twelve hours since Maddy's disappearance—the longest twelve hours of Sam's entire life, feeling even longer than the weeks he'd spent in jail back in high school. At least then, he'd only had to worry about himself.

If only he had asked Maddy for her phone number eons ago. They needed it to find her phone, and therefore *her*. Sam's impulse to ask Lyle Scott for Maddy's phone number had been vetoed by Commander MacDougal for the following reasons: The longer Lyle Scott remained ignorant of Maddy's situation, the safer Maddy was. The candidate for Senate wouldn't be able to keep the news to himself, and soon the press would know. If Hezbollah realized what a prize they held, there was a good chance that they'd ship her out of Paraguay on the first plane to Beirut, where she'd be held as a bargaining chip for the release of high-profile terrorists currently in U.S. captivity. She would become a political pawn, never to see the light of day again.

"We'll call GEF to request her cell number," Mad Max had suggested. But after an hour of trying and failing to reach a live human being on a weekend, the CO had given up.

In desperation, Sam had dashed across the street to beg Lucía for Maddy's number. Lucía had referred him to Ricardo, who still lay in the hospital recovering. At precisely 0600, the soonest that visitors were permitted to see patients, Sam had burst into Ricardo's room.

"Maddy's gone," he'd announced without preamble.

"What the hell are you talking about?"

"The terrorists took her. I guess she never told you that she was in the lab when they killed the security guard and stole the nitric acid, did she? Well, she was," he added, as Ricardo's eyes had widened in horror and the implications had registered on his swarthy face. "They threatened to kill her if she told anyone."

Ricardo had started struggling out of bed, and Sam had ordered him to lie back down. "She had her phone with her," he'd explained. "But we need her number so we can use the phone's GPS to find her."

Ultimately, Ricardo had offered him more than just a number. He'd informed him that Maddy had registered her phone with AccuTracking, which meant that anyone in law enforcement could find the phone by plugging in her number.

Sam had taken that encouraging news straight to his leaders. Lt. Lindstrom had promptly called his wife, an FBI special agent. Pledging to keep Maddy's kidnapping a secret for the time being, Hannah Lindstrom had used AccuTracking to provide the SEALs with the exact latitude and longitude of Maddy's satellite phone. JSOTF then linked them to a satellite perfectly situated to send them live images of the area where her phone was located—eighteen miles north of Mariscal Estigarribia.

"Got 'em," Master Chief said, opening the first image. Sam sat forward in his seat, straining for a better view. The pixelated images focused abruptly, showing the top of a white van amidst sand and scrub brush.

Master Chief toggled in, and a few more details came into view, like the broken taillights. He toggled way out. There was nothing but a rolling savannah and a couple of palm groves for miles in any direction. If Maddy was in the same place her phone was, then she was out in the middle of fucking nowhere.

Subsequent photos taken five and ten minutes later showed no movement, no signs of life whatsoever. Moreover, there was no option of seeing what had happened earlier, as the satellite had just begun to sweep over the area.

It was Bronco, a trained tracker, who pointed out a faint set of tracks leading south. "Someone walked away," he stated. "Headed back to town."

"That's a long walk," Kuzinsky observed.

"She could have been dropped off anywhere along the way, and just her phone was left behind," Jeremiah suggested.

*Or she might still be lying in that van with a bullet in her head.* Sam thrust the unwanted image from his mind. "Can AccuTracker trace the route she took?"

The Ops officer shook his head. "Not unless she made a call along the way."

Sam's hopes for a quick recovery hit another wall. He looked back at the screen, his eyes burning for lack of sleep. *Lyle Scott is going to blame me for this,* he thought with a guilty conscience. *And I deserve every ounce of the man's condemnation. I should have protected Maddy myself, not left it up to a SEAL with limited experience.*

He sent the CO an imploring look. "What are we waiting for, sir? We know where to start searching."

Mad Max's long stare made him regret asking. "Nightfall, Lieutenant," he said in a voice that managed to be both condescending and sympathetic at the same time. Straining the joints in his chair, the CO leaned back and folded his arms across his chest.

"Operation Anaconda was supposed to be a purely

military operation," he reflected, chiding the group in general, though Sam knew the man's words were directed at him. "Now that there's a civilian involved—a high-profile *American* civilian—our activity down here is going to fall under scrutiny, especially if we fail to handle this situation effectively and quietly."

In other words, if they failed to liberate Maddy, the whole world was going to hear about the SEALs in Paraguay. Their agenda would be discussed over dinner tables all across America, which was not a good thing as everything SEALs did was supposed to be clandestine. Sam's temples throbbed with self-condemnation.

"Get some rest," the CO added, thumping the table with both hands as he pushed to his feet. "You can expect to head out at sunset. Charlie Platoon remains here unless you require them for backup."

The only reason they would need backup was if they found Maddy too well-protected to be wrested away by one platoon.

Sam rolled to his feet. As tired as he was, he couldn't imagine falling asleep right now, not with his imagination spawning vignettes of Maddy being raped and tortured. Meeting the gazes of his leading petty officers, he sent them a nod, knowing he could count on them to alert the lower enlisted to the situation. He didn't have the heart to relay the situation himself.

"We'll find her, sir," Bullfrog assured him, laying a comforting hand on Sam's shoulder as they moved out the door and up the hallway.

"Thanks," Sam muttered. Seeing the exit ahead of him, he muttered an excuse and darted out of it.

Pushing into sunshine, he was caught off guard to find it just another ordinary day. On the other side of the military installation's wall, the townspeople of

Mariscal Estigarribia went about their daily routine, unaware and apathetic to Maddy's plight. Sam put his back to the sunbaked brick hoping the warmth would drive away the chill deep inside him.

He'd been a SEAL for seven years, and in that time he'd seen a lot of scary shit. But there'd never been a circumstance that frightened him like this did. A possessive shudder traced his spine.

*Maddy is mine. Those terrorists had no right to steal her.*

Why had it taken her being kidnapped for him to see the truth? And just when, exactly, had he started thinking of her as his? Was it when he'd kissed her on the little bridge in her father's backyard? Or did it go back even further, to that first night in Matamoros, when he'd shielded her breasts from the leering eyes of the DEA agent? She'd definitely been his the other night when he'd brought her to climax.

And now this had happened. The fear and dread swirling inside him made it hard to breathe. He reminded himself that he'd never faced a challenge he couldn't overcome. But this time, so many matters were out of his hands. Only one thing was certain. If she survived this latest travesty, he wouldn't want to let her out of his sight again. He'd want to keep her safely by his side forever.

Convincing her to let him shelter her? Now that would be the real challenge.

# CHAPTER 11

Maddy struggled to make sense of the argument raging downstairs, immediately below the closet in which she'd been locked all day. Her captors yelled at each other in Lebanese, practically at the top of their lungs.

She'd been let out only once since Salim had videotaped his interview with her that morning. Harsh punctuations of sound coming from the lower level had wakened her from a fitful sleep. She'd scrambled to her feet, putting her ear to the crack in the door in an effort to make sense of the words, but their dialect, so distinct from any Arabic she had ever heard, was completely unintelligible to her.

She could only think of one reason why they would bicker so heatedly: Hezbollah leaders were demanding access to the hostage.

Her heart thudded with dread at the likelihood. She'd been kept away from them since they'd seized her the first night. How long before her ransom video was delivered to GEF? How long before her father learned of her captors' demands? She couldn't live like this, trapped in a closet for hours on end.

*Save me, Sam.*

Don't be stupid, she immediately scolded herself. Don't put your faith in an outcome unlikely to happen. Who knew how far away her phone had been driven? Instead of leading the SEALs to her, it might actually be sending them on a wild goose chase.

A sudden shout and the crack of a bullet had her leaping away from the door, hand clapped to her mouth to stifle a scream. Over her pounding heart she could hear Salim speaking in the commanding voice he had used at the lab, and she sagged against the wall, relieved to know that he hadn't been shot. Without his protection, she knew she was doomed.

The sound of steps on the stairs kept her motionless in the closet. What would happen now? The knob jiggled and the lock released. She backed into the corner. Would she be dragged downstairs and forced to face the others?

The door cracked open, and Salim's brilliant orbs rested on her frightened visage. "Come," he ordered, his tone still gruff with anger. He held out a hand for her to take.

Operating purely on instinct, Maddy placed her hand in his. He drew her briskly out of the closet to where his brother stood, guarding the top of the stairs with a rifle now braced across his chest. Sweeping Maddy into his dark room, Salim shut and locked the door. Then he flicked on a light, powered by the generator grinding away outside.

His stormy gaze went straight to her uncovered head. "Where is the scarf you are supposed to be wearing?" he asked sharply.

His misdirected anger made her blanch. "I'm sorry. I took it off. It was so hot in the closet—"

Her voice trailed off as his gaze dropped to her bosom, molded by the otherwise shapeless *chapan,* then slid to her bare, slender feet peeking out below its hem. The assessing quality of his gaze kept the breath wedged in her lungs. Had he brought her into his bedroom to protect her or were his intentions less chivalrous?

With a stabbing gesture, he ordered her to lie down on the nearest bed. Maddy stiffened, her blood running cold. She shook her head, no.

"Go to sleep." His impatient tone suggested he was not about to rape her.

Still mistrustful, Maddy lowered herself across the thin mattress. Her muscles tensed as Salim whisked off his shirt. His naked torso, comprised of lean muscle and matted with black hair made her think of Sam, whose chest she'd felt but never seen bare. A wave of longing swept her in its relentless path. *Where are you, Sam?*

Her pulse sped up as Salim unbuckled his gun belt and dropped his pants. Horrified, she turned her head toward the wall and squeezed her eyes shut. It took every ounce of willpower not to curl into a protective ball. *This isn't happening.* The pillow under her head gave off an odor she had come to associate with him  a blend of gun oil and sandalwood.

A vision of Sam hovering tenderly over her, his body taut with desire, eyes alight with passion, drove a shaft of remorse through her so fierce that she had to catch back a sob. *Oh, Sam.* If only he'd finished what he'd begun the other night! How could she have known that might be their only chance to make love, their last night together?

She started violently at the feel of a blanket sliding over her rigid body. Whipping her head around, she brought up her hands to fend Salim off. Only then did she realize he had covered her.

"Rest," he said, mocking her frightened response with a bitter smile. Straightening away from her, he turned toward the other bed and snapped off the light.

The springs on the second bed creaked as tears of relief slid from the corners of Maddy's eyes. Through spiked leashes, she watched Salim stretch out on his moonlit bed, drape his gun belt across his stomach, and notch his hands behind his head.

"Thank you," she whispered, speaking as much to her mother's ever-present spirit as to him.

"Do not thank me yet," he replied in a grim voice that prophesied trials to come. "From now on, you must wear the scarf and do exactly as I say."

"I will," she promised.

A taut silence fell between them, filled with the sound of Salim's deep sigh as he wrestled with weighty thoughts. Maddy closed her eyes and willed herself to sleep.

If only a pair of SEALs would come sneaking through the window as they had in Matamoros to whisk her away.

The beleaguered van resembled a harpooned, white whale beached on a solitary shore. Sam had sensed the instant he first viewed it through his NVGs that it stood empty. He sniffed the breeze tentatively, dreading the scent of death, but smelling only fresh, savannah air. The good news was that Maddy wasn't lying dead inside the van. The bad news? They had no earthly idea where she might be.

Sam signaled for Carl Wolfe to approach the vehicle first, just in case it was booby-trapped. Carl peered inside with a penlight. Then he went down on all fours, twisted onto his back and disappeared beneath it. Coming out a minute later, he declared it clean, and Sam reached for the door handle, sliding it open.

Bullfrog joined him, crawling into the cargo area while Bronco searched the seats up front and the remaining platoon formed a perimeter around them, just in case the terrorists had lured them there. They all searched high and low for Maddy's satphone.

"Found it." Bullfrog held up a rectangle. "Still has some battery left," he observed passing it to Sam.

Resisting the urge to put the phone to his nose, perhaps to catch a trace of Maddy's essence, Sam powered it down, preserving whatever battery power it had left and sliding it into his thigh pocket. "Bronco, you see any registration papers?" he called up front. "Anything with an address on it?"

Bronco had just torn through the glove box. "Negative, sir."

Sam swallowed down his disappointment. The van had been their only lead. "Any chance you can follow the tracks we saw on the photos?"

They climbed out of the van to look for them.

"What do you see?" Sam asked as Bronco bent to study the sandy ground through his NVGs. He flipped them up and looked again. In his youth, he'd been trained by a Crow Indian to track game. His blue eyes seemed to burn through the preternatural darkness. He stood up slowly and shook his head. "I'm sorry, sir, but the wind's blown them away."

Mother Nature had conspired against them. With a bitter taste in his mouth, Sam admitted defeat. "Haiku," he called to his communications specialist, "tell the head shed to come and pick us up."

Their search for Maddy had hit another wall.

"Why do you work for GEF when your father owns Scott Oil Corporation?" Salim's question, coming at the heels of their luncheon the following day, made Maddy set aside her pita and hummus as she deliberated what to say.

In the day and a half that she had remained in his

room, guarded either by him or by Nasrallah, she had lost any lingering fear of ravishment or torture—at least at their hands. Only the others, whose restlessness she sensed and could sometimes hear, remained a threat. But for the time being, the warm upstairs chamber felt as secure a place as any. If only she were free to leave it.

"Well, I've always fretted about the impact of fracking on the environment," she answered honestly. "I studied environmental policy in college, so the work is a good fit."

"But what if you discover that the wells have corrupted El Chaco irrevocably and that the region will never be the same again?"

Maddy shrugged one shoulder. "Actually, I was expecting to find that to be the case, but our tests have shown no significant levels of toxins anywhere."

Salim's expression grew disdainful. "Really. None whatsoever?" It was obvious he didn't believe her.

"What are you implying?" she challenged him. He seemed to be suggesting, as Ricardo had once implied, that Scott Oil had planted her at GEF so she could manipulate the testing to make the oil industry look good.

He startled her by whipping out his cellphone, the same Motorola with which he'd filmed her ransom video. "I have pictures to show you," he announced, thumbing his keypad. He scooted closer, holding his phone before her eyes and scrolling through a number of pictures that made Maddy's eyes widen and her heart grow heavy.

"Where did you take these?" she asked, dismayed by visions of dead cattle, rotting under a hot sun and a swarm of flies.

"Twenty kilometers south of the Guaraní village, not far from the Pilcomayo River. The toxins have built up there. They've seeped into the surrounding soil, poisoning the flora which these cows have eaten. Now they are dying. The people eat the cows and drink their milk. What will happen to them?"

Maddy thought of the elders' complaints about gastro-intestinal trouble and dizziness—were those early symptoms of encroaching cancers? If so, then it was just as her mother feared. She shook her head in dismay. "I've only seen something like this once," she admitted, recalling the hapless cow belonging to the native ranchers.

Salim sat back, putting his phone away. "Perhaps you've been directed to run your tests in the wrong areas. The effect of the oil wells is obvious if you ask the residents where to look."

Was it possible that GEF had directed them to collect soil and water samples in the wrong places? She didn't speak Guaraní. Perhaps, if she had, she would have known where to look. But why would GEF not want the truth about the toxic waste to be known? Unless they'd been bought off by Scott Oil, she considered. Or even the U.S. government. Salim's accusing gaze seemed to suggest that was the case, and that he believed Maddy to be in on it.

She seized his forearm, gripping it hard. "I am not working for my father," she insisted. "My mother was an environmentalist like me. She opposed drilling in El Chaco ten years ago, and I have issues with it myself. If I find out that Scott Oil has bribed GEF in any way to keep them from finding the kind of destruction that you've seen, I swear to you, I will expose the corporation and force Scott Oil to make restitution."

The tight accusative expression on his face softened toward conviction and then gratitude. "I believe you," he replied.

The intimate and emotional energy arcing between them propelled Maddy to her feet. Confused, feeling that in some strange way she was betraying Sam, she crossed the room to one of the two barred windows. She had peered out of this one many times before, praying each time for Sam and his SEALs to materialize out of thin air and rescue her.

Her captors' home stood in a grassy area, with no adjacent neighbors, but with several houses behind their own walls, not too far away. If she ever managed to escape this room, this house, she would run to them for help.

"Madison."

Salim's voice sounded practically in her ear, making her jump. She hadn't heard him get up. His hands settled gently on either of her shoulders. She could feel the heat of his palms burning through the cloying fabric of the *chapan* he made her wear. If she hadn't ever met Sam, hadn't known the roaring power of their physical attraction, she might have thought herself drawn to Salim's gentle touch. It didn't frighten her the way it ought to. If anything, she felt comforted by the physical contact but, to her, it wasn't sexual. She let him turn her around so that she faced him.

"I think we have more in common than you realize," he said. His striking eyes roamed her face centering on her lips.

She realized he was poised to kiss her when he started to incline his head. "Please don't," she whispered, her spine stiffening.

His gaze reflected puzzlement. "I won't hurt you," he swore. "You and I were meant for each other. Don't you see? With your help, my protests have credibility. Together, we can keep El Chaco untainted. We can expose the corporation exploiting her purity."

His words mesmerized her, for she would like nothing better than to leave the children of Paraguay such a legacy, but his offer came with an unspoken implication. She would have to become his woman to accomplish such a feat. "I can't." She shook her head, picturing Sam's brooding gaze.

"Why not?" Salim pressed, still patient. "I'm well educated. I come from a good family. Is it my religion?"

She could have cared less about his religion. "Of course not." She shrugged his hands, catching them in hers to show her willingness to be friends. "You're a good man, Salim. But I've given my heart to someone else."

Until that moment, she hadn't fully realized that was true. She'd wanted so badly to remain a free spirit, a woman on a mission. But the truth was, she'd belonged to Sam since the night he'd kissed her on the bridge behind her father's house. Whatever mysterious claim he had on her, it had begun there if not sooner. No wonder she hadn't been able to get him out of her head!

But seeing the disillusionment harden Salim's handsome face, she both regretted the truth and resented it. Why Sam? Why couldn't she just banish him and all the complications that a relationship with him entailed and accept the offer of something more with Salim? Well, for one thing, Salim associated with some questionable characters. His radical efforts to eject North American enterprise frightened her.

"If you help me escape, I will help you," she promised him steadily.

Getting no immediate objection, she pursued her proposal. "My father is a reasonable man. If he saw your pictures and received lab reports to corroborate them, he would address the situation immediately."

"You said your uncle now runs the company,"
Salim countered on a flat note. The idealistic flame
burning in his eyes earlier had fled, making him look
suddenly older than his twenty-something years.

"Yes, but he'll do whatever my father asks him." At
least she hoped that to be the case. "Please," she
added, dismayed by the distant way in which he held
her hands. "Let me go, and I swear I will rectify these
issues with the environment. Nothing would please
me more."

A thin smile curled up the edges of Salim's mouth.
"It's too late for that," he said. Dropping her hands, he
turned his back on her, and Maddy's hopes crumbled
to dust. She watched him cross the room where he
gathered her plate of half-eaten food, carried it to the
door, and let himself out. She heard him mutter orders
to Nasrallah, no doubt to alert him if he heard
anything suspicious.

By kidnapping the daughter of Scott Oil
Corporation, he had set the ball rolling toward some
unknown catastrophe. Maddy held little hope of her
situation ending on a positive note—not for her, not
for Salim, not even for the country he loved.

Sam let himself into Maddy's condo using a credit
card. The scent of lemon cleaner blended pleasantly
with her one-of-a-kind fragrance, just the scent of
which made his stomach churn with desperate
wanting. The sun reflected brightly off her kitchen
countertops and table. Everything looked so neat and
orderly.

Drawn to her bedroom, he stood at the door to
regard the bed where they'd lost themselves to
passion. While neatly made, the coverlet bore the
impression of Maddy's body. She'd lain there,
perhaps reading the leather bound book, lying face-

down on her nightstand.

Curious, Sam crossed the room to pick it up. The realization that it was a journal had him sinking down on the bed, instantly intrigued and thinking he'd stumbled upon Maddy's diary. Except the dates at the top of each entry were ten years old. He skimmed several passages, absorbing the words of an intelligent woman on a passionate mission to improve the environment. It sounded just like Maddy talking, except Maddy had been a teenager at the time, which meant this journal was probably her mother's.

Sam looked up, thinking back to what he'd read in Maddy's file about her mother. An avid environmentalist, Melinda Scott's plane had crashed into the Pantanal region of Brazil on her way home from Paraguay a decade earlier. Understanding dawned like a sunrise in his mind. Maddy had made it her life's mission to fill her mother's shoes.

Suddenly he understood her—so clearly that it took his breath away.

No wonder she cared so little about her personal safety, her own comforts. She was chasing after a spirit, perhaps hoping to be reunited with her eventually.

A shiver coursed Sam's spine.

A knock at the door had him setting down the journal with a guilty start. Certain it was one of his leading petty officers, whom he'd instructed to fetch him the moment the SEALs got news, he hurried to answer.

Bullfrog's half smile beat back Sam's foreboding. "We've got a lead," he said. Dimples flashed on his lean cheeks.

"What lead?" Sam joined him on the stoop, locking the door from the inside and shutting it behind him.

"GEF received an email with a video link to

YouTube. The terrorists posted a ransom video online, probably figuring it couldn't be traced."

Hope vied with dread at the prospect of seeing Maddy in her captor's clutches. On YouTube, a video like that wouldn't stay secret for long.

"The CO's waiting so we can all watch it together."

Sam leaped off the stoop with Bullfrog right behind him.

In the TOC, he found every SEAL in the task unit already seated, eyes glued to the Internet browser projected on the large monitor.

"There you are," the CO boomed as Sam joined them, muttering an apology. "Have a seat."

Sam dropped into the only empty seat left in the room. Someone cut the lights. Mad Max clicked the link, and Sam found himself staring at Maddy wearing Middle-Eastern garb, even a scarf over her bright head. A lump of helplessness swelled in his throat as the camera focused on her luminous eyes, wet with tears she refused to shed.

The window behind her was barred. He could hear a rooster crow. Then a male voice declared in a cultured, British accent, that Madison Scott, an employee of the Global Environmental Fund, would remain a hostage of the National Liberation Army of Paraguay unless Scott Oil Corporation met their demands.

Sam catalogued clues as he listened to the terrorist's demands. The speaker had obviously been educated in England, and sounded polished. Given the view through the window, Maddy was being held on a second floor. A crowing rooster suggested the location was set in a rural area, not in the heart of town.

"Our demands are simple," the voice continued. "We require Scott Oil Corporation to cease operations entirely until a majority of its shares are owned by Paraguayan investors. The sale of shares must be offered before closing hours Friday or the hostage will be put to death."

Sam flicked the CO a look of disbelief. Those were the only demands? Aside from the threat of death, it sounded all too reasonable, not like the radical demands for which Hezbollah was famous. Surely Lyle Scott would do whatever it took to get Scott Oil Corporation to offer shares to Paraguayan investors. But wait. Lyle Scott wasn't the CEO of Scott Oil Corporation anymore—Van Slyke was.

The screen flickered and the video ended at just over a minute in length.

"How has GEF responded?" Sam wanted to know.

"They haven't. But I understand they're in touch with Lyle Scott, who has already spoken with General DePuy. SOCOM wants us to locate the hostage and neutralize the situation ASAP before the terrorists realize whose daughter she is. JSOTF is deliberating. Once Hezbollah realizes her political value, they'll leverage it for all she's worth. The FBI's been authorized to help."

Sam swallowed hard. Why couldn't Scott Oil just make this easy by meeting the terrorists' demands?

"The problem is keeping news of this YouTube video from leaking to the media. Chances are they'll identify the hostage as Lyle Scott's daughter and it'll all be over."

Worse and worse, Sam thought.

"The FBI is working with Google now to get the video taken down. But there is one plus to having it posted on the Web. You want to tell them, Luther?"

The towering ops officer cleared his throat. "Based on the Internet Service Provider's IP address and cashing servers used to upload this video, the FBI narrowed down the estimated location of the upload to a region on the northeast side of town."

Hope stormed Sam's heart like Marines assaulting a beach.

"We're getting closer." Lt. Lindstrom gestured to the blank screen. "Adding clues from the video, like the fact that she's being held on a second floor—there aren't that many two storied structures on the northeast side—we can narrow down her location to maybe half a dozen buildings within a five-square-mile area."

Kuzinsky, who'd been quiet up to that point, stood up at the CO's nod. "Here's what we're going to do," he began.


A shout downstairs jarred Maddy from a light slumber. She sat up slowly on the spare bed. Salim hadn't returned in the wake of the proposal she'd rejected. Left alone in the room for hours, she'd finally succumbed to sleep after the sun went down.

With Nasrallah presumably still outside her door, armed to the teeth, she heard Salim downstairs with the Hezbollah volunteers. Earlier, the sound of a television show suggested that they may have mended their differences, a circumstance that had reassured Maddy sufficiently to fall asleep. Now, however, the angry accusations floating through the floorboards suggested the truce was over.

Straining to hear over her pounding heart, she wondered how the current disagreement might impact her safety. Aside from a hint of moonlight patterning the tiled floor, the room stood in darkness. The faint hoot of an owl floated through the barred window. Salim's voice, familiar to her now, was the easiest to discern. He sounded defensive, angry. She put her feet to the cool floor, crossed to a window, and peered longingly outside. The buildings she could see—so close yet impossible to reach—tormented her.

The sudden thunder of footsteps, accompanied by a warning cry, had her whirling toward the door in alarm. Salim barked urgent instructions to his brother. The lock released, and he burst into the room, stepping through a wedge of moonlight that illuminated his furious expression as he locked the door behind him. Breathing hard, he surveyed her standing by the window.

"I'm so sorry," he said on a wrenching note.

It brought her closer. "What's wrong? What's happening?" she asked, knowing an urge to comfort him. Foreboding put a vice grip on the muscles at the base of her neck.

"The others have discovered who you are—who you *really* are. It was on the news, word of your kidnapping. My mistake. The media identified you as the daughter of the founder of Scott Oil. I should never have posted the video online. Now that Ashraf and Musa know, they want to take you back to Beruit with them. Tonight. I forbade them," he added with a tremor in his voice. Apprehension seemed to ooze from his pores.

Doubt and fear speared her. "Will they listen to you?" she whispered.

He took a sudden step forward capturing her hands. She could feel his fingers trembling, and it did nothing to ease her rising terror. "I will protect you with my life," he promised.

Shock ricocheted through Maddy's body. *This is it.* Counting on Salim's protection, she had hoped that she would ultimately be spared, but his portentous words betrayed uncertainty. His colleagues had turned on him, denied his status as their leader, and were making plans to wrest her from his control.

The sudden bark of gunfire from the bottom of the steps startled them both and confirmed her fears. Salim drew her swiftly toward the bathroom. "Stay inside and do not come out," he said, pressing an object into her hand.

Maddy looked down, recognizing the dagger Nasrallah had used to cut off her cuffs the other day. Frozen in terror, she stared as Salim started to draw the door shut then hesitated. She knew what he would do next and made no move to stop him this time. Catching her jaw in his hand, he dipped his head and pressed a heartfelt kiss to her lips. His soft beard tickled her face. His gentle lips tasted of fear and farewell.

"I'm sorry," he repeated, stepping back. The door closed behind him, and Maddy quickly locked it, acknowledging with a sick lurch in her stomach that it wouldn't keep anyone out for long.

# CHAPTER 12

Sam held up a hand, signaling for the men ghosting him to hold their position. Leaning into the shadows of a stucco wall he thumbed his mike. "Did you hear that?" he whispered.

"Gunfire," Bronco corroborated. "Couple of blocks west."

Relying on Brantley Adam's excellent judgment, Sam directed the majority of his platoon west, while sending two scouts in the opposite direction. They shouldn't put all their eggs in one basket.

Every dwelling on the northeast side of Mariscal Estigarribia looked the same—a squat cinderblock or adobe structure surrounded by a yard and an eight-foot wall. Their primary objective was to locate and map every structure with two or more stories and leave two men observing it. They'd encountered four two-story structures so far, which left six men including him and two more on the prowl.

Keeping his footfalls stealthy, Sam turned down a narrow road pitted with pot holes. *Where are you, Maddy?* He swore that he could smell her somewhere close by, or was the fragrance of climbing Bougainvillea playing tricks on his senses?

The majority of the homes stood in darkness, their occupants sleeping. His toe made contact with an aluminum can, and it rolled into the street, prompting a dog to bark. Sam stilled. That was when he heard it, another spate of semi-automatic gunfire.

"Talk to me, Chief," he exhorted Bronco.

"Dead ahead, sir. Coming from across the field, on the other side of those palm trees. See the light? Right there."

"Everyone, pick it up," Sam ordered, breaking into a run.

The *rat-tat-tat* of semi-automatic gunfire sounded like cannons going off.

Maddy pressed herself into the corner of the tiled shower, one hand clamped over an ear, the other gripping the dagger for dear life. The thud of a body hitting the floor brought a whimper to her lips as she pictured young Nasrallah sprawled in the hallway, imagined the scarred devil and his companion stepping over him to throw their shoulders into the bedroom door.

They fired at the lock, instead. An answering volley came from inside the room as Salim sought to defend himself.

*Thud.* Another body hit the ground on the other side of the wall as one of the assailants fell.

Then a voice—not Salim's—shouted threats from the hall into the bedroom. Salim called back what was clearly a refusal to surrender. Maddy's heart thundered into the silence that followed.

Then an angry roar preceded an equally violent exchange of gunfire. Eyes closed, teeth gritted, Maddy cringed, praying for the noise to end, for Salim to be the victor. Something hit the bathroom door and slid down it, and in her mind's eye she pictured her protector, his eyes open, blood sliding from one corner of his mouth as he gasped his final breaths. *Oh, no.*

Fury edged aside Maddy's terror. She drew herself upright. How dare the Hezbollah volunteers betray their leader, their host! She would *not* let them take her. She would *not* become a hostage of Hezbollah! *Never!*

Her lungs expanded on an indrawn breath. Adrenaline galvanized her rigid muscles. Over the thundering of her heart, she could hear the ceramic lamp crackling under the footsteps. Salim's killer stopped before his victim. Hissing ugly words, he shoved the body aside. It fell like a sack of potatoes. The doorknob jiggled.

Tucked behind the door in the shower stall, Maddy begged her mother's spirit for strength. The door shuddered as the terrorist threw his shoulder into it. The frame gave a crack. Another hit, and it would give. Maddy tightened her grip on the dagger.

*Crack!* The door flew open, blocking her view of the intruder. She held her breath. Timing meant everything. She could sense him plumbing the dark room with his eyes, searching for her. The snout of his semi-automatic pistol slid past the door. If she waited too long, he would sense her presence right beside him.

*Now!* Maddy stepped from the shower, grabbed the barrel and yanked, pulling her assailant into the room and straight into her outstretched hand, the one gripping the dagger. The blade met resistance in the form of his clothing, but then it slid with astonishing ease into his abdomen. She gave it an extra shove.

With a choked exclamation, the terrorist stepped back, pulling on the trigger. As Maddy leaped back into the shower out of harm's way, bullets spewed the sink and mirror, shattering porcelain and glass, sending shards flying. The assailant staggered, let up on the trigger, and turned to regard her in astonishment.

In the uncertain light she recognized him as the scarred devil who had slapped her, the one who had most likely killed Enrique. The dagger poked obscenely from his midsection.

He weaved on his feet, raising his weapon to shoot her at point blank range.

"No you don't," she snarled in a voice that raised the hairs on the back of her own neck. Jackknifing one leg, she shoved off the shower wall and struck her heel into his groin, sending him crashing into the wall opposite. Bullets strafed the tiles next to her shoulder, then the ceiling as he lost his balance. With a click, he ran abruptly out of ammunition.

Maddy didn't wait to see if he would die. Darting past his listing form, she dashed into the room, only to draw up short at the sight of Salim, sprawled across the rug, his torso glistening with bullet wounds.

He turned his head, miraculously still alive, and looked at her.

"I'll go get help," she promised, her heart in her throat. "You'll be all right."

He whispered something unintelligible as she sprang up again. Legs unsteady, she lurched for the door. *I'm free!* Horror usurped her giddiness as she stumbled upon Nasrallah, lying face down in a pool of his own blood, the second Hezbollah volunteer draped over him.

With a sob, she edged around them. Down the stairs she flew, terrified of encountering more terrorists, relieved to find the house empty. A small TV lit the lower level, filling it with the discordant sounds of a television game show and canned applause.

Disoriented, it took her a moment to find the exit, situated in the kitchen.

She threw herself outside without looking first, running into fresh balmy air, a dark yard, and the arms of a stranger who sprang out of the shadows to grab her.

"It's me! Maddy, it's me," Sam exclaimed, hushing her scream of terror.

She focused wild eyes on him. Gasping a breath of relief, she buried her face against his shoulder, shaking silently as he dragged her away from the house, behind the wall that circumscribed it. There, he tabbed his mike. "Target recovered. I say again, we have the target."

Across the field separating this house from the others, lights blinked on in several of the adjacent buildings. The firefight had awakened the neighbors. They were bound to draw attention to themselves.

Maddy shuddered against him. He pulled her closer, holding all her weight as her legs seemed to give out.

"You're okay," he crooned. Sweeping a palm over the silky fall of her hair, he wrestled back the urge to break down and sob—he was that relieved to have her back alive, but they'd yet to secure the area. "Tell me what's going on," he requested, prying her gently off him so he could see her face, ascertain whether she was hurt.

She peered back at him, visibly shocked, and he took quick inventory of her injuries—a cut on her forehead, another on her lip. She was still wearing the *chapan* she'd worn in the ransom video. It covered her from head to toe, but she appeared otherwise unharmed.

"There are two still alive," she whispered, her horror evident. "I stabbed the scarred devil, but he's not dead yet."

No sooner had he keyed his mike alerting his platoon than a spate of semi-automatic gunfire hailed down from the second story window, peppering the other side of the wall and sending Sam sprawling over Maddy just in case.

"He's still alive!" she cried, stiffening with fear beneath him.

"It's okay. We can take him, Maddy." Craning his neck, he could see Bronco waving platoon members into position.

Carl Wolfe pulled the pin out of a smoke grenade and launched it over the wall where it rolled in the sand before spewing a lovely violet cloud that concealed the SEALs as they scurried furtively toward the entrance, skirting the path of the bullets and preparing to storm the house. But before they stepped so much as a foot inside, a single shot rang out, and the semi-automatic gunfire ceased.

What the hell just happened? Sam wondered.

In his earpiece, the scuffle of rapid footsteps announced the SEALs' push into the house.

"What's going on?" Maddy asked in a frayed voice.

"It's almost over," he crooned, wanting to wipe that haunted expression off her face forever.

"Bullfrog, we need you up here," Bronco said over the inter-team radio.

Apparently, the medic's services were needed, telling Sam that someone was alive, but who? "Sit rep," he demanded, unwilling to get up and check for himself.

"We've got two dead and two men down, both bleeding out. One is definitely that Al-Sadr motherfucker, the other one unknown."

"Salim," Maddy whispered, making Sam wonder if she could overhear his chief.

"Try to keep them both alive," Sam retorted, recalling Kuzinsky's orders.

"Not gonna happen, sir. Al-Sadr was shot in the back by the guy we can't identify. Bullet's in his heart."

"What about the other guy?"

"Multiple gunshot wounds to the chest. Weak vitals. He's on his way out."

*Damn.* Sam had wanted to try at least one of the bastards for putting Maddy through hell. The silhouettes of neighbors coming out of their houses wrested his attention toward other matters.

"Haiku, call for immediate extraction," he ordered. Shifting his weight to his knees, he drew Maddy to a seated position. "You okay, *querida*?" The endearment slipped out of him as naturally as breathing. Tipping her chin so she was forced to look into his eyes, he added, "Christ, I am never letting you out of my sight again."

He halfway expected her to protest his assertion. Instead, she fastened her clear wide eyes on him and declared, "I don't ever want you to."


Maddy sat curled up in a ball in her bathtub while the shower rained down on her in a steady warm stream.

*It's over*, she told herself as she'd already done about a hundred times in an effort to subdue the shudders that still wracked her naked frame. Minute by minute, the horror of her captivity and the shock engendered by the violence she'd witnessed trickled down her limbs, out of her hands and feet, and swirled down the drain.

Sam's colleague, a medic with large gentle hands and empathetic eyes had looked her over. "Name's Jeremiah," he'd told her, declaring her to be in good shape. "You're one lucky lady," he'd added.

She boasted a cut just above her eyebrow and another on her lip, but the rest of her had emerged unscathed. And when he'd tactfully inquired whether her captors had hurt her in any way, she'd been able to reply in the negative because Salim, who'd been dead by the time they'd slid his stretcher into the back of one of the Humvees, had kept his word. He'd protected her with his life. With his final gasps, he'd even shot the scarred devil trying to hamper her escape.

A wave of grief pegged Maddy in the chest. Her face crumpled and hot tears mingled with the water that was slowly turning colder. She would never forget Salim's gentleness, nor his apology accompanied by the bittersweet kiss he'd planted on her lips. A vision of Nasrallah, who could not have been more than eighteen, lying in a pool of blood made her sob suddenly. She let herself weep quietly, to honor them both for their willingness to die for a cause they believed in. In that regard, they were kindred spirits, she and the brothers.

By degrees, the low timbre of male voices penetrated Maddy's awareness. Someone, probably Sam, had joined the medic Jeremiah in her living room. With a sharp sniff, Maddy pulled herself together. She couldn't let the men think the trauma of her captivity had broken her spirit. Not at all. If anything, Salim's quest to hold Scott Oil accountable for the slow poisoning of El Chaco bolstered her own resolve.

Shutting off the water, she pushed to her feet, wondering how long she'd dawdled. It was time to shake off recent horrors and move forward. There was work yet to be done.

Toweling off, she girded herself in a thin cotton

robe and ventured out of the bathroom. At the sound of the door opening, Sam and Jeremiah both turned to look.

Sam cast a protective gaze over her.

"There she is," the medic said. When neither Sam nor Maddy acknowledged him, he added, "I'd better be heading back." He tossed a knowing smile over his shoulder as he pulled her front door shut behind him.

In some form of silent agreement, Sam and Maddy split the distance between them, meeting in the middle of the room. "I called your father," he volunteered, his unwavering gaze still fixed on her face, possessive, concerned. "Have you ever heard a grown man cry?"

"He does that all the time," she assured him, noting that Sam had scrubbed his face, removing all traces of the dark paint that had covered it earlier. "He's really a big softy."

"He wants to talk to you, no matter how late it is. You can call him. Look." He led her over to the kitchen counter where her phone sat charging.

"You found it," she exclaimed, picking it up and hugging it to her chest—her lifeline to civilization.

"Sure did. That was good thinking hiding it in the van," he praised. "Might have worked, too, if they hadn't abandoned the vehicle out in the middle of nowhere."

She put the phone down, thrusting away the memory of that awful night. "I'll call my father tomorrow," she decided. He would expect her to come home right away, and right now she didn't have the heart to verbally defy him. Looking up at Sam, she found him hovering protectively. His unwavering gaze made her sharply conscious of her nakedness under the thin robe.

"How are you doing, *querida*?" His gruff, gentle tone had a curious, tingling effect on her nipples. His astute gaze took in everything about her face, from her red-rimmed eyes to the cuts that gave testimony to her nightmare.

"I'm good," she said breathlessly.

A spasm of pain hardened his features briefly. "I thought I'd never see you again." He shook his head. "You're so damn lucky to be alive."

"It wasn't luck," she told him, sharing a part of herself she rarely shared with anyone. "It was fate. My mother's spirit watches over me. She kept me safe so I could finish the work she started."

His torn expression made it clear he didn't fully believe her. "Maddy." Her name sounded as if it were torn from his chest. His warm hands gently cupped her face. With a slight tremor in his fingers, he caressed the cut on her lip with his thumb, the one above her eye with his index finger. "Please," he implored, his voice rough with emotion, "please don't put me through anything like this ever again."

If he'd said it any other way, she might have taken exception to his request. But how could she resent his desire to keep her out of harm when he begged her so honestly?

"I'll try not to," she promised. She had no intention of ever being kidnapped again, if that meant anything.

Tears of what might have been relief put a sheen in his eyes. "You must be tired," he said, dropping his hands to her upper arms. "Would you like to rest?"

She glanced thoughtfully toward her bedroom. Honestly, she was too keyed up to sleep.

"I can just hold you if you'd like," he said, stroking her arms through the sleeves of her robe, stirring her desire unintentionally.

"I don't want to sleep," she said, hearing his breath suspend as he waited for her to say more. "But I would like to go to bed," she hinted, boldly.

Comprehension lit his green eyes from the inside out. He gave her one last chance to change her mind. "By yourself or with me?" he asked.

"With you, silly." Sliding her arms around his neck, Maddy rolled up on her tiptoes and carefully touched her lips to his. His indrawn breath and the tightening of his arm around her waist emboldened her to deepen the kiss, parting her lips in invitation. Desire warmed her blood, banishing the last remnants of shock that had congealed in her belly.

With infinite gentleness, Sam accepted her offer. The sweet, seductive glide of his tongue against hers made her moan into his mouth.

In the next instant, he was sweeping her up into his arms, carrying her with long strides into the bedroom where he promptly kicked the door shut. Keeping the light on, he deposited her gently in the center of her bed before stepping away to draw the curtains shut. "I want to see you this time," he explained. "Do you mind?"

She shivered with expectancy. "Only if I get to see you, too." The last time they'd gone this far, he'd left his clothes on. "Is anyone going to knock on the door and interrupt us?"

"Not if they value their lives," he grated, tackling the buttons on his BDU jacket. He shrugged it off before stripping off the tan T-shirt under it with equal expedience. She feasted her gaze on what lay beneath it—olive-toned skin, a flat abdomen rippling with defined muscles, raised pectorals with a dusting of dark hair between them, broad shoulders and powerful arms. A vision of Salim's hairy chest flashed briefly through her mind before she banished it.

"You look good," she admitted, focusing her attention on the black-ink tattoo that adorned his right arm from bicep to shoulder. "What's your tattoo about?"

He turned his shoulder to show it to her. "It's my grandmother's family crest. When Castro took over, her family was forced to flee. She still takes pride in her heritage."

"So do you," she pointed out. "It looks really sexy on you."

He shot her a grin. "Thanks." And then the show continued as he shucked off his boots. With an intentional slowness, he unbuttoned the fly of his desert-pattern cammies then pushed them down and off his legs, discarding his boxer briefs in the same fluid movement. Maddy's mouth went dry at the vision of him, completely nude, blatantly aroused, enduring her wide-eyed scrutiny with mixed confidence and vulnerability. "How do I look now?"

If she told him the truth—that she'd never in her life seen a man as gorgeous as he was—he'd get an overblown ego. "I think I'm overdressed," she said simply, sitting up to take off her robe.

"Oh, no, that's my job," he protested, pushing her gently back and coming to kneel over her.

She watched him undress her, studying every nuance of his reaction as he did so, all but panting with anticipation as he tugged at the belt that kept her gown closed. With reverence in his expression, he peeled back the two halves the way a kid would take the wrapper off his favorite sweet, only more slowly.

"*Dios,*" he muttered, inspecting every curve and indent now exposed to him. And then he looked her in the eye. "Do you know how much I've regretted not making love to you the last time?" he asked thickly.

Unexpected relief clogged her throat. How gratifying to know she wasn't the only one who'd entertained that regret.

"I was so afraid I'd never get the chance again.

Maddy, you're the most beautiful, most sexy, most *maddening* woman I've ever met."

"Hence the name?" she teased. Her close call had brought them to the same realization. They were meant for each other.

Desire drew his face taut. Stretching his frame over hers, he settled his weight over her body and claimed her mouth with a kiss that promised heaven. Tears of gratitude that she had lived to experience this moment slipped from the edges of her eyes. He caught sight of them, raising his head with a frown of worry.

"I'm okay," she said before he could question her. "I'm more than okay." And she pulled him down to kiss her again, adjusting her body so that their skin touched from shoulder to ankle, a perfect fit.

And then his lips seemed to be everywhere at once—on her mouth, her neck, her breasts, back to her mouth—inciting a craving to be utterly consumed by him. She touched him, in turn, filling her hands with his dense muscle, his smooth skin.

A scar pinched the muscle under his left arm, another slashed his forearm. Envisioning the type of injuries he'd sustained to cause them only increased her gratitude for this life-affirming moment. They had both survived perils in order to arrive at this place in time, a connection that might possibly alter the course of both their lives.

He slid his hand down the plane of her belly between her hips, pressing the heel of his palm into the valley between her pelvic bones. She arched in welcome, inviting his fingers to furrow through her honey-colored hair into the moist cleft below.

Her soft cry of encouragement urged him to repeat the caress, centering his attention on the swollen nubbin there, so sensitive that each glide of his fingers threatened to send her toppling off a cliff.

"Please," she implored, not wanting to take that plunge alone. She caught his tumescence in her hand, stroking him, marveling at the flagrant masculinity of his form, encouraging him with wanton words to take her now, to take all of her.

He shot her a scalding look that promised that and more, spread her legs with his knees, and settled himself between her thighs. The head of his sex nudged her opening and retreated. Maddy gasped, bracing herself for his possession, for the torrid pleasure she sensed about to consume her. He encroached again, studying her face in the lamplight as he slowly and intently filled her.

*Yes. Oh, God.* She fought to keep her eyelids from drifting shut as ecstasy stormed her senses. *This moment,* she thought, committing it to her memory forever, *will sustain me no matter what the future holds.*

Sam had never seen anything so sexy in his life— Maddy's gaze unfocused, her moist lips parted so enticingly that he longed to kiss her, but then he wouldn't be able to watch her response to his possession.

She yielded in a way that enthralled him, their bodies moving in perfect sync, in a dance as old as time. Breaths mingled in a duet of delicious discovery, muscles tightened in a relentless compulsion to pursue this insatiable wanting to its ultimate destination.

"Sam," she breathed. A sheen of sweat glinted between her swaying breasts. She coiled her legs around his back, using them to pull him harder, deeper into her.

"Yes, baby?"

"I always knew this was going to happen."

He gave a pained laugh. He'd been terrified something bad would happen to her to prevent it. Gratitude overwhelmed him suddenly, compelling him to bow his head and catch that kiss he'd been craving.

His senses immediately overloaded. The dance of their tongues in tandem with the sinuous movements of her body hurtled him toward climax. He tried to hold it off, to bring Maddy to release first, but then he realized that her keening cry and the pulsing of her inner muscles signaled her timely arrival at the finish.

With a loud groan he relinquished control, panicking for a split second at the realization that he wasn't wearing a condom—hadn't even given it a thought. He tried to pull out, but it was a little too late. He had spent most of himself inside of her. Christ, he'd better not do that again.

He collapsed onto his side, pulling her over to rest against him. Their chests rose and fell together, their heart rates slowly subsiding. Sam adjusted the pillow under his head and looked down. A secret smile, so utterly feminine in its form, curved the lines of Maddy's mouth.

"I was afraid you'd get yourself killed before I got the chance," he said, picking up the conversation where they'd left off.

She arched an eyebrow at him. "Is that why you didn't want me heading overseas? Afraid you'd never get me into bed?"

"Something like that," he admitted. Actually, his fears went way beyond that, but why bring up a sore subject? Only, he couldn't avoid it. "Maddy, I'm not going to be here much longer. Now that the threat to the oil wells has been pretty much eliminated, we're going to write our reports and head home. The CO wants us gone before the media finds us."

A troubled expression crossed her face.

"Did you...have plans?" he asked, keeping his question vague for fear of offending her and ruining this blissful moment.

Her gaze slid off to one side and he just knew he wasn't going to like what he was about to hear. "I think I'll hang out in McLean for a while," she said, surprising and relieving his fears. "But first I have to run a few more tests." His momentary relief gave way to nagging concern.

"Why?" he asked as gently as possible. "Can't GEF find someone else to take your place?"

"I can't trust GEF to take samples from the right area." She explained her suspicions that someone— Scott Oil, perhaps, or the U.S. government itself had influenced GEF to avoid sampling the area of El Chaco where Salim had taken his photos.

Earlier in the Humvee that transported them from the terrorists' house back to the military facility, she'd told Sam how Salim and his brother Nasrallah weren't members of Hezbollah. They were leaders of the National Liberation Army, Paraguayan patriots who had fought to keep El Chaco free from exploitation, to keep Scott Oil from profiting off the natural resources that belonged strictly to their adopted country.

The truth hit Sam like a sledgehammer: She wanted to prove Salim's allegations and then insure that Scott Oil kept its promises to Paraguay by making restitution for the damage done.

"Maddy, your dad's not the CEO anymore," he pointed out.

She frowned intently. "I know that. But just because my uncle's the CEO, that doesn't mean he doesn't still have a say in the company."

"Van Slyke is your uncle?" He pulled his head back to regard her in surprise. No wonder the man's eyes had reminded him of Maddy's.

"On my mother's side," she affirmed with a quizzical expression. "You make it sound like you know him."

"Yeah, I met him the other night. He's living in the big house on the hill."

"Seriously?" She had no idea her uncle was even in Paraguay. That might make her objective easier. She could convince him in person to open his doors to foreign investors, taking steps to undo the damage the wells had caused.

"Maybe you should stay with him," Sam proposed, warming to the idea. "Especially if you're still here after we pull out. I don't like the thought of you living alone."

"I'm not alone. Ricardo should be out of the hospital soon. Besides, I'm not staying long, maybe a week at the most."

He didn't know what else to say. Persuading Maddy to abandon a task she'd set her heart on was impossible—he already knew that. "When you get back to Virginia, we can get together," he proposed, confident that she'd say yes.

Her answering smile was nothing short of radiant. "I'm counting on it."

"Good." He knew he was grinning like an idiot.

She sat up a bit, propping her chin on her elbow. "I kind of like you, Sam Sasseville." The declaration ended on a great big yawn.

Christ, she was adorable. "I kind of like you, too, Maddy Scott," he admitted. "And I could probably make love again right now, but you need to rest."

A spark of interest lit her drooping eyes. "I'm not that tired."

"Yes, you are. Come on. I'll tuck you in."

"You can't stay with me?"

The fear lacing her voice had him rushing to reassure her. "I'll stay until dawn," he promised. "Like I said, we'll be busy tomorrow tying up loose ends." And he'd get maybe two hours of sleep, but who cared? He would gladly stay awake the rest of his life if it meant he could watch over Maddy.

He helped to situate them both under the covers. Maddy snuggled closer, releasing an exhausted but content sigh.

*I'm in paradise*, Sam reflected closing his eyes and savoring the silky length of her body tucked against him. *Paradise in El Chaco Boreal*. He supposed it was fitting. And if Maddy managed to hold Scott Oil Corporation accountable for the waste it was spilling into the soil, it might just remain a paradise forever.

# CHAPTER 13

—◆—

"Maddy!" Sam waited for a car to streak past him before darting across the street to where she was helping Ricardo step out of the Jeep. She swiveled toward his call, her smile putting the sub-equatorial sun beating down on his head to shame. It flooded him with giddy warmth.

"Hey, you're still here!" she exclaimed.

"We're on our way out," he admitted, and her sunny smile immediately faltered. He felt the same ambivalence about his leaving. Sensing someone watching their exchange, he turned his head to find Ricardo using the door of the Jeep to hold himself upright. "Need a hand?" he offered.

Ricardo waved him off.

"You know, I never did hear how you two know each other," Maddy stated, her eyebrows pulling together in a frown of confusion.

Lucía saved Sam from having to answer as she rushed out of the house to assist her husband. Sam turned his attention to Maddy. "Can we talk?" he added, gesturing toward her front stoop.

"Of course. I'm so glad I got to see you again."

The roof's eave cast a blessedly cool shadow over

them. Maddy visibly struggled to keep her smile pinned in place as she took both his hands in hers, squeezed them, and looked up at him. They said nothing for a moment, just gazed into each other's eyes. Sam thought of everything he'd been through with her and how damn lucky she was to be alive.

"Have you gone out and run your tests yet?" he finally asked.

"Not yet. I need Ricardo's help to talk to the Guaraní. They're the ones who can lead us to the right place. He's handy with a gun, too." She wet her lips with a little glide of her tongue that jolted his pulse and fueled his libido.

"Good. I didn't like the thought of you doing it alone," he admitted. Her scare with the terrorists had apparently left her with a modicum of common sense, thank God.

She tucked a strand of hair behind her ear in a careless-looking gesture. "So, you're leaving—like, right now?" Her plaintiff tone betrayed her actual disappointment.

He felt a little better hearing that she was as dismayed to let him go as he was to leave. "Yeah," he admitted. "In a couple of hours."

"It seems like you just got here."

To Sam, it had felt like an eternity—especially those three days in which Maddy had been held hostage.

"Do you have time to come in?" she asked earnestly.

He cast an assessing glance at the facility across the street. It was impossible to tell through the thick brick walls and narrow windows how frantically the SEALs were packing up their equipment, preparing to go wheels up before the press arrived looking for answers. He looked again into her lovely face.

"My CO wants me to ask you to abstain from

talking to the press if they request an interview," he said.

"Okay." She gave a visible shudder. "I'd rather not relive that experience anyway."

"Thanks." He stole a peek at his watch. He was supposed to come right back. But Bronco and Bullfrog would cover for him for at least another ten minutes. "I guess I could come in. I've got a couple of minutes, at least."

Brightening, she pulled her keys out of her pocket and unlocked the door for them.

As the door swung open, he swept her into the cool entryway, shut the door behind them and pressed her up against it, not wasting a second. Catching her sweet lips beneath his, he kissed her with all the desperate hunger that burned inside of him. He couldn't get enough of her, certainly not in the short amount of time they had.

Luckily for him, she seemed to feel the same way. Delving both hands under his T-shirt, she lightly scraped and kneaded his chest, arousing him so thoroughly that the bedroom seemed impossibly far away. He hauled his T-shirt over his head and divested her of her tank top. To his gratification she wasn't wearing a bra. He didn't have the patience or the time to deal with tricky little latches.

Gathering her beautiful breasts in his hands, he bent his head to feast on the firm, velvety buds. She slid her fingers through his hair, guiding his mouth from one nipple to the other, arching with visible pleasure. "Oh, Sam."

*Oh, Sam, what?* There seemed to be more words hovering on the tip of her tongue. He sank slowly to his knees, laving and nibbling a path down her hourglass shape. He released the button on her shorts and peeled them over her hips, kissing every inch of pale skin as he exposed it.

"Have mercy," she panted, sounding on the verge of bursting into laughter.

He speared his tongue into the curls at the apex of her thighs.

"Oh, God."

He did it again and again, causing her to moan and fall back, her shoulders propped against the door. Looking up the length of her luscious body, Sam watched with fascination as she visibly melted—eyes growing limpid, her dewy lips parting. Heat radiated off her body while that scent that had driven him crazy since he'd first met her rose into his nostrils, robbing him of all logical thought.

"Sam, please," she begged, tugging at his hair to get him to rise. "I need you. I need you with me now."

Her fingers went straight to his fly the moment he gained his feet. She released his arousal with sure hands and guided him between her legs in a blatant request to be filled—right here, right now. Hands on her bottom, he lifted her against him, found her slick entrance and slid home in one deep thrust.

Her cry of exhilaration inflamed him. She locked her arms around his neck, her legs around his hips and matched his frenzy as he drove himself into her. His mouth slanted over hers as they raced forward, trying to keep pace with cruel time that, even now, seemed to be pulling them apart.

Suddenly Maddy tensed, shouting his name on such a rapturous note that it unraveled him completely. Ecstasy exploded in Sam, rupturing like a volcano that sent magma spewing in all directions. He pushed his face into her neck with a muted roar, his knees threatening to buckle under the torrent of bliss that rained down on him. Holy God, that was…

*Unprotected, again*, his conscience pointed out.

Shit, he had a condom in his pocket and he'd totally forgotten to use it.

Reality sobered him at once. With his heart still racing, he let Maddy's feet slide down to the floor. Her legs nearly folded before she caught herself. Her suspiciously bright eyes wrested his thoughts from his deplorable lack of self-control.

"Don't be sad," he ordered, speaking as much to himself as to her.

"I'm not," she said, but she averted her face, bending down to pull her pants up.

"I'll come up and see you as soon as you get back to McLean," he promised, alleviating the weight on his own chest. "I've got your number now." After the effort it had taken to secure her number in order to find her phone, he'd promptly memorized all ten digits.

She sniffed lightly, wiped her nose, and looked up, sending him a brave smile. "Okay. I'll see you soon then," she added.

He loved how brave she was, how independent. She didn't cling to him like other women he'd been with—women who'd chased after him for the status it brought them to date a Navy SEAL. Maddy didn't seem to give a damn about status, perhaps because she already had it.

Cupping her face in his hands, he memorized the pattern of blues and grays in her irises, the cut above her eyebrow—it might leave a scar. Her freckle-dusted nose, the curve of her irreverent mouth. Just looking at her and knowing how much he would miss looking at her made his heart hurt.

"My uncle asked me to dinner tonight," she volunteered. "I'm going to take up Salim's complaints with him."

Sam envisioned Paul Van Slyke's charismatic smile

with inexplicable reservation. On the one hand, he was glad Maddy had family in this region, someone influential to turn to if she needed help. On the other, he still resented the man for presuming the SEALs were here to protect his interests, not American interests. "Something tells me he won't be very receptive."

She shrugged. "Probably not, but when did a little resistance ever stop me?" She shot him her one-of-a-kind grin.

"True." Resistance only doubled her determination. They were rather alike in that regard. "Wow, I just realized something," he admitted, giving voice to his discovery.

"What's that?"

"When you told me on the aircraft carrier that we're the same, you were right." He regarded her, dumbstruck. It was suddenly so clear to him. "We're exactly alike."

She play-punched him in his bare abs. "Now you admit it!"

He caught her wrist as she went to hit him again. "Hey, I'm just a little slow when it comes to these things," he confessed. "But then you don't listen so well yourself."

Her eyebrows snapped together. "How do I not listen?" she demanded.

He pointed a finger at her. "I told you to stay out of the hot spots."

She glared for a second at the finger then snapped her teeth as if to bite it off, and he drew it back with a laugh. "Okay, no lectures. Just a kiss, then."

Her eyes floated shut as she offered her lips up to him. He memorized the texture, the taste of her and then lifted his head regretfully. Her eyes opened again, misty with emotion, but she kept her mouth shut, withholding words she might regret, the same way he was.

Time would tell if they'd started something that could last.

"See you around, Lieutenant," she finally said, in a husky voice. He immediately recognized the parting words as the same farewell she'd tossed at him aboard the aircraft carrier.

A smile overcame his despondency. "I'm counting on it, Miss Scott." With that, he scooped his shirt up off the floor, glancing surreptitiously at his watch as he tunneled into it. Bronco and Bullfrog were probably hating him right now.

Chucking Maddy under the chin, he took one last look at her and let himself out.


Maddy leaned against the cool wood of the door, eyes closed, replaying her last few minutes alone with Sam. Unconsciously, her hands strayed up to cup her bare breasts as she relived the passion between them—passion attested by the sticky moisture seeping out of her.

Her condo seemed suddenly empty with him gone. She hadn't felt this lonely since her mother's death.

For once, she looked forward to going home to her father, but only because Sam would come and visit her there. As long as some new assignment didn't whisk him away, as long as she didn't feel compelled to address another global concern, they would date each other.

*What will that look like?* she wondered. Virginia Beach wasn't situated particularly close to northern Virginia, which meant they'd have to invest in a long-distance relationship.

With a shrug, she told herself they'd cross that bridge when they got to it. For now, the prospect of a relationship was exciting and new. And Sam had finally realized what she'd known all along—that they had more in common than met the eye.

With a sad but stoic sigh, Maddy snatched up her top and carried it to her bedroom in lieu of putting it back on. Her uncle's bodyguard was scheduled to pick her up at 5 PM. She had two hours in which to shower and dress and find something presentable to wear.


"Master Chief, what time did we tell the liaison officer we wanted the bus here?"

With an impatient stride, Mad Max paced the cafeteria where all thirty five members of his task unit waited with their gear to be taken to the runway. The room was packed with bodies and gear, and not nearly enough air coming through the open windows.

Kuzinsky stole a peek at his watch. "Half an hour ago, sir, but we're on South American time, remember?"

In South America, any scheduled event was going to run about an hour behind. As Mad Max muttered an oath and resumed his pacing, Sam went back to staring out the window at the Paraguayan Special Forces members wrestling in the yard behind the cafeteria. But he wasn't really watching them. He was missing Maddy, worrying that something would happen to her before they got together again.

A hand settled on his shoulder. "You okay, sir?"

Sam looked over to find Bullfrog standing behind him. Damn, and here he'd thought he was fooling everyone, even himself, by behaving outwardly cavalier about leaving her behind. "Yeah, sure," he said, turning slightly to acknowledge Bullfrog's concern.

Hazel eyes, so intelligent and discerning, studied his face with empathy that only magnified Sam's private despair.

Bullfrog sent him a pained smile. "Sucks to be in love," he observed before moving away.

Sam stared after the petty officer's retreating back and wondered what his medic knew about love. He'd never seen Jeremiah do anything but share polite conversation with the women at the club. He didn't go out and party, didn't go through girls like they were candy the way Bronco did. Sam had even wondered once if Jeremiah might be gay, except he'd never caught him staring at guys the way he stared at girls. *Sucks to be in love,* he'd said, making Sam wonder if Bullfrog wasn't committed to some woman he'd never mentioned. On the heels of that realization came stark and scary self-discovery.

Oh, hell. I am in love, he acknowledged. In love with the daughter of a billionaire. And I don't even like rich people.

The squeaking of the cafeteria door drew the attention of everyone in the room, including Sam. Instead of the liaison officer they were all expecting, Bamm-Bamm rushed into the room, a barely contained grin on his face. The CO and Kuzinsky regarded him with confusion, then looked over at Sam and Bronco, who headed in Bamm-Bamm's direction under the guise of chewing him out. Poor kid, he'd only been doing what his platoon leader had instructed—to make sure Maddy got safely into her uncle's car when he came to pick her up.

"Sir!" Bamm-Bamm exclaimed, his brown eyes dancing with excitement.

"Dial it down, PO3," Sam growled, blocking the CO and Master Chief's view by standing between them and the young SEAL.

"But you won't believe it," he gushed. He bounced on the balls of his feet, too excited to be still.

Bronco threw an arm around his shoulders to constrain his exuberance. "Believe what?" he demanded.

"The guy driving the car—her uncle's bodyguard. He's The Annihilator!"

"The what?" Bronco said.

"Who?" Sam asked.

"The 2005 World Wrestling Federation champion!" Bamm-Bamm practically bellowed. "Elliot Koch, The Annihilator."

Sam frowned at him. Okay, so maybe that was why Van Slyke's bodyguard had looked familiar. He used to be on TV.

"Is that a joke?" Bronco demanded with mock seriousness. "Elliot Cock, as in penis?"

"No, chief. It's a German name."

"Spell it for me."

"K-O-C-H." Bamm-Bamm rolled his eyes, clearly aware that Bronco was having fun with him. "I know it was him because I saw his championship ring—size of an egg—right there on his right hand."

Something in Sam's head went *click*. A vision of the bejeweled fist arcing toward his jaw had him sucking in a gasp of astonishment.

"What'd it look like?" he demanded, but he didn't really need to hear Bamm-Bamm's description of a thick gold band topped with a topaz the size of a small boulder. He'd already known in his bones that Van Slyke's bodyguard was Lyle Scott's would-be assassin. That was why he'd looked familiar. And— oh, shit—Maddy was having dinner with the man who'd probably ordered Elliot Koch to shoot her father. But what the hell? Why would a member of Lyle's own family want him dead? The motivation became appallingly apparent. With Lyle Scott out of the picture, Van Slyke would be the real CEO of Scott

Oil, not just a puppet or a stand-in.

"Sir?" Bronco queried at the look of horror that Sam couldn't have hidden if he'd tried.

He dragged his fingers through his hair, considering his options. With no time to explain himself to Bronco, he broke away and hurried up to his CO and Kuzinsky. "Sir, there's a situation," he announced with a tremor in his voice. Bronco and Bamm-Bamm had come up behind him.

"What kind of situation?" Mad Max's expression conveyed an unwillingness to acknowledge any situation that potentially delayed their departure.

"You remember the assassination attempt on Lyle Scott?"

The CO nodded. "The one you thwarted?"

Sam had been forced to share the details when the FBI contacted his CO for witness verification purposes.

"Yes, sir. I just realized who the shooter was—it's Van Slyke's bodyguard. I knew the man looked familiar, but I didn't know why until Bamm-Bamm mentioned that he used to be a famous wrestler. That's how he flipped me over and got the better of me, sir. And now Maddy's alone with him and the uncle who wants her father out of the picture so that he can own Scott Oil outright."

"Slow down, Sam." The CO's deep-set eyes had narrowed into slits. "You're telling me that the CEO of Scott Oil, that pompous cowboy we met the other night, wants the old CEO, Maddy Scott's father, dead?"

"Yes, sir. That's exactly what I'm saying. She can't be safe with him."

Mad Max stroked his walrus-like mustache, saying nothing. In desperation, Sam turned to appeal to the master chief. "I can't leave her with her uncle, Master

Chief. I have a really bad feeling about this. Please," he looked back at the CO. "Just give me permission to stay behind."

"Denied," said the CO flatly. "How would you get back?"

Sam thought fast. "Through our CIA contact, Ricardo Villabuena. I'm sure he's got connections."

But the CO simply shook his head. "Forget it. We don't leave men behind."

"Unless they're on leave," Kuzinsky finished.

Mad Max slanted him a funny look.

"I have a leave-chit in my briefcase," the master chief volunteered, picking up the hard-shell case at his feet and laying it on a nearby table. His poker face betrayed no emotion whatsoever as he thumbed the combination lock and popped open the tabs on either side. "Something told me you might need a few more days here," he added pulling out the sheet in question. "All it requires is a signature," he added, handing it to the CO.

Sam didn't know who was more amazed by Kuzinsky's forethought—him or Mad Max. His heart thudded painfully as the CO slowly took the sheet and read it over. Picturing Maddy in the clutches of her uncle was making his heart race. *Just sign it already*, he willed the CO.

"Says here that you're taking five days of leave." The CO's squinty eyes jumped up from the paper he was holding. "You'd better get your affairs in order in that time, Sasseville. You work for the United States Navy, not for Lyle Scott."

"Yes, sir," Sam replied. *Sign the fucking paper*. Beads of sweat were gathering on his forehead. Wouldn't it just suck if Maddy came to harm at the hands of a family member after surviving abduction by known terrorists? Nausea roiled up in him, making him swallow hard.

"Fine." Taking the pen Kuzinsky held out silently, the mustached commander scrawled his signature on the line, handing it back to the master chief who signed his own before passing it off to Sam to sign on the third line.

"Maybe in your free time you could look into that little matter you were wondering about last week," Kuzinsky suggested, as Sam handed him the form.

It took Sam a second to realize what matter he meant—the possibility that Scott Oil resided in SOCOM's back pocket and was manipulating the military to act on its behalf.

"Of course," he said.

"You need a copy?" Kuzinsky inquired, holding up the leave chit.

Sam scanned the document, noting the date and hour he was due to report back to Dam Neck Naval Annex, SEAL Team 12's headquarters. He didn't have time to wait for Kuzinsky to find a copier. "No, thanks, Master Chief." He sent him a silent nod of thanks, held a salute up to the CO, and waited with years melting off his life for Mad Max to set him free.

The commander finally acknowledged him with a tossed-off salute. "I want you back in one piece."

"Yes, sir!" Sam had already slung his duffel back over his shoulder.

Bronco followed him all the way to the exit. "You're going without us?" He sounded incredulous, like they were Siamese twins recently separated.

"Look, I don't have a choice. Just keep the guys in line for me, and I'll see you in six days." He backed out of the door, making eye contact with Bullfrog next, then sending a nod at Bamm-Bamm, who might have just saved Maddy's life. And then he took off running.

# CHAPTER 14

"I'm telling you," Maddy insisted, carving into her steak with a dull steak knife, "the proof is out there, and I'm going to find it this week."

She had thought her uncle would object to her insistence that Scott Oil's waste barrels and containment walls weren't doing their job, that the flora and fauna of El Chaco were being negatively affected. To her surprise, he'd listened to her intently while forking up bites of his entrée, a rib-eye steak, deliciously prepared by an unseen cook, while two young servers scurried about filling their glasses and bringing in the next course.

"You should do whatever your heart dictates, Maddy," he declared when her objections came to a close. Sitting back in his chair, he stifled a burp, and reached for his wine. "Whether you succeed in proving your mother's objections to drilling or not, she would be proud of you."

Maddy basked in his unexpected compliment. "Well, thank you." She tolerated Uncle Paul for one simple reason only. It wasn't because she fell for his insincere smiles and zest for the good life. It was because he could talk about her mother without plunging into grief the way her father did.

"I miss her, your mother," he said with a ponderous sigh.

A lump formed in Maddy's throat, keeping her from taking another bite. "Me, too," she admitted.

A faraway look entered his eyes as he sadly shook his head. "Funny how we take people for granted until they're gone. Have you tried the wine?" he asked, switching topics abruptly and holding up his glass. The burgundy liquid caught and held the light of the gaudy chandelier.

Everything about the mansion her uncle admitted to purchasing was heavy and ornate, even the long table at which they sat, hewn from dense, gleaming *quebracho* wood. "This is Screaming Eagle Cabernet from Napa Valley," he informed her on a proud note. "One bottle cost me almost three grand."

Maddy stared in astonishment at her uncle's proud statement. "Three thousand dollars for a bottle of wine?"

"Nearly," he amended, putting his glass down.

Her opinion of his character sank to a new low. "You do realize that a well can be dug in Somalia for three thousand dollars—providing fresh water to mothers and children, keeping them from having to walk miles and miles in either direction, toting jugs on their heads?" she asked, fighting to keep her tone even.

Her observation had him throwing back his head in a spate of laughter. After a moment, he wiped a tear of mirth from the corner of his eye and said, "Now, *that's* why I enjoy having you around, Maddy. That's exactly something your mother would have said."

The compliment caught her off guard, mitigating her condemnation of his values. "Tell me one of your memories of her from when you were young," she requested. "What was it like growing up together?" She could never hear enough about her mother to satisfy her yearning.

Uncle Paul pursed his full lips as he thought back. "Okay, I'll tell you," he promised, "but first try the wine since I went to the trouble of opening it for you."

"Actually, your serving boy opened it," she pointed out with a jab of her fork.

He wagged a finger at her. "She would have said that, too." Then he gestured at her glass. "How is it?"

Lifting the long-stemmed glass to her lips, she took an obligatory sip. Yes, the wine was good, but no better in her estimation than her favorite seven-dollars-a-bottle Chilean malbec. "Lovely," she replied, putting down the glass and eyeing him expectantly.

Her uncle drummed his fingers on the table top. "A memory, huh?" He thought another minute. "Okay, when she was little, say six, and I was eight, she used to follow me everywhere—very annoying from a brother's perspective. I remember one day when I was hanging out with my buddies up in a tree—a huge oak tree in our front yard in Dallas, and she joined us. She didn't say anything, mind you, but I could tell my friends didn't like her there, so I gave her a nudge."

Maddy gasped in horror. "You pushed her out of the tree?"

He held up a hand to ward off her condemnation. "She wasn't that high up, and she survived the fall with just a sprained wrist. What impressed me, however, was that she never told on me. Most little sisters would have told, don't you think?"

"Definitely," Maddy agreed, picturing her blonde mother clutching her injured wrist and marching stoically away. "What about when you were older?"

"Hmm. Our relationship remained strained. You

know what it's like in high school, how important it is to be one of the popular kids?"

Maddy acknowledged his statement, though in her case, coping with her mother's death had been her biggest preoccupation back in high school.

"I was a junior when your mother was a freshman," her uncle recalled. "There I was, trying my best to look cool and to maintain the status I'd earned as an upper classman. Your mother joined me at the high school and nearly ruined me."

"How so?"

He gave a self-disparaging laugh. "She didn't play the games everyone else played. Didn't give a fig for social mores. Instead, she collected misfits. Every new kid, every fat kid, every foreign kid or immigrant became her friend," he said on a droll note. "I had to pretend we weren't related."

Picturing her uncle's quandary, Maddy grinned. Her mother had had it right. People were just people. To Melinda Scott, there were no distinctions of race or appearance or judgments based on popularity. Admiration toward the teenaged Melinda for defying peer pressure made her yearn more than ever for her loving presence. How she wished her mother were alive still, so she could tell her just how much she admired her. And so she could introduce her to Sam.

"She watches over me, you know," Maddy heard herself admit.

Uncle Paul sent her a startled look. "What do you mean, darling?"

She explained how she could feel her mother's spirit sometimes, usually in dangerous situations or when she had a decision to make. "I think she's the reason I survived being kidnapped. Most people aren't that fortunate."

The sudden appearance of Uncle Paul's bodyguard

kept her from elucidating. The taciturn giant who entered the room with a scowl on his face hadn't bothered to introduce himself when he'd knocked on her condo door two hours before and escorted her to her uncle's Mercedes. Throughout the twenty-minute ride to the mansion at the top of the hill, he'd kept silent, ignoring her questions and observations. It wasn't until her uncle greeted her in the foyer that she'd learned the bodyguard's name—Elliot.

He'd apparently been a former wrestling champion. And the reason he didn't speak, her uncle had explained, was because he'd bitten his tongue so badly in a wrestling match that he couldn't talk without a terrible lisp.

Maddy would like to feel sympathy for the man, but Elliot's oily regard had made her skin crawl. She'd found herself missing Sam, mere hours after their farewell. Sam would never have put up with the man's rudeness.

Uncle Paul looked annoyed at having their dinner interrupted. "What is it, Elliot?"

The gargantuan man marched up to his employer and handed him a scrap of paper. Her uncle scanned the words scribbled on it, and his expression grew shuttered.

"Well, let him in, then," he said with a forced smile. As Elliot exited the dining room, Uncle Paul looked down the table at Maddy. "It seems you have a fan," he said.

She blinked at him, not comprehending.

"Your colleague Ricardo has a message for you, apparently," he explained.

"Ricardo," she repeated, looking toward the door in concern. "Something must be wrong."

"I'm sure everything's fine," her uncle assured her. "Don't you like the wine?" he added, directing her attention back to her glass.

She was too distracted, however, by the sound of the heavy front door opening in the foyer to take another sip. Training her ears to the tread of footsteps, she kept her gaze glued to the doorway until Ricardo stepped into the room followed by Elliot.

Her colleague's intent, dark gaze had her gripping the arms of her chair, preparing to rise. But then she glimpsed the pistol Elliot aimed at Ricardo's back, and her mouth fell open. "Oh," she exclaimed.

"Elliot, put that away," her uncle ordered on a long-suffering note. "I'm so sorry, sir," he added, rising belatedly to greet the newcomer. "My bodyguard is overzealous in his duties. Please, join us." He beckoned Ricardo closer to the table. "Have a seat. I'll have a servant bring you a plate."

"Thank you, but that won't be necessary," Ricardo replied. He approached Maddy's seat, and the light of the chandelier fell on his taut features. Maddy didn't know if it was pain bracketing the edges of his mouth—after all he was barely out of the hospital—or whether he conveyed bad news. "Maddy, GEF is trying to get a message to you," he relayed, explaining the reason for his presence though her phone should have rung if they'd been trying to call her.

"Your father has suffered a stroke," he added gently.

"No." She shook her head in denial.

"I volunteered to get word to you and to fly you to Asunción immediately, so you can get back to him as soon as possible."

Through her shock Maddy heard her uncle protest, "But that's impossible. I just spoke with Lyle less than two hours ago. He sounded perfectly fine."

"He suffered a massive stroke about an hour ago. His state is critical," Ricardo insisted. "Maddy must leave with me as soon as possible."

His urgent stare drove home the seriousness of her father's condition. Maddy pushed her chair back and came unsteadily to her feet. The food she'd just swallowed threatened to return.

Ricardo caught her elbow, steadying her on her feet and drawing her inexorably toward the door.

Her uncle remained seated, a frown of deep concern upon his face.

"I'm sorry, Uncle Paul." Maddy met his gaze over her shoulder. "I have to go."

He sent her a faint nod. Still in his seat, he watched as Ricardo hurried her out of the room.

Ricardo's stride lengthened as they entered the hallway and headed for the home's enormous double doors. Hearing footsteps behind them, Maddy pulse leaped to see Elliot stalking them, a scowl on his face, his pistol trained on their backs. Ricardo pulled the door open and pushed her outside, where the sky had already darkened to a bruised hue.

"This way," he hissed, shutting the door in Elliot's face and tugging Maddy across the semi-lit yard toward the exterior wall and the wrought iron gate. It stood open, with the Jeep parked just inside. Someone was sitting in the driver's seat.

Behind them, the door of the house creaked open, and Ricardo pulled Maddy into a trot.

"Run," he urged, but dread had turned her legs to rubber leaving her less than coordinated, and her thoughts swam in confusion. Why was Elliot pursuing them?

At last they reached the Jeep. Ricardo snatched open the passenger door, threw the seat forward, and all but tossed her into the back before hopping up front.

As she settled into the rear seat, Maddy recognized the man behind the wheel. "Sam!" she exclaimed.

Mystification undermined her delight at seeing him so unexpectedly. "What are you doing here?"

"Keep your head down," he warned with the barest glance over his shoulder.

Ricardo hadn't even shut the door behind himself before the engine whined and the Jeep flew into reverse, shooting out of the gate tail-first.

Maddy groped for her seat belt. Why on earth was Sam even here? And why were both men behaving like their very lives were in danger?

The Jeep braked abruptly then lurched forward, tires spinning on the dirt road before gaining purchase and shooting them swiftly away. Maddy braved a peek through the rear window and caught a glimpse of Elliot at the gate, pistol raised as if to shoot.

But they were safely out of range now, barreling down the winding hill that she'd traversed in her uncle's car two hours earlier.

"What is it, Elliot?" Paul demanded. He sat at the table, cellphone pressed to his ear, willing Lyle to answer his call. Something about Maddy's abrupt departure smacked of conspiracy.

Elliot's pen had run out of ink. Giving up on scribbling a note, the giant tossed the implement onto the table and spoke with his pronounced lisp. "I daw dat navy deaw in da caw."

For once, Paul understood right away what his bodyguard said. "You saw the Navy SEAL? The one I recognized from the party photos on Facebook?"

They'd shared a similar conversation the night Paul had met with the SEAL task unit about the plight of Well 23. Elliot grunted his assent.

"Damn it!" Paul thrust an accusing finger in the former wrestler's face. "This is your fault," he declared. "I told you he might have recognized you the other night. I should have known your fame would be a liability. What if he suspects who's behind the shooting?" Paul shoved back his chair and pushed to his feet. "Why are you just standing there?" he bellowed. "Go get the car ready. We have to stop them before that man's testimony ruins everything!"

Elliot gave a nod and bolted in the direction of the five-car garage.

With a heavy sigh, Paul leaned his weight onto the table. His thoughts raced before him. Had the SEAL conveyed his suspicions yet to Lyle Scott? Why else would Lyle not be taking Paul's calls? They'd been best friends for decades. Hell, they would have been equal partners but for the fact it was Lyle's money that had financed their oil business.

Paul, however, had been the one to find the most lucrative areas for drilling, including the untapped energy stores of El Chaco, Paraguay. Without his instincts, Scott Oil Corporation would never have prospered and flourished the way it had. In the back of Paul's mind had lurked the certainty that, one day, his devotion would pay off, and Lyle would pursue his political aspirations, leaving him in charge.

Sure enough, he had. And now that Paul's power and wealth were unparalleled, he had discovered an unyielding determination to retain what he had earned, no matter the cost.

He could never relinquish the reins of control back to Lyle. Just as he could not have allowed his little sister to persuade her husband *not* to drill in El Chaco simply because it would harm the stinking environment. Some things had to be done, regardless of the hardship it placed on others, especially if a profit might be made. Paul refused to let his newfound elevated status slip from his grasp when he had labored all his life to make Scott Oil as lucrative as it could possibly be.

He sought to reassure himself. How likely was it that the testimony, practically hearsay of a stranger, could threaten a lifetime bond? Not likely at all. Still, Paul couldn't take the risk. Whatever it took to stop the SEAL, he had to do.

"What is going on?" Maddy demanded as they sped pell-mell down the dark road. "I thought you left Paraguay today," she said to Sam.

Before he could answer Ricardo twisted in his seat to look back at her. "Maddy, I lied to you. Your father didn't have a heart attack."

Relief blended with confusion, putting her thoughts in a tailspin. "He didn't? Why—why on earth would you make that up?"

Sam answered on Ricardo's behalf. "To get you away from your uncle."

"My uncle?" Was that why he'd stayed behind? "What's wrong with my uncle?"

Tension seemed to radiate from Sam's stiffly held body as he guided the Jeep down the dark, winding road. "Remember the man who tried shooting your father at the party?" he asked.

"Of course." How could she forget?

"He's your uncle's bodyguard."

It took Maddy a minute to associate Elliot with the shadowy figure Sam had wrestled with in the woods.

"I thought he looked familiar when your uncle met with my task unit last week," Sam continued. "But it took some extra intel to make the connection."

They all braced themselves as he took a hair-pin turn on two tires.

Goose bumps stitched over every inch of Maddy's skin as she paused to consider his words. If her uncle's bodyguard had tried to kill her father, then that would mean...

"I don't believe you," she said. His allegation threatened the very foundation of her existence. It just wasn't possible.

He tore his gaze from the road to glance into the mirror at her. "I wouldn't make this up, Maddy," he said with pity in his voice.

"No." She shook her head, still refusing to accept his claim. "My uncle would never harm my father. They were friends even before my parents met. And he's my mother's brother. He was just telling me how much he misses her. Why would he want my father dead when Daddy's given Uncle Paul everything he has?"

"Why do you think?" Sam asked, on that same pitying note. "With your father out of the picture, he's in charge of Scott Oil forever. The only person who could threaten his succession is you."

"Me?" Maddy exclaimed.

"Who inherits Scott Oil when your father dies?" he challenged.

Another rash of goose bumps sprouted on Maddy's skin. "I don't know. I never thought about it." Had her father made her his primary beneficiary? "But you're wrong, in any case. Uncle Paul would never hurt my father. And he would certainly never hurt me."

"How do you know?" Sam's tone had hardened subtly.

"Because we're family!"

A weighty silence followed her declaration, alleviated only by the sound of wind whistling through the cracked windows as they careened toward the brightly lit town.

"What does my father say about all this?" Maddy demanded. Surely *he* didn't believe Sam's ridiculous allegation.

"Let's just say he wasn't willing to risk your life tonight," Sam clipped. "Unlike you, he hasn't rejected my testimony out of hand. He's bringing the FBI with him, and we're meeting him in Asunción tomorrow to discuss Van Slyke's motives."

"You seriously think my uncle was going to harm me tonight?" Maddy couldn't fathom it. "*You* knew I was having dinner with him. My father knew it. If my uncle had tried to kill me, he'd go straight to jail and end up with nothing. Besides, I wasn't in any danger whatsoever. I was actually enjoying myself!"

Sam set his jaw and kept silent. Slowing at the approaching intersection, he ignored the stop sign and swung them out onto a trafficked main road, speeding them toward town.

"I'll be flying you to Asunción tonight," Ricardo said into the crackling silence.

Maddy sat forward, her blood flashing to a boil as she shifted her glance between the two men. "You know what? I've had it up to here with being told where I'm going next!"

Sam gripped the wheel so hard his knuckles stood out in silhouette. "And I've had it up to here with you resisting what's in your best interest," he retorted.

Ricardo emitted a chuckle of genuine amusement. "You two are birds of a feather."

"I am nothing like her," Sam bit out.

"That's not what you said the other day." Maddy threw herself back in her seat and folded her arms across her chest. Scowling, she glared outside at the darkness while the sweet memories of her and Sam's last encounter raked her heart. "I don't want to leave the area," she insisted, focusing on her immediate plans to do more testing. "I have critical work to do here."

"You can come back after the FBI investigates your

uncle," Sam promised harshly. It occurred to Maddy that he was perhaps as tired of rescuing her from peril as she was tired of being rescued.

With growing disappointment, she watched the lights of Mariscal Estigarribia brighten as they entered the city limits. Elliot couldn't possibly be the shooter in McLean, she told herself. All big, burly men looked the same, didn't they? And now Sam's confusion was leading to her premature departure when there was work yet to be done.

It was like Matamoros all over again.

"Oh, hell, what's this?" Sam groused, focusing her attention on the road before them.

Looking up, Maddy saw that both lanes were clogged with traffic, mostly vans with strange contraptions mounted on their roofs. A large number of people seemed to be standing on the street. Even in the dark, she could make out a dozen individuals milling around her condominium, some of them on cell phones. One woman stood under a hand-held spotlight with the wall of the military installation at her back and a microphone in her hand.

"It looks like the press," Ricardo replied.

"Maddy, don't let them see you," Sam requested. "Keep your head down."

"I'll find a way around it," Ricardo promised, reaching out to program the GPS. "In the meantime, turn down this alley." He pointed to the narrow side street next to them.

"I can't even go home first?" Maddy protested. She'd intended to call her father in private and discuss the situation with him first. Who knew? He might relent and let her stay another week.

Ignoring her question, Sam turned down the alley headed away from her condo.

In sullen silence, Maddy watched the beams of their

headlights bounce before them as they progressed awkwardly through the roads more fit for foot-traffic than for cars. A sense of unreality enveloped her as Sam continued to drive and Ricardo tossed out directions.

In her line of work, she had always remained vigilant against such threats as terrorism, violence, anti-American sentiment, even disease. Danger had never taken on this particular specter.

What if Sam was right and her uncle was behind the shooting in McLean? Doubt pricked her briefly. *No way.* Uncle Paul would have to be utterly without a conscience to turn on his best friend and brother-in-law.

Her heart accelerated suddenly, pounding like pistons in a high-octane engine.

She clapped a hand over her jumping breastbone. *What on earth?* It had to be a belated adrenaline rush. Or maybe this disagreement was Sam was taking a toll on her emotions. If they were going to attempt a relationship after this, they were going to have to get past this rather serious hiccup.

Given the way Sam was behaving now, his mouth clamped shut as he focused on getting her to the airfield as swiftly as possible, continuing a relationship with her seemed to be the last thing on his mind.

# CHAPTER 15

Even with GPS, Ricardo managed to get them lost in the web of unmarked streets. After twenty minutes of driving in what seemed like circles, they finally lurched back onto the highway, well north of the town and the clamoring press. Soon they were nearing the airfield where the SEALs had landed less than two weeks earlier.

Had it really only been ten days? Sam marveled. It felt like a lifetime ago.

Ricardo pointed out the lumpy silhouette at the other end of the airfield. "There's the hangar."

"No one's here," he heard Maddy observe. Her angry tone made it clear that she thought Sam's suspicions regarding her uncle completely bogus. She sure as hell resented having to leave Paraguay before her work was done.

But Sam didn't question what his gut was telling him. And even though it looked as though their escape would be unhampered, he couldn't shake the uncertainty nipping at him. Raking the flat terrain with a naked eye, he wished fervently that he carried a pair of NVGs in his pack. Anyone could be lying in wait, hidden in the shadows.

A few stunted palm trees and tufts of coarse savannah grass grew on either side of the runway. An armadillo scuttled across the tarmac in front of them, its eyes shining in the dark as Sam veered around it. At least the place looked deserted.

But he wasn't willing to bet on it. "You two stay put," he said, parking next to the hangar. "Let me take a look around."

"I'll go," Ricardo volunteered. "I have the key," he added, snatching the key ring out from the ignition and jingling it.

Reluctant to let Maddy out of his sight, Sam deferred to Ricardo's wishes. The case officer climbed stiffly out of the passenger seat, a reminder to Sam that he was still recovering from surgery. With a prick of guilt, Sam watched him let himself into the door at the side of the hangar. Silence filled the interior of the Jeep, stretched to the snapping point as Maddy continued to simmer in the back seat.

That comment she had made about Uncle Paul being family had set off warning bells in his head. It had reminded him exactly what kind of family Maddy came from: a rich and powerful family that used their influence to control other people's lives—people like him.

Her refusal to believe that Elliot was the shooter he'd wrestled with in McLean rankled. She had chosen loyalty to her so-called family over him. How well did that bode for a future relationship?

Suddenly, the enormous doors at the front of the hangar rumbled open, and there stood Ricardo, waving them inside.

"Here we go," Sam said.

Exiting the Jeep, he escorted Maddy out of the back seat. Keeping a firm grip on her arm—no hand-holding—he drew her briskly toward the hangar. The *tack-tack-tack* of her high heeled shoes echoed off the concrete. The certainty that something wasn't right assailed him suddenly. His free hand sought the butt of his holstered pistol. Every nerve in his body twitched in anticipation of trouble, but he could see no cause for his concern.

"This way," Ricardo urged, gesturing for them to follow him farther into the huge metal shelter. "The place has electricity, but I say we keep the lights off."

"Agreed," Sam murmured. With his ears open, his eyes peeled for danger, he drew Maddy past two midsized, privately owned planes to an even smaller one.

A faint crackling sound had him swiveling toward the sound while drawing his pistol with the speed of a Western gunslinger. "Did you hear that?" he asked Ricardo.

The whites of the case officer's eyes shone in the shadows as he looked around. "A bird, perhaps?" he suggested. "There are several nests in the rafters."

It could have been a bird. All the same, Sam kept his gun at the ready. At least Maddy was cooperating, though they'd make less noise if he carried her—like she'd go for that.

They waded deeper into the hangar where the ghostly outline of a Cesna-182 took shape before them.

"This is it," Ricardo announced, bending to inspect the exterior. Sam recognized the four-seater, single-engine airplane as one commonly used by skydivers. Its respectable safety record helped to ease some of his inexplicable fears. The flight to Asunción was only 530 kilometers—330 miles—or so. How dangerous could it be?

Ricardo unlocked the door for them, and Sam helped Maddy clamber up and into the cabin. To his relief, she went right in, sinking down in one of the back seats. "Need help?" Sam called to Ricardo.

"No, I've got it," the case officer assured him, waving him inside.

*Do I sit up front?* Sam wondered, *and brood over Maddy's lack of faith in me, or sit in the back with her?* Like a moth drawn to a flame, he chose the back. She'd donned a strappy royal blue dress to wear to her uncle's dinner. Cut similarly to the red cocktail dress she had worn at her father's soiree, it hugged her lithe figure, showing her long legs to advantage.

She had better be wearing underwear, he thought with a scowl.

A minute later, Ricardo joined them, locking both doors and taking up residence in the pilot's seat.

"You sure he knows how to fly this?" Maddy asked. The fight appeared to have gone out of her. She now sounded distinctly uncertain.

Ricardo reached back to pat her knee. "Maddy," he said. "Once again, I've deceived you and I'm sorry. My job with GEF was just a cover for me. I'm not actually an environmentalist, which you intuited. I work for the CIA. And, yes, I can fly this plane."

Even in the plane's shadows Sam saw Maddy's mouth fall open. Her incredulous gaze swung in his direction. "So that's how you two know each other. You work together," she guessed.

Chuckling, Ricardo faced forward again. This evening's adventures were apparently proving highly entertaining to the case officer. He flipped the master switch, lighting up the panel, then hit the auxiliary fuel switch. After several seconds, he turned the ignition handle to start.

The plane's single engine roared to life, drowning out any comment Maddy might have made and sounding inordinately loud inside the hangar. Under normal circumstances, they would have pushed the plane through the doors first and out onto the tarmac before starting the engine, but they were in too much of a hurry for that.

With a lurch, they rolled forward, turning slightly to sweep through the bay doors. The wings cleared the opening with ample room to spare. They were just easing onto the moonlit tarmac when a faint flicker of light and an accompanying *plink!* drew Sam's head around.

"What was that?" he called. It sounded to him like a something had struck the wing of the plane, but Ricardo, who was wearing a radio headset, looked at him and shook his head. Sam glanced back at Maddy, who shrugged at him.

His heart beat an uneven tattoo as Ricardo lined them up with the long runway. Without waiting as standard operating procedure dictated for the oil temperature to rise, he pushed the throttle forward, causing the little plane to accelerate. Faster and faster they rolled, the tarmac streaming under them like a dark river. Then, without warning, they were weightless, climbing up, up, up into the star dusted sky.

Gazing out of the plane's large windows, Sam watched the town's lights shrink to pin-sized specks of illumination in an otherwise pitch-black void. He could see no reason for the tension still gripping his neck and back. It had to be Maddy's earlier assertion—*Because we're family!*—keeping him so agitated.

If it wasn't galling enough that her work consistently put her in harm's way, she was and would always be the daughter of a billionaire who thought nothing of asking Sam to rescue her yet again. It was more than Sam could tolerate.

Paul Van Slyke watched the lights of the Cessna retreat into the night sky until they blinked and were gone. Then he lowered his gaze to where Elliot was making his way back from the hangar toward him, as he sat in his Mercedes hidden in a grove of trees.

He'd instructed Elliot to fire a single shot into the plane's gas tank, and minutes earlier, he'd heard the shot being fired. It was done, then. The plane would run out of fuel before the pilot had the chance to turn around and make it back to the runway. He would be forced to land on rugged terrain where the plane would break into hundreds of pieces the way Melinda's plane had done. And everyone on board would die.

A peculiar taste lingered on Paul's tongue.

He hadn't realized when he'd made the decision to eliminate the Navy SEAL that he would end up sacrificing his niece in the same way that he'd dispatched his sister. The coincidence worried him. What if someone made a connection? Not that he regretted having to kill Maddy. If she'd drunk enough of that poison-laced wine, she'd have died eventually, anyway. He could not afford for her to inherit what rightfully belonged to him—ownership of Scott Oil Corporation. Still, he hadn't meant for her to perish in an ugly plane crash.

Luckily, he wasn't burdened with what others called a conscience. But logic alone dictated that Maddy should die a painless death. After all, over the course of her life, she'd provided Paul with countless hours of entertainment. She'd reminded him so many times of his sister, that he'd scarcely even mourned Melinda's passing. Certainly, life would be dull without Maddy.

He heaved a sigh that his plans had veered off

course, if only slightly. With the SEAL out of the way, Lyle would eventually forget about the man's allegations—if he'd even heard them in the first place. Besides, he'd be so distraught over his daughter's death that he'd have no choice but to lean on Paul as he'd done in the past. Paul would surely remain at the helm and continue as CEO indefinitely.

The heavy tread of Elliot's feet reminded him of one last thread that required snipping. His bodyguard had proven to be too much of a liability. And now he had outlived his usefulness. It was high time that Paul dispatched Elliot, too.

Glancing over at Maddy, Sam did a double take. Not only was she hugging herself hard, but her chin was tucked to her chest in an attitude of uncharacteristic terror. "Hey," he called out. "What's wrong?"

When she didn't answer him, he wondered whether she was playing games—acting terrified to break through the barrier he'd erected. With a sigh of resignation, he put a hand on her shoulder and realized she was trembling. He cupped her chin, forcing her to look over at him. Her panicked gaze sent a shaft of uncertainty through him.

"What's wrong?" he repeated.

"I don't like small planes," she said in a thin voice.

It took him a second to realize why. Her mother had gone down in a plane like this. Comprehension and compassion edged aside his lingering annoyance. "You're not going to die," he insisted.

She nodded, clearly just to placate him, as she still looked terrified.

Reluctantly, he scooted closer on the bench seat and put an arm around her, knowing it would undermine his resentment the instant they touched. Sure enough, when she leaned into him, laying her head against his chest, he had trouble remembering why he was so mad at her. She'd been enjoying her uncle's company, hearing stories about her mother, whom she clearly missed every day of her life. He'd have to be an ass to hold it against her for wanting to stay.

Reaching for his bag, he unzipped the pocket and reached inside. "I stopped by your condo earlier and picked this up for you."

Maddy gasped, clutching the small book to her heart. "My mother's journal," she exclaimed. She sent him a searching look.

"Something told me you wouldn't want to be without it."

"I wouldn't. Thank you," she softly said, summoning a weak smile for him.

Putting himself in her shoes, Sam could appreciate why she wouldn't want to believe her mother's brother could have targeted her father, let alone that he would seek to harm her, as well. His resentment frittered away, allowing him to turn his head and kiss her temple.

"It's going to be all right," he assured her. His gaze strayed to her lap where the hem of her dress had ridden toward the tops of her thighs. He was dying to put a hand down there to assuage his curiosity.

He was just about to venture a bold attempt when Ricardo uttered a virulent curse. Sam felt Maddy go tense at the pilot's tone.

"What is it?" Sam asked, sitting forward.

The case officer shook his head while staring at the display. "One of the tanks must have a leak. It was full when we took off."

A suspicion wormed its way into Sam's thoughts. He leaned across Maddy's knees to peer out of the side of the plane where that strange sound had come from earlier. Cupping a hand to block the light from the cockpit, he spied a thin trail of gasoline weeping from the wing where he knew the fuel bladder to be located.

"It's not a leak," he relayed with a tickle of foreboding. Giving Maddy's leg a reassuring pat (he would rather have groped her higher up), he stood up to lean over Ricardo's shoulder so he could discuss the problem without having to shout. He didn't particularly want Maddy to overhear, but Ricardo still had on a headset.

"I think someone took a shot at us as we were leaving. Do you think Van Slyke could've beaten us to the airfield?"

"It's possible." Ricardo studied the display with a grim expression. "We could turn back," he suggested.

"That's probably what they're hoping we'll do." Sam glanced back at Maddy and found her hugging herself again, her face twice as pale. There wasn't any question she'd heard what he'd said. "What other options do we have?"

Ricardo sighed. "The second tank is full, but based on the mileage we've gotten so far, we won't make it all the way to Asunción, not with the wind in our face."

"Are there any landing strips between here and there?" Sam asked, but he already knew the answer.

"No. We'd be forced to make an emergency landing."

Sam's intestines knotted. The terrain could be worse. They could be flying over a jungle instead of a desert-like Savannah, but the odds of none of them getting hurt weren't good. He didn't fancy being battered to death in a crash any more than he'd wanted to be buried alive in a tunnel.

"You two could jump," Ricardo suggested, "but

I've only got one parachute. You'd have to share it somehow."

"Shit!" Sam swore, not liking any of the options.

Ricardo snatched up the radio handset. "Let me advise air control at Asunción. Maybe someone has a better suggestion."

Sam listened to him hail the air traffic controller at their destination field. The radio crackled and hissed, its reception poor at best. Ricardo tried again, speaking in fluent Spanish and receiving a broken reply.

Seeing Maddy's face in her hands, Sam dropped down next to her. "Hey, we're going to be okay," he said.

She dragged her fingers down her cheeks, revealing impossibly wide eyes. "This is exactly what happened to my mother. Except there was water in her tank, not a leak. And no parachute. My God, Sam," she added with horror in her voice. "It makes me wonder…"

"What?" he pressed her.

She shook her head. "Nothing. Nevermind."

Whatever she was thinking it had put her into shock.

"I won't let anything bad happen, Maddy," he insisted. *Oh, hell, no.* After the trouble he'd gone to snatching her out of Matamoros, then wresting her from the terrorists, he sure as hell was not going to let her die at her uncle's hands. "I've jumped out of a plane hundreds of times. If we go that route, we'll be just fine, even sharing a parachute."

"I think I'm going to puke," she managed to choke.

He snatched a vomit bag out of the pocket in front of her and shoved it in her hands. But she didn't throw up. Instead, she fixed her lagoon-like eyes on him and said, "What if Uncle Paul sabotaged my mother's plane, too?"

He considered it a distinct possibility, but he wasn't

going to tell her so. "Don't think about that right now. We're not going to die, Maddy. We've got plenty of fuel left. We can make an emergency landing if we have to."

Only Ricardo wasn't having any luck getting through to Asunción.

"Something's wrong with the radio," the case officer called, ripping off his headset and tossing it aside with disgust. "The antenna's been compromised."

They would have to set the plane down without any input from air traffic control, then, counting on topographical maps to find the best place for a landing. There'd be no emergency vehicles lying in wait to tend to them if anyone got hurt. At least they had Maddy's satphone. Once they were down, their location pinpointed by Accutracker, they could summon help.

He made up his mind. A SEAL never abandoned his teammates. "We're staying with you, Ricardo. I guess we'll see how good a pilot you really are," he added, needling the case officer playfully. "Maddy, switch seats with me," he added, moving her farther from the leaking wing.

She slid over wordlessly and buckled herself back in, her movements stiff with fear.

"We'll be all right, *querida*," he promised her, pausing to stroke the top of her head. Then his training kicked in. Rifling through the cabin, he came up with a fire extinguisher and a first aid kit. He laid the single parachute at his feet, just in case. He didn't let himself dwell on the odds of all three of them arriving back on the ground safely. That was something only God knew the answer to, right along with whether he and Maddy had a shot at a future together, considering their very disparate pasts.

Maddy closed her eyes and prayed. The plane was going down—not in the theatrical way she'd envisioned her mother's plane floundering, but a smooth descent disturbed only by occasional air pockets that launched her stomach repeatedly into the air.

Through her haze of panic, she gleaned that Ricardo had chosen a place for them to land by studying a map stored under his seat. The area lay two hundred kilometers outside of Asunción. After they landed, they could call for help using her satphone, which Sam had taken from her purse and put in the first aid pack for protection.

At least the terrain wasn't marshy here, like it was in the *Pantanal*, where her mother's plane had ripped open the instant it hit a swamp.

"Two thousand feet," Ricardo called, announcing their altitude so they wouldn't be caught unawares. "Fifteen hundred," he added minutes later.

Sam remained with Maddy in the back seat. "Hug your legs, Maddy," he instructed, grim but calm. "Keep your head as low as you can."

Obeying, she thought of Lucía and baby Isabella and prayed for Ricardo's safety.

*Is this what it was like for you, Mom?* Had her mother prayed for deliverance only to perish the instant her plane struck the earth? *Don't let that happen to us, please.*

She stole a peek at Sam, wondering if this was the end for them. Would she never get to hear him say her name again or, for that matter, the words *I love you, Maddy*?

Unlike her, Sam wasn't braced yet in a crash position. He watched their descent out the window, a first aid pack on his back and a fire extinguisher on his lap—poised for whatever calamity came their way. There wasn't any question he would do everything in his power to get them out of this predicament alive. Her mother hadn't had Sam to protect her, but Maddy did. Once again, her mother seemed to be watching over her.

"I see the ground," he announced, preventing her from saying anything.

"Roger that. I see it, too," Ricardo countered, his tone unnaturally calm, though she was sure he was praying and thinking of his little family back in Mariscal Estigarribia.

Maddy forced her body to relax. The impact would hurt more if she was all tensed up.

"We're looking good. I'm going to bank and come back around so the wind's at our back," Ricardo warned. "Two hundred feet."

The little plane abruptly listed, causing Maddy to flash out a hand and grope for Sam. He caught it and held onto it, his grip reassuring.

The plane slowly righted itself. Even though she couldn't see outside in her present position, she could sense their descent, could feel the land rising up under them, rough and unpredictable.

"Any second now," Ricardo announced controlling their descent.

Maddy stole a peek at him, saw only the tense line of his shoulders, and squeezed her eyes shut.

"Easy, easy," Sam called out to Ricardo, his tone full of warning, like he'd suddenly caught sight of something in their way.

*Ka-BAM!*

In the next instant they slammed into the earth, rebounded into the air, and crashed again. The top of Maddy's head struck the seat in front of her as their momentum kept them careening forward, bouncing hard and landing again. The sound of hydraulic brakes combined with the thunder of wheels reverberating over brush and sand.

The wing on Sam's side caught on something unseen—a small tree, perhaps—and the plane spun around, its back end lifting into the air. Maddy screamed. The tail described an arc in the air and the entire plane flipped, striking the ground with such force that Maddy's world went black.

It took several seconds to surface to reality. She roused to silence that had her gasping in horror and peering into the dark in fear. She hung practically upside down while Sam lay in an unconscious heap against the window, now below her, his head and shoulders outlined by the lighter expanse of Plexiglass window.

"Sam!" she cried his name, stretching out a foot to nudge him, but he didn't stir.

"Sam, wake up!" she repeated in a voice hoarse with fear. What about Ricardo? Turning her stiff neck, she realized that the nose of the plane was crumpled, leaving the pilot squeezed between the instruments and his seat. The engine, built inside of the nose, was smoking. Wisps of it rose through vents like thin ghosts, conveying a chemical smell.

The pilot stirred. "Ricardo!" Maddy cried, sobbing in relief when he released his seatbelt and slipped out of the deathtrap. A larger man might have been crushed to death.

Groaning, Ricardo righted himself, bracing his feet on the side of the plane which was now beneath them. His dark eyes took stock of their situation. "Sam!" He crouched down with a grimace, picked up the fire extinguisher and gave Sam a shake.

Sam lurched to wakefulness, freeing Maddy to breathe again. "What happened?" His gaze locked on her. "You okay?"

"We're both okay," Ricardo answered for her. "But the engine's smoking, and even though the fuel is in the wings, we should probably get out of here." Reaching over Maddy's head, he released the lock on the door and tried to throw it open, groaning in defeat when it didn't budge.

Maddy's heart lurched into a painful trot, the way it had in the car earlier. My God, what if they were trapped inside and the plane caught fire?

Sam rose to a vertical position then stepped in front of her to help Ricardo. The door yielded with a moan, and cool air wafted in. Maddy filled her lungs with the fresh scent and her pulse subsided.

It was Sam who released her from the seatbelt that strapped her in. She fell into his arms with a grateful sob. Ricardo exited first, climbing out of the opening onto the side of the plane. Sam hoisted Maddy through the opening next. She sat a moment on the slick hull then slid into Ricardo's waiting arms. Sam leaped lightly down beside them, taking Maddy's hand as Ricardo carried the fire extinguisher to the damaged engine.

The smell of low leaded gas permeated the air, competing with the clean grassy fragrance of the savannah. Sam drew Maddy to a safe distance as Ricardo hosed the engine with foam. Maddy's heels sank into the soft ground. Tough, calf-high grass scratched her bare calves, but she had never been more aware of the steady flow of blood through her veins, the gentle warmth of Sam's big hand as it cradled hers.

Fifty feet from the fallen plane, they stopped and looked back. A crescent moon hung low over the horizon highlighting the single white wing that jutted upward. The plane lay in an endless field, without any sign of civilization visible in any direction.

But Maddy wasn't afraid. Her gaze rose in gratitude to the brilliant and innumerable stars glittering in the sky above them. *I'm alive,* she marveled. Her entire life still lay before her, brimming with possibility, blessed with the potential of love.

She tugged at Sam's arm to get his attention. "After that, I think we can handle anything that comes our way, don't you?" she asked.

Rubbing a spot on the back of his head, he spared her a distracted glance. "I like your optimism," he said, sliding the pack off his shoulders. "Everything's easy after that. Just remember that in the hours to come."

A splinter of uncertainty slid beneath her skin. "Who can we call for help?" she asked. "My father's not going to get to Paraguay until tomorrow."

He glanced up at her sharply. "Do you always call your father when the going gets tough?"

Something in his tone had her taking a closer look at him. "Not if I can avoid it," she retorted. "But you've got to admit, my father has contacts."

"No doubt about that," Sam clipped. "I'm sure Ricardo knows someone who can help us," he added on a kinder note.

As it turned out, Ricardo did have an idea. Using Maddy's satphone, he contacted an asset living in Asunción. Maddy's number provided their exact coordinates. The asset instructed them to walk due east about five kilometers until they ran into Highway 12. He would pick them up in two to three hours.

By the first kilometer, Maddy's feet had begun to protest. "I should never have worn heels tonight," she lamented, but who could have guessed how her dinner with her mother's brother would end? She stopped to shake sand out of her shoes. "Can I walk barefoot?"

"Not a good idea. Here, have a seat." Sam laid the first aid kit on the ground and patted the earth beside it. "We'll put some bandages on your feet to keep you comfortable. Just remember, it's mind over matter. Everything's easy after that crash, right?"

"Right," she agreed, helping him to locate and cover up all the spots that were rubbing raw. Then he took each shoe in his hands and snapped off the four-inch spikes.

"How's that?" he asked when tried on the new flats and stood up. Ricardo had gone ahead of them a short ways, giving them a modicum of privacy.

"Much better," she said, resolving not to complain again, regardless of how bad it got. She was alive, in one piece—they all were. That was what mattered most.

To distract herself from her discomfort, Maddy hummed a folk song she had learned in Thailand.

"You've got a nice voice," Sam commented with surprise. "What's that tune?"

"It's just something I picked up in Thailand when I helped clean up after the tsunami. The villagers used to sing it to keep their spirits up."

"Sing it louder," he invited.

"I'm faking half the words. My Thai is very rudimentary."

"Just sing," he said. So she did, and then she sang a song that a little orphan girl had taught her back in Haiti.

"Music is a gift from the gods," she reflected. "It gives us all a tool for coping, don't you think?"

"Absolutely. We even use it in the military."

She pictured Sam and his SEALs singing folk songs. "You're teasing me, right?"

"Not at all. What are cadences if not songs?"

"Oh, I guess you're right. What's a good cadence? I

need something to keep me going," she huffed, her toes and heels burning.

"All right. Here's one we use for the War on Terror:

*Some say freedom is free*

*Well I tend to disagree*

*Some say freedom is won*

*Through the barrel of a gun*

*My daddy fought in Vietnam*

*Went to war with the Viet Cong*

*My granddad fought in World War Two*

*And gave his life for me and you*

"There's another six or seven verses, but I've never memorized them all."

"I hate to say it," Maddy interjected, "but the premise is all wrong. There wouldn't be a War on Terror in the first place if we treated our neighbors as we treat ourselves." She warmed to her argument. "Put an Afghan and an American on an island in the middle of nowhere and you can bet they'd become the best of friends."

"Yeah, but the world's not an island. You can't change a thousand years of hatred by being kind to your neighbor."

"You'd be surprised," Maddy replied, panting with the effort it took to slog across the soft soil. "The schools and hospitals we've built in Afghanistan and Iraq have done more good for the people than either war has."

"I agree with that," Sam said, without a hint of defensiveness. "That's why I like being a SEAL. Precision targeting means we take out only the bad elements and leave the rest. Plus we work closely with tribal and religious leaders to help them oust the Taliban who terrorize their villages. There are some things SEALs can do for people that humanitarian aid workers can't."

She considered the laments she'd heard from Bosnian refugees asking where help had been when their family members were being raped and killed. NATO military intervention had put an end to the bloodshed, not the Red Cross.

"I think you've got a point," she admitted, casting him a sidelong glance. "So we're both doing our best to make the world a better place."

His teeth flashed in a brief smile. "Like a tag team," he agreed. "We're here by the way," he added, pointing to a spot ahead of them where Ricardo stood staring down an endless expanse of highway.

"Thank God," Maddy sighed, quickening her pace to get there. The heat was still rising off the asphalt from the previous day's warmth. It heated Maddy's backside as she collapsed on the edge of the road along with her companions. It had been 11 PM when Ricardo first called his colleague for assistance. They'd walked at least another hour over the rough terrain. She wished fervently that she was back in her condominium safely tucked into bed.

Sitting next to her, Sam and Ricardo had fallen silent, no doubt taxed by the ordeal of crashing and the lateness of the hour. Sam scooted closer, shielding her from the breeze that whipped at her hair.

"Have some water," he invited handing her a bottle from the pack. He handed Ricardo a second bottle.

Maddy assessed Sam's thoughtful expression as she tipped her head back to drink. "Are you okay?" she asked, handing back the bottle for him to share. Something seemed off about him.

"Hit my head pretty hard in the crash," he explained. "It's nothing."

Concern shot through her. She lifted a hand to feel the spot he'd pinpointed, and her fingertips encountered a lump behind his ear the size of an egg. "Oh, Sam," she exclaimed. "Is there something in the pack for that?"

"It's nothing a little Tylenol and sleep can't cure."

"There's got to be Tylenol in this pack somewhere." She sifted through the contents until she came up with several foils containing acetaminophen. "Here, swallow these," she instructed, handing Sam a packet. "What about you, Ricardo?" she asked, turning toward her former colleague. He'd stretched his entire body out across the concrete. "Would you like pain pills?"

"Maddy, it would take a full bottle of rum to kill the pain I'm in," he rasped.

"I'm so sorry, Ricardo." Stretching out a hand, she clasped his ankle. "I'm sorry about your plane, too. I'll get my father to buy you a new one."

Sam snorted with derision practically in her ear.

She focused her attention back on him. "It's the least he can do after Ricardo saved my life," she insisted.

"I thought you still believed your uncle was innocent."

"Well, it's hard to believe that after what just happened to the plane, isn't it?"

"You could have just taken my word for it." He rubbed his forehead tiredly, not even looking at her.

"I'm sorry," she said, realizing her lack of faith in him had nearly pushed him away forever. "It's just so hard for me to accept that my uncle could turn against his own family." And if he'd turned against his own sister as she now suspected, his crimes were beyond forgivable.

"Some people have no conscience, Maddy. Your uncle is a psychopath."

Oddly, she still had to squelch an impulse to defend her uncle. *Blood runs thick,* she realized. Sam was right, though. Uncle Paul probably was a psychopath. After all, what normal brother would push his sister out of a tree, let alone cause her plane to crash?

Exhaustion overwhelmed her suddenly, and she lay back on the road the way Ricardo was doing and shut her eyes. With Sam nearby to protect her, she didn't fear that a snake or tarantula or even a jaguar would creep out of the wilderness to threaten her. The greatest threat came from within her own family, she ruminated, reeling inwardly. Miraculously, they'd all survived her uncle's heartless endeavor to end their lives.

*Thank you again, Mom. I love you so much.*

# CHAPTER 16

Maddy cringed, turning her head instinctively from the source of bright light and the corresponding sound of a curtain being whisked open.

She rolled over, groaning at the stiffness in her neck and spine. Memories of the plane crash chased the pleasant dreams from her mind and brought her fully awake. She found herself in a hotel room in the queen-sized bed Sam had tucked her into at the crack of dawn that morning.

"Rise and shine, *querida*," he called out, sounding far more energetic and looking fully recovered.

As he came to stand over her, she noticed that he'd swapped his military attire for a pair of jeans and a green T-shirt that matched the color of his eyes. His tolerant smile gave her hope that he'd truly forgiven her for not believing him right away the previous night and for defending her uncle until the evidence became too overwhelming to ignore. "Feeling a little sore, I bet," he wagered.

She gave a tentative stretch and groaned. "Every inch of my body hurts."

"That's normal," he assured her.

"But you don't look like you hurt." If anything, he

looked rested and bright-eyed.

He shrugged. "I'm used to crashing," he explained.

Her eyes widened. "Is that supposed to make me feel better?" She sat up slowly.

He shrugged. "Better get used to it. We both face danger as part of our jobs."

Excitement bubbled inside at the implication that a long-term relationship was now in the works. She sniffed the air catching a whiff of something delicious. "Do I smell breakfast?"

"More like brunch." He turned toward the desk where she caught sight of a tray heaping with food. "I took the liberty of ordering room service."

"Good. I'm starving." Putting her feet to the floor, she found herself completely naked which was, of course, how she normally slept. "When did I lose my dress?" she asked, a tad self-consciously.

"When you passed out on the bed the minute we got into the room. I was glad to find you wearing underwear," he added on a dry note.

"So pleased to have met your expectations," she countered sweetly.

"Don't worry, I snagged a change of clothes for you before we left town yesterday. They're in the bathroom."

Touched by his thoughtfulness—he'd grabbed her most sacred keepsake, too, her mother's journal—she thanked him as she moved into the bathroom. She showered briskly and scrubbed her teeth with the complimentary toothbrush. A pair of her most practical pants and a cotton blouse hung on the back of the door. The prospect of making love kept her from putting them on, however. Instead, she donned the fluffy white robe, courtesy of the Marriott and rejoined Sam in the bedroom. He'd already laid their meal on the desk and drawn up the recliner so they could both have a seat.

"This is cozy," she remarked, shivering privately as his gaze lingered on her plunging neckline.

Two steaming cups of coffee filled the room with a delicious aroma. He'd ordered them fresh fruit, a crepe, and an omelet, all piled onto a single plate. Casting the bed a regretful glance, she took a seat in the recliner and he pushed her closer before sitting next to her in the chair.

"Thanks," she said, picking up a fork. "Where are we again?" The final hour of their adventure was nothing but a blur.

"Near the Asunción International Airport. Which would you prefer, the omelet or the crepe?"

"I'll take the crepe if that's all right with you."

He carved a piece off the omelet by way of an answer.

"And Ricardo stayed with his contact?" she inquired, taking her own first bite from the assorted fruit.

"Yes, his friend was going to drive him back to his wife and baby."

"Now, that's dedication," Maddy mused.

"That's the kind we're going to need," he gravely informed her. As he chewed his first bite, he studied her face intently. "You know the odds are stacked against us, right? A long-distance relationship is one thing. My being a SEAL and you being a global environmentalist doesn't make things any easier."

Only slightly daunted, she selected a melon wedge. "Trying to get out of it?" she inquired, arching an eyebrow at him.

"Actually, I thrive on challenges." A glint of determination shone in his green eyes.

"So do I," she insisted with a determined smile. "But I hardly know anything about you, whereas you've been told everything there is to know about me," she pointed out. "I hardly think that's fair."

"There was nothing in your files about your propensity for going commando," he objected, working on the omelet.

"But you found that out on your own."

"Yes, I did." His gaze dropped again to her cleavage, now visible between the two halves of her robe.

"You're trying to distract me," she realized, hunting down another piece of fruit. "What makes you love challenges so much?" she asked him, wresting his gaze from her cleavage.

He chewed thoughtfully. "Being born without privileges, I guess. When I realized hard work and determination actually got me somewhere, I didn't want to stop."

Intrigued, Maddy waited for more, but that was all he said. "Why are you being so vague? You can tell me specifics, Sam. I'm not going to judge you. That's not my style."

His expression remained shuttered. "You want to know where I come from?" he asked on a harder note, but he didn't look up at her. He played with his food, instead.

"Yes. I want to know every hardship and obstacle you ever overcame," she insisted.

He blew out a long breath. "That could take a while." He glanced over at the clock beside the bed. "And your father is due at the airport any moment."

*Darn.* So much for making love after breakfast. She relinquished that hope while pursuing the topic more avidly. "Sounds to me like you're making excuses. What are you afraid of, Sam?"

She knew he wouldn't like the inference that he was afraid of anything. Putting down his fork, he sat back and crossed his arms in a defensive posture. "Fine," he said, staring hard at her. "I'm the grandson of a Cuban refugee."

"Really?" Maddy smiled her delight. "I love Cuban food," she asserted. "And Cuban music. And Cuban poetry."

"José Marti," he tossed out with a hint of a smile. "You've read his works?"

"Plenty of times, but we're talking about you," she reminded him.

He lifted his chin in the air. "I was born a bastard," he stated.

Maddy just looked at him. "If you're waiting for me to run away screaming, I can save you some time."

He loosed a reluctant laugh at her droll remark. "My mother was fifteen when some college boy at Miami U got her pregnant. We lived in a poor Cuban neighborhood with my grandmother, who raised me while my mother finished school. She met my stepfather when they were in college, and a year later we moved to a single-family home in the same neighborhood."

"Did you like him?" Maddy asked, referring to his stepfather.

He shrugged. "We got off to a rough start, but now I can see he's the best thing that ever happened to me. He always told me if I didn't want to be thought of as a Spic and a gangster then I needed to work hard in school and get the hell out of there. It took a while to get that message through my thick head, but I finally got it. I did what he said."

"Good for you," Maddy interjected.

"Don't patronize me."

Her smile froze at his harsh admonishment. "I'm not, I'm cheering you on," she insisted on an equally firm note.

"Sorry." He shook his head. "I'm a little sensitive about my history, that's all."

"I can see that. Sam, you're a self-made man. You should be proud of how hard you've worked to get where you are."

"I am proud of it," he replied.

"Good. So am I. Is that okay? Can I be proud of you?"

He looked uncomfortable with the mere idea. Suddenly her phone gave a shrill ring. Maddy leaped up and immediately regretted moving that fast as she hobbled toward the bed where her phone lay.

"It's my father," she relayed, recognizing the number. With a tremulous smile and no small amount of relief, she greeted him. "Hi, Daddy."

Sam listened to their exchange with only half an ear. An unaccustomed mishmash of emotions held him in thrall. Having told Maddy about his humble past, he felt naked but also oddly liberated. Just as she'd promised, she hadn't seemed to judge him. If anything, she'd been proud of him, but that only made him feel inferior, which he hated feeling.

"We're at the Marriott right by the airport," he heard her relay. She surprised him by not mentioning their brush with death last night. "Oh, great," she said instead, though she sounded vaguely disappointed. "We'll see you soon then." She ended the call and met Sam's gaze. "He'll be here in twenty minutes."

*Just perfect.* Annoyance competed with the other confusing emotions running amok inside him. He'd been hoping for a chance to part the two halves of the robe that had been tantalizing him over breakfast. "You didn't mention our forced landing last night," he pointed out as she took her seat beside him, phone in hand.

"There's time for that later," she said with a careless shrug. "Right now I'm more interested in hearing about the rest of your life." She sat back down in the seat she'd just vacated.

Suddenly, he wasn't in the mood to relive his past. "There's not much to tell. I joined the Navy out of high school, went to night school to earn my degree—"

"In what?"

"International politics."

Her eyes brightened. "That's a lot like my minor in global studies." She cut off a corner of her crepe and stuck it in her mouth.

"Except that I took my classes online. I didn't go to a prestigious college like Rice." His tone mocked her choice of universities.

"You know what college I attended?"

He shrugged. "It was in your files. The detail stuck with me."

"And when did you decide to become a Navy SEAL?" she asked.

He thought back. "At OCS, Officer Candidate School. I didn't like the Senior Chief telling me I wasn't officer material. Wanted to prove that not only could I lead, but I could kick his ass to the next planet."

Maddy searched his face with a thoughtful expression.

He ducked his chin self-consciously and worked on putting away the fried potatoes. They'd been overcooked, not nearly as good as his mama made them.

"Now that you've proven the world wrong, you should be able to relax and bask in your accomplishments," Maddy reasoned.

He considered her logic with cynicism. "It doesn't

really work that way," he replied. "Better drink your coffee before it gets cold," he added changing the subject.

She wisely let the topic drop. They moved on to other matters, like what would happen next and when she might be allowed to return to Mariscal Estigarribia to finish her research. She polished off half of her crepe then retreated into the bathroom again, this time emerging in the clothes he'd brought for her—not nearly as sexy as her dress but somehow still sexy on her remarkable frame.

"I hope Daddy takes me shopping soon," she muttered, grimacing at her reflection.

Sam stiffened at the telling comment. She was obviously used to being pampered. How was he supposed to compete with a billionaire on his modest salary?

Her phone rang as if on cue. She took the call with the same brightening of her expression. She loved her father—that much was clear. "He's waiting in the lobby," she announced, looking for Sam's feedback. He pushed the tray away. "We'll be right down, Daddy," she added.

Three minutes later, they emerged from the elevator to find a weary-looking Lyle Scott in a rumpled suit, his thick head of silver hair mussed, dozing on one of the lobby's sofas. Three bodyguards stood at a discreet distance, looking rested and vigilant, along with a familiar-looking older gentleman. Where had Sam seen him before?

"Daddy!" Maddy roused her father by shaking him gently awake then lowering herself into his lap.

Sam felt like a third wheel as he sized up Lyle Scott's watchdogs out of the corners of his eyes. Paul Van Slyke didn't stand much of a chance of killing his brother-in-law now.

Lyle returned his daughter's embrace with a hug so fierce Sam feared he'd snap Maddy's ribs. "Sweetheart, I'm so glad you're safe!" His bloodshot gaze traveled over her shoulder to where Sam stood with his hands in his pockets. "Lt. Sasseville."

Without releasing his daughter, Lyle Scott managed to come to his feet. Keeping Maddy anchored by his side, he extended Sam a forceful handshake, one that showed no sign of easing up. "Son, looks like I owe you again," he said with a throb of real emotion in his voice.

"Not at all," Sam muttered, seriously concerned that Maddy's father might start to cry.

"Daddy, we think Uncle Paul sabotaged our plane last night," Maddy gently inserted, regaining her father's attention.

Lyle's brown eyes widened in horror. "What?"

"He put a bullet in one of the wings, causing us to lose fuel," she explained. "We had to crash-land in a field two hours from here, but we're fine, thanks to my colleague Ricardo who was piloting the plane and found us a ride to this hotel."

Her father turned to the man Sam had recognized but hadn't identified. "Did you hear that, Harry?" he demanded. "The bastard tried to kill my daughter. With a plane crash!" he added, visibly blanching.

"Sit down, Daddy," Maddy urged, reading his shock accurately.

The man named Harry moved closer to them and also urged Lyle Scott to sit. "Special Agent Hodges," he said to Maddy, including Sam in his introduction. "FBI. We met the night of the shooting in McLean."

How could Sam have forgotten? Hodges was the one who'd tried suggesting Sam was in cahoots with the shooter. "Mr. Scott tells me you believe you've identified the shooter as Van Slyke's bodyguard?"

"I'm sure of it," Sam said. "He fits the description from the ring he wears to the wrestling move he pulled on me."

Hodges nodded. "I've accompanied Mr. Scott to Paraguay to question Van Slyke in person. It's apparent that he's got a motive for wanting your father out of the way," he said, addressing Maddy. "And you believe he sabotaged your plane?"

They spent the better part of the next hour hashing out the details of Maddy's escape from Mariscal Estigarribia. "Honestly, I think my uncle might have intended to poison me over dinner with the wine he was serving."

Sam blinked and stared at Maddy in disbelief. "Why didn't you mention this before?"

"Because I didn't drink it. No worries," she assured him with a shrug.

"What makes you think it was poisoned?" asked the FBI agent and her father at the same time.

"He kept foisting it on me, trying to make me feel guilty if I didn't drink some."

"We'll look into that," the agent promised, but his tone remained skeptical.

"And I think maybe..." She swallowed hard, darting an uncertain look at her father who looked more haggard by the moment. "When our plane was going down last night, it occurred to me that...my uncle might be responsible for my mother's death as well," she said quickly.

"Maddy!" her father exclaimed in horror.

"Just let me finish," she begged, squeezing his hand in a gesture of sympathy. "We know the cause of her crash was water in the fuel tanks, correct?"

"Yes, we know that. It was an unfortunate circumstance caused by a downpour the day before. Someone must have left the fuel cap open. Those planes are notorious for their faulty caps."

"But what if it wasn't an unfortunate circumstance? I've read Mom's journals, Daddy, including the one we recovered from the wreck. I know you haven't read them because it's too painful for you. So maybe you never knew how much she opposed drilling in El Chaco. She wrote down all of her objections in the journal, and she was flying home to beg you to stop the prospecting. She didn't want Scott Oil drilling in Paraguay; however, I'm certain Uncle Paul did."

Lyle Scott's brown eyes glazed over as he retreated into dark thoughts.

Special Agent Hodges eyed her dubiously. "I'd say that's a bit of a stretch," he drawled. "I can't imagine Van Slyke would attempt to murder his own sister."

"He pushed her out of a tree when they were children," Maddy argued. "What kind of brother would do that?"

"We'll look into it," Hodges said again. "There is no statute of limitations that would prevent us from charging him with murder if we find there's evidence," he added reassuringly.

"So what happens now?" Maddy asked. "When can I go back? I've got work to finish."

"Not yet." Her father, although clearly exhausted, shook his head implacably. "Until your uncle is in custody and denied bond, you're staying as far away from him as possible."

"Who's running the company?" she inquired.

"For the time being, it's the board of directors. I'll have to name a replacement for Paul, but if the man I trusted most in the world has turned on me, who can I trust?" he wondered out loud. His stricken expression made Sam feel sorry for him.

Maddy rubbed his arm encouragingly. "I'm sure there's someone." She turned to the FBI investigator.

"How long is it going to take to arrest my uncle?" she queried.

He shrugged. "Might not take so long. Could be just a matter of days, if the bodyguard cops a plea to save his own hide."

"Where do I stay in the meantime? Here?" She cast a glum look around the tasteful lobby.

Her father roused from his thoughts to pat his pockets. "Well, I thought about that, actually," he admitted, pulling a folded piece of paper from his breast pocket. "It occurred to me that Sam has a few more days' leave, and you don't want to spend more time than necessary flying from one continent to the other, so perhaps you two would like to take a vacation."

Sam blinked at the unexpected offer. He'd told Lyle Scott he was on leave when he'd shared his revelation about Elliot Koch.

"A vacation?" Maddy repeated, saying the world like it was something alien and reprehensible.

"Honey, you need it." Her father held her gaze with a benign but firm look. "You've given everything you have to helping other people. When do you ever take the time to pamper yourself?"

"I do that every time I visit you in McLean," she protested. "Vacations are boring."

"Not this one," her father insisted, handing her the printout. "You're going to love Curacao," he avowed. "I've booked you at an all-inclusive resort on the beach. There's horseback riding, golf, a spa, tennis— all the recreation you can imagine. And best of all, it's right next to a forward operating base for the U.S. military. Sam can fly out of there and back to Virginia Beach with just his military ID."

Maddy looked visibly torn. She looked to Sam for his opinion. "What do you think?" she asked.

He had trouble finding his tongue. A vacation with Maddy at an all-inclusive resort in Curacao, a Netherland's owned island just off the cost of Venezuela, sounded like paradise. On the other hand, her father had arranged is, which made Sam feel manipulated. Taking Maddy on an island vacation was something Sam would have had to scrounge to afford. He could probably do it at least once, but only for a super special occasion. Like a honeymoon—the thought popped into his head. It didn't hold nearly the same appeal when her father had arranged all the details. Then again, Sam would be earning his keep, wouldn't he, acting as Maddy's bodyguard?

A kernel of resentment heated and popped inside of him. "And what happens when my leave runs out?" he demanded. "I just fly off and leave Maddy alone?"

"I'll take your place in Curacao when that happens. Or perhaps Paul will have been arrested by then," Lyle Scott replied.

"And then I can go back to Paraguay to finish my work," Maddy said hopefully. She bit her lower lip, her gaze sliding back to Sam. "What do you think?"

A hint of anticipation sparkled in her lovely eyes. He was helpless against it. "Why not?" he answered, revealing just a trace of bitterness. But in the back of his mind he was thinking, *If this is how it's going to be with her father controlling our lives, we're never going to make it.*

He reminded himself what a remarkable woman Maddy was, how great sex was between them, how well their world views meshed. Any normal man would be thrilled to have a girlfriend whose rich father loved to spoil her. Bronco and Bullfrog would be sick with envy when they heard where Sam had spent the majority of his leave time. "Sounds like fun," he forced himself to add. "When do we leave?"

# CHAPTER 17

From the vantage of a horse's back, Maddy took in the view with a gasp of wonder. The trail had led them to the height of a promontory overlooking the Southern Caribbean Ocean.

"Oh, Sam," she marveled, slowing her mare so that his horse could get abreast of hers. Impossible shades of blue—sapphire, then tourmaline, then aqua— lightened by degrees as it approached the horseshoe beach below them. This would be the highlight of their horseback riding tour, a gallop in the surf. She held out a hand so they could share this moment. "Isn't it breathtaking?"

The gentleness of the hand clasping hers completed her happiness. They'd spent three unforgettable days so far exploring the island—visiting the sea aquarium, spelunking in the Hato caves, swimming with dolphins at the Dolphin Academy. Their two evenings here brought romantic strolls, dishes to die for, and hours in bed getting to know exactly what pleased each other.

"It's like a dream," Sam agreed, but his gaze wasn't on the view. She could see him out of the corner of her eye watching her response to the vista.

Tearing her gaze from the water, she took in his tanned visage with an unmistakable melting of her heart. "I love you," she stated, prompting a look of startled pleasure. There had been no premeditation on her part, simply a certainty that demanded articulation and conveyed the enormity of her joy in this moment.

A flicker of uncertainty lowered the flames in Sam's eyes as they searched her face. "You love me or you love this vacation?" he inquired.

"Sam!" Not only had he ripped the rug out from under her declaration, but he'd even doubted the veracity of her words. "How can you ask that? I wouldn't say I love you if I didn't mean it. Of course this vacation is fabulous." She threw out an arm to encompass their playground. "I've had the time of my life here. But that wouldn't be the case with any other person. It's you who have made this experience so special. I'm not imagining things."

He hung his head for a moment, pretending to adjust the reins that had fallen over the pommel of his saddle. If not for the smile playing at the edges of his lips, she might have grown nervous that he didn't return the sentiment. At last, his curly lashes swept upward and he met her gaze directly. A hint of ruddy color stood out on his cheekbones. And then he lunged in the saddle, catching her head in his hand to press a brief but blistering kiss on her lips.

"I love you, too," he said, so softly that his words seemed to blend with the crash of the surf below them.

Pleasure flowed through Maddy's veins, prompting that same thready racing of her heart that unnerved her for its unexpectedness. There wasn't any reason for her heart to act like it was struggling to pump blood through her body. She automatically pressed her palm to her breastbone, taking deep breaths to strengthen the fast, feeble beats.

Sam hadn't noticed. He'd pointed down the beach where their guide, a tanned, shirtless youth, galloped through the mild surf below them, kicking up water in his wake. They'd turned out to be the only two guests on this tour, and after their guide discovered they were both competent riders, he'd kept his distance, giving them plenty of privacy.

"You ready for this?" Sam gestured with a grin for her to lead the way.

Maddy's pulse had yet to even out. "You first," she invited, reluctant to ruin this moment by complaining that her heart was acting up again. The last time she'd mentioned it, at the Dolphin Academy, Sam had made her get out of the water in front of everyone. He'd gotten the medics to take her blood pressure which had been a little low, but nothing life-threatening. In another few seconds the odd episode would be over, anyway. It only ever lasted a few minutes at a time.

Sam hesitated, searching her expression with eyes that missed nothing. "It's not that steep," he promised, mistaking the reason for her hesitancy. The trail winding down to the beach looked more precarious than anything they'd traversed so far.

Maddy could have pointed out that she'd taken horseback riding lessons from the age of five, but Sam would probably think her an elitist snob. "I'd rather you went first," she said with a tremulous smile.

Eager to reassure her—she knew he would be—he guided his horse down the trail ahead of her. Maddy fixed her gaze on the twitching chestnut tail in front of her as her mare automatically followed his gelding. To her relief, her heart resumed its normal steady beat, but then a peculiar numbness settled on her tongue, making it feel swollen and immobile. The odd sensation had her wondering if she'd drunk enough water. She reached into the pack hanging off the side of the saddle, grateful to her mare for negotiating the winding decline without direction.

As Maddy untwisted the cap on her water bottle, her fingers began to tingle. Razor-like pain shot up her fingers into her wrists. Growing increasingly concerned, she tossed back a quick sip only to sputter and cough when swallowing proved difficult. The bottle slipped suddenly out of her hand, tumbling into a patch of sea grass.

"Sam, wait!" she called, but her tongue could barely form the words, and her voice failed to carry over the rush of the waves on the sand.

Sam glanced back with a grin of anticipation as he reached the open beach. Without noticing her stricken expression, he jabbed his heels into his horse's flanks and spurred it into a gallop. Maddy's mare took her cue from the gelding and lurched into a trot, catching Maddy off guard. She squeezed her knees to keep her seat. She could feel the wind in her hair, the roll of the saddle beneath her bottom, but that was all she could feel as numbness stole over her in an implacable tide.

What's wrong with me? her mind cried.

The mare headed straight for the water, where the sloping beach threatened to upset Maddy's balance. She felt herself teetering in the saddle and fought to right herself, but her arms proved uncooperative and gravity won.

She listed toward the water, hoping to jump clear of her horse in lieu of falling. She managed to swing her right leg over the horse's rump. She started for the water feet first, but then her left foot tangled in the stirrup, upending her even as it kept her attached to her horse.

Arms flailing, she failed to catch hold of the saddlebag before her head and shoulders plunged into warm salt water.

If Sam had wings, he was certain he'd be airborne. Even without them, he felt weightless, kept aloft by the powerful beast vaulting him repeatedly into the air. *She loves me!*

He hadn't realized how profoundly Maddy's confession would affect him. Plenty of women had said those words to him in the past. But none of them held a candle to Madison Scott. Despite his initial cynicism, he'd *felt* her tenderness; he'd *seen* the passion and wonder that filled her eyes when their heated bodies came blissfully together. They'd connected on every level—mentally, emotionally, and physically. She *did* love him. And in defiance to the voice whispering in his head that their backgrounds were too dissimilar to make a relationship last, he'd said he loved her, too.

Because he did—probably from the moment he'd clapped eyes on her. He'd tried to fight it, not wanting to face his hatred and disgust for the wealthy. He'd even tried telling himself these feelings were an illusion conjured by her billionaire father in some wily plan to put a Navy SEAL in his back pocket by marrying him off to his daughter.

But it wasn't the setting that sealed their commitment to each other. It was the knowledge that in spite of their hugely different socio-economic backgrounds, they were meant for each other. Always had been.

With peaceful resolve, Sam slowed his mount so that Maddy could catch up with him. He could hear the thunder of her mare's approach, but she was slowing down, not speeding up. As he twisted in the saddle to look back, their guide gave a shout and wheeled his horse around. Sam's soaring heart plunged at the sight of Maddy hanging by one stirrup, her upper body being dragged from the surf onto the sand by a horse that hobbled uncertainly toward them.

"Maddy!" With a strangled cry, Sam wheeled about, upsetting his docile mount with the unexpected command. For an agonizing moment, the horse resisted but as the guide went tearing past him, it shot forward, nearly unseating Sam who clung to his seat.

Closing the short distance between them and Maddy, both men vaulted off their horses at the same time. Sam went to free Maddy's ankle from the tangled stirrup while the guide paused to calm the shaken mare. Once freed, the lower half of Maddy's body fell lifelessly onto the sand.

"Maddy!" Sam dropped to his knees and gave her a shake.

She stared back at him, as still as a corpse.

"Maddy, can you breathe?" he asked, falling back on his training to assess the seriousness of the situation. When she didn't answer, he put an ear to her mouth, relieved beyond words to hear a wheezing in her throat. "She's breathing. She must have had the air knocked out of her," he decided, glancing at the guide for corroboration. The kid just looked back at him. Obviously, nothing like this had ever happened on a guided tour before.

"You're going to be okay," Sam said, catching Maddy's cold face in his hands. He tilted her head back, opening her airway. The way she stared at him made his skin shrink. Her hair was wet. Maybe the horse had dragged her through the water and she'd inhaled some. But he was afraid to roll her onto her side lest she'd suffered a spine injury. "Are you just stunned?" he asked, searching her huge frightened eyes for clues. "Blink your eyes if you're just stunned."

She stared at him, not blinking.

*Christ.* "Maddy, blink your eyes if something's really wrong." It sounded like someone else was talking.

She gave a slow, deliberate blink and every possibility in the world occurred to him at once, from a broken back to an epileptic seizure. He glanced helplessly up at the tour guide who was fetching something from his horse. "We have to get her to a hospital, now!" he shouted.

The kid nodded and showed him the cell phone he'd pulled from his pack. "I'll call the ranch," he said in Spanish—thankfully not in Dutch which many of the white islanders spoke. "They'll bring an ATV to pick us up."

"Okay." Sam looked back at Maddy whose stare hadn't wavered. "*Querida*, what's wrong?" he demanded, embarrassed to hear his voice crack. He'd kept a level head under far worse conditions. At least there wasn't any blood pouring out of her, no gaping bullet wounds, no limbs ripped off her body. He'd seen all that and never been as scared as he was now.

Her tongue moved slightly as if she was trying to talk, but the roar and retreat of the waves and the cry of a seabird were the only answers he got.

Maddy roused by degrees. With her heavy eyelids still shut, she listened to the rhythmic beat of a heart monitor, the low-pitched murmur of many voices. Someone not too far away from her seemed to be moaning in pain. A thin blanket covered her chilled limbs, and she could tell that she was naked. The tangy-sweet smell of betadine and the pinching sensation on the top of her right hand had her prying her eyelids open with alarm.

She lay in a cubicle of sorts, surrounded on all sides

by sheer curtains.

"Sam?" she called. Footsteps drew closer and one of the curtains slid open. A bright-eyed nurse marched over to smile down at her.

"You're awake and talking," she exclaimed, as if the two actions together were unheard of. "Doctor Troost," she called over her shoulder. "Miss Scott's alert."

A lean, balding doctor joined the nurse by her bed and studied her through his spectacles. "How are you feeling?" he asked with a faint Dutch accent.

Maddy queried her body. "Fine," she decided. "My ankle hurts a little."

"It's a sprain, nothing serious. We were more concerned with your paralysis and stabilizing your vitals." He flicked a glanced at the heart monitor. Took a penlight from his pocket and shone it in her eyes. "Make a fist for me?" he requested.

Maddy did as he requested, using the hand that wasn't attached to the IV tube. "What happened to me?" she asked. "Where's Sam?"

The doctor looked up. "Your boyfriend's in the waiting room. Only family are permitted in the ER. After we transfer you to a regular room, he may join you." His grave, puzzled expression kept her from drawing a full breath as she waited for him to answer her first question. "It appears that you were poisoned, Miss Scott," he added, not mincing his words.

"Poisoned?" Maddy's thoughts went straight to the glass of wine her uncle had insisted she drink. Her instincts had been right.

"By a plant that grows in the Amazon—*cojungali.* When consumed, chemicals in *cojungali* block the neurotransmitter acetylcholine, required by your nerve cells if you're to control the actions of your muscles. You're extremely fortunate that I am familiar with this poison from time I spent with the Amazon Conservation Team."

Interest licked through her—she would love to ask him more about his experience.

"And even luckier for you, I also know the antidote, an enzyme that destroys the protein blocking the neurotransmitter. In a North American hospital, your symptoms would have been treated, but the poison would have continued to attack your nervous system, eventually killing you."

The enormity of the doctor's words tore through Maddy's consciousness like the shockwaves of an earthquake. "I'd be dead right now," she reiterated, thinking of how both Sam and her father would have reacted to her unexpected death. It was never more apparent that her mother's spirit had saved her again, connecting her with the one doctor who recognized her symptoms and suspected the true cause. Tears of profound gratitude rushed into Maddy's eyes.

"I'm required by law to inform the police," Dr. Troost added, sobering her instantly.

She huffed out a bitter laugh. "The FBI's already investigating the man who most likely did this," she admitted. In the next few minutes, she sketched for the doctor an embarrassing account of her family drama.

A phone conversation with her father the day before had informed her and Sam that Paul Van Slyke had disappeared from Paraguay by the time Lyle Scott showed up at his mansion in Mariscal Estigarribia. Interpol had pounced on him when he'd arrived at customs in Switzerland, but without corroborating proof of any wrongdoing, no confession on Paul's part, and Elliot Koch nowhere to be found, the FBI had instructed Interpol to let him go. By the time Maddy finished her explanation, Dr. Troost's eyebrows had risen to where his hairline ought to have been.

"I see," he said faintly. "You will still have to explain all this to the police when they come visit you."

*Whatever,* Maddy thought. "Can I see Sam?" she pleaded.

"As soon as you are moved to a private room. I'll clear you for transfer shortly," he promised. Picking up a clipboard from the end of her bed, he checked his way through it, paused and looked up. "Is there any chance you could be pregnant, Miss Scott?"

The question caught Maddy off guard. The memory of making love with Sam those first two times brought a flood of heat to her cheeks. They'd both been too enraptured with each other, too caught up in the moment to think about safe sex. Ever since then, Sam had been scrupulous about using a condom. "I don't...think so," she slowly replied.

Keen blue eyes probed her uncertain expression. "Your HCG levels are normal," he informed her, "which suggests that you're not, but perhaps it's too soon to tell. Should you find yourself pregnant, I would advise you to abort," he added gently. "There's no telling how the neurotoxin might have affected an embryo."

Maddy swallowed against a dry throat. "I'm sure I'm not," she told him quickly. Sorrow swamped her at the thought of having to abort a baby conceived in love.

"Very well. It was remarkable to meet you," Dr. Troost added, extending a handshake. "I have this strange feeling it was meant to be."

"I know it was," Maddy said with certainty.

"Good luck finding your uncle," he added. "Here is my card," he added, slipping her a business card from the pocket of his white coat. "You may share it with law enforcement personnel should they require a statement or copies of your medical files. I'd be happy to testify on your behalf."

Maddy glanced down noting his email address. "Thank you, doctor. Perhaps I could ask you more about your experience with the Amazon Conservation Team? I'm a conservationist myself, working with the Global Environmental Fund."

"Are you, now?" he exclaimed, becoming less stiff and more relaxed by the moment.

They chatted for several more minutes until an orderly appeared to wheel her out of the ER and down a hall into an elevator. Maddy caught a glimpse of Sam behind a wall of glass. "Oh, there's my...boyfriend," she said, the words sounding strange to her ears. She pointed him out to the orderly. "Please get him for me."

"It's against hospital regulations, lady," said the orderly kindly. "The doctor will tell him in a moment where to find you."

"Sam!"

Sam lifted his face out of his hands, wondering if he was hearing voices. He'd been lost in thought, praying every prayer he could remember from his childhood and reliving the gut-wrenching helplessness he'd experienced from the moment he'd seen Maddy being dragged by her horse.

The guide and a representative from the horse-riding tour had helped him transfer Maddy's limp body into a four-wheel drive vehicle. They'd raced to the only hospital on the island, seven miles away. Every second of that ride, Sam had clung to Maddy's hand and begged her to hang on.

A vision of Lyle Scott bursting into the ER's

waiting room brought him back to the present. The billionaire looked even more careworn and rumpled than the last time Sam had seen him in the Marriott lobby in Asunción. The tail of his light-weight cotton shirt was untucked. His fair skin had been burned by the sun; his hair was windblown. Sam pushed to his feet to greet him.

"Where is she?" Maddy's father demanded, not bothering to shake Sam's hand or embrace him as he had in the past. "Where's Maddy?"

Sam glanced at his watch, though the sky's pink hue outside the windows had already informed him how much time had passed. "She's still in the ER. I brought her in about five hours ago," he conveyed, too worried to feign optimism for her father's sake. "They won't let me see her."

"Well, that's about to change," Scott growled, turning toward the check-in desk.

Just then, a gaunt doctor with intelligent blue eyes that shone behind his spectacles approached them. "I'm Dr. Troost," he said with a hint of an accent. "You're both here for Madison Scott?" He looked them each in the eye.

"Yes," said her father before Sam could speak. "How is she?"

"Recovered," said the doctor simply. "At first I thought her a victim of sarin poisoning, but the symptoms were slightly different. I'd seen something similar in my work in the Amazon."

Sam's incredulity rose as he heard the doctor say that she'd been poisoned by a plant unique to South America. Luckily, the antidote to the poison was a simple enzyme, one that reversed the effects immediately. Relief turned Sam's bones to liquid, making it hard for him to stay standing.

"She will need to be monitored another twenty-four

hours, but she appears fully recovered," the doctor added into their stunned silence.

"Poison," Lyle finally repeated, clearly as shocked and dumbfounded as Sam was.

"She said something about her uncle forcing her to drink some wine?" One of the doctor's eyebrows rose over the other.

Lyle looked at Sam, his eyes wide with remorse. "She mentioned the possibility back in Asunción, remember? None of us took her seriously."

"Because she said she didn't drink any," Sam recalled. "Apparently, she did. Why didn't we see any signs of this earlier?" he asked the doctor.

Troost grimaced. "The poison has a delayed response," he explained. "It takes a day or two to affect the nervous system. If she consumed very little, it would have taken even longer. Still, without the antidote, her heart may eventually have stopped beating. She is lucky to be alive."

"My God," Lyle Scott exclaimed, putting his hands to his pale face.

"She's in room 213. You may visit her now." The doctor gestured to the elevator.

"Thank you." Lyle spared a second to pump the doctor's hand before charging toward the elevator. Sam followed on his heels, his knees still distinctly squishy.

Her heart may eventually have stopped beating.

Shock seeped into his bloodstream, forcing him to lean against the elevator wall as he went suddenly lightheaded. Over the ringing in his ears, he could hear Lyle Scott's ragged breathing. The man was having as hard a time digesting the news as he was. He regarded him sidelong. "I'm sorry," he started to say.

"This should never have happened," Lyle said at the

same time.

While Sam knew none of this was his fault, and while Lyle's comment hadn't been directed at him, guilt burned a hole in his gut. He felt as though he'd let her father down.

Room 213 stood across from the elevator. Lyle gave a swift knock before pushing his way inside. Sam followed more slowly.

"Daddy!"

He hung back, giving father and daughter time to reunite—*again*. This was starting to be a trend.

Maddy looked none the worse for wear, though she now wore a hospital gown in lieu of the bikini that had driven him wild for what it didn't reveal. Under the gown, she had to be wearing a heart monitor because he could see her heartbeat blipping on a device mounted to a shelf behind her. Her tangled hair was still probably full of sand. Christ, he'd never get over the shock of seeing her being dragged by her horse, as limp as a ragdoll.

She clung to her father, patting him consolingly on the back as he clung to her, white-knuckled, clearly fighting to keep his composure. "It's okay, Daddy. I'm okay," she crooned.

Catching Sam's eye as he lingered near the door, she sent him a smile that warmed him clear to his toes and compelled him to shuffle closer. "Sam, I'm so sorry," she apologized, taking the blame for what had happened. "It must have been the wine at Uncle Paul's. I only had a sip or two at most."

"That son of a bitch," Lyle railed, pulling his haggard face from Maddy's shoulder standing at his full height. Sam could see him trembling suppressed rage. "I swear to God I'm going to make him pay for this!"

"Can't we get him on attempted murder now?"

Maddy asked. "It's obvious he tried to kill me."

Lyle shrugged and shook his head. "Only how do we prove it was the wine? You could have ingested poison by eating something here that was tainted." He glanced in Sam's direction causing Sam's gut to tighten reflexively.

"What evidence do we have so far?" Maddy asked.

Lyle Scott visibly reined himself in. "No, no. We're not going to talk about this now." He patted her hand. His gaze swung to the heart monitor pulsing quietly and steadily. "You've just been through hell, honey. The doctor said your heart could have stopped."

"It's been beating funny for days now," she admitted, glancing guiltily at Sam, whose jaw muscles jumped as he clenched his teeth. "I didn't want to alarm anyone, but I started having symptoms the night Ricardo pulled me out of Uncle Paul's house." She looked back at her father. "Why don't you have a seat and we'll discuss what you've found."

Lyle heaved a sigh then went to collapse into the arm chair. Sam sat on the end of Maddy's bed, unable to tear his gaze from her beloved face, still reeling at the thought of her heart stopping. He laid a hand on her knee, which was covered with a blanket. Every inch of her body was now branded in his memory. He knew every freckle, every small scar, every pleasure point.

"Elliot Koch's body was found just this morning," Lyle Scott announced, wresting Sam's attention back to him. "It was lying in an alley behind that bar in town, *La Cantina*. No evidence of foul play. The coroner thinks he had a heart attack."

"That's terrible," Maddy murmured.

"Especially since the FBI was counting on him to inform against Paul, and now he can't," her father added grimly. "According to witnesses, he'd been hanging around town, cursing Paul for giving him the sack."

"Why would Uncle Paul fire him now?" Maddy mused.

Lyle turned his gaze on Sam. "When you retrieved Maddy from Paul's home that night, he must have guessed our suspicions. Maybe he realized that you recognized his bodyguard from the night he tried to shoot me."

Sam thought back and nodded. "That's distinctly possible. He caught me staring at Elliot when he met with my task unit to discuss the explosion. But I can't believe Elliot actually died of a heart attack. That doesn't sound right." The wrestler had been too active, too young to succumb to a heart attack. Another alternative occurred to him and, in light of what had just happened to Maddy, it made perfect sense. "What if he was poisoned, the same way Maddy was?"

"What if he was?" Maddy repeated as they gaped at each other. Sam hadn't thought that father and daughter resembled each other at all until that minute.

"It may have looked like a heart attack, but what if his heart just gave out like mine almost did?" she added.

Excitement coursed through Sam's veins. "If you can prove he was poisoned the same way Maddy was, the FBI can probably make a charge stick."

"Dr. Troost gave me his card," she recalled, reaching for the white rectangle next to her bed. "You can get the name and the characteristics of the poison from the doctor, then tell the medical examiner in Paraguay to look for them in Elliot's blood."

Her father rolled out of the chair to take the card. "I'll do that," he agreed. "Can't hurt to try." Hope smoothed some of the lines from his careworn expression. "And if his bodyguard was poisoned the same way, we can charge him with attempting to murder you, also."

"And then I can go back to Paraguay and finish my work," Maddy said, her words prompting utter silence.

In that moment, Sam felt as sorry for her father as he did for himself. Letting Maddy flit off to other continents to do her work was going to be the hardest part about being in a relationship with her, especially since his own job had him doing pretty much the same thing.

Dismay wreathed Lyle's face, making him once again look every one of his sixty-five years. "Maddy," he said, dragging the armchair closer so he could sit in it while still holding her hand. "You don't need to finish your work with GEF," he said gently. "I'll send my own people to take a closer look at the situation. Any significant pollution being created by my wells will be cleaned up and contained for good, I swear it on your mother's name."

"Daddy, you're not the CEO anymore. You're not even in charge of the board of directors," she pointed out. "You can't guarantee that they'll agree to that expenditure."

"Of course they will. They're all still loyal to me."

"Even if they will, this is something Mom would have wanted me to do," Maddy insisted, knowing that argument would win him over.

Lyle fell silent. "Fine," he gruffly relented, "but you're not going back to Paraguay until your uncle is arrested," he insisted.

Maddy rolled her eyes. "What's he going to do to me from Switzerland?" she reasoned. "Nothing. He knows the gig is up. Killing me now won't make a lick of difference. Just let me go, Daddy."

"We'll talk about this later," he said on a sterner note.

Maddy fell quiet. Sam could tell by the way she pursed her lips together that she was going back soon, regardless of her father's wishes. And where would he be when that happened? Either training in Virginia Beach or in the mountains of Nevada or even in Alaska—it all depended on the terrain of the task unit's next big Op.

The conversation shifted to concerns that were far less controversial. Maddy regaled her father with the highlights of her and Sam's time together. Her happy smile reminded him of her declaration of love. Their feelings for each other were strong enough to merit a commitment.

*We're going to do this,* Sam thought, rubbing her calf through the blanket. On one hand it felt perfectly right; on the other, he was petrified. What did the future hold for them? Could they really nurture the feelings they shared while spending so much time apart?

He knew he had to try. He couldn't let Maddy slip out of his hands a second time. It had been hard enough to put her from his mind after Matamoros.

"When do you have to head home, Sam?" Lyle Scott asked him, as if reading his mind.

"I have to report in tomorrow by noon," Sam replied, fighting the weightiness that shackled his heart, threatening to drag him into despondency.

Maddy's mouth immediately drooped at the corners, letting him know that his imminent departure saddened her, as well. He found himself wishing Lyle Scott had stayed in Paraguay so he and Maddy could spend their last night alone together, even if it was in a hospital. But then Maddy's situation had been critical. In any case, her father had been planning to collect his daughter when Sam's leave was over.

Lyle Scott stood up. "Well, I'll leave you two alone while I go find a bite to eat. I'm famished," he declared, proving himself more astute than Sam had realized. He bent down and gave Maddy a swift kiss on the cheek. "Could I speak to you for a minute in the hall, Sam?" he requested as he headed for the door.

Sam glanced at Maddy for permission then said, "Sure," and trailed him out into the hall.

He found Lyle Scott clenching and unclenching his hands, looking totally overwrought. "Sam, I have a proposition for you, and I hope you'll give it some serious consideration."

Sam suffered the certainty that he wasn't going to like what he was about to hear. "What is it?"

Lyle heaved a weary sigh. The halogen lighting drew attention to the dark circles under his bloodshot eyes. "I know my daughter's work means a lot to her, the same way it did to her mother. But the stress is killing me," he admitted. "I can't focus on my platform when I'm worried for her welfare."

Sam slid his hands into his pockets. "What do you want me to do?" he asked warily.

"I'd like to ask you to try to convince her to stay in the States for a while, maybe get a job in Virginia, close to you. You seem to have a strong pull on her. Maybe if you got engaged or something," he hinted, avoiding Sam's incredulous stare.

"If she still won't quit," Lyle continued, clearly uncomfortable with Sam's continued silence, "I'd like to make you an offer. If you would leave the Teams and guard my daughter fulltime, I'll pay you twice your current salary. I know that sounds presumptuous. I just—" His voice cracked with emotion. "I can't *stand* the thought of anything happening to her."

A ten ton tank might as well have rolled right over Sam. The offer had floored him. Presumptuous? Hell, yes, it was presumptuous. It smacked of elitism and superiority and all those disgusting attributes he associated with the filthy rich. "You want me to give up my career to be your daughter's security detail?"

A stricken look entered Lyle Scott's eyes as apparently it occurred to him that he'd gone too far. "No, no, of course not." He swept away the offer with a wave of his hands. "I'm sorry. I'm so overcome with fears and doubts right now that I don't know what I'm saying."

"But you said the words," Sam insisted, his heart hardened to the man's obvious distress. "Can I ask you something?"

"Of course." Lyle sounded eager to make amends.

"Did you lean on General DePuy and therefore SOCOM to get the SEALs sent to Paraguay to defend your oil wells?"

Lyle's eyes widened with guilt. "Well, I might have suggested it. But he told me SOCOM has no say-so over your foreign operations. That was strictly up to the Joint Special Operations Taskforce."

And so it was. But there was no telling how much influence SOCOM had in JSOTF's decision making.

An awkward silence fell between them. Sam stood taller to counteract the feelings of inferiority and indignation sluicing through him. Here was this man thinking he could be bought, thinking he had a right to sway the military to protect his interests. This wasn't only about Maddy and her safety. This was about Lyle Scott believing that his wealth gave him the right to manipulate others, even to the point of suggesting Sam get engaged to Maddy and give up his career for her sake.

*Hell, no.*

"I think I've said enough," Lyle acknowledged, lowering his gaze. He turned away with a nod. "I'll go get some food."

In a tumultuous frame of mind, Sam watched him walk away until he'd disappeared from view. And then he turned and looked at Maddy's door.

A memory surfaced suddenly. He had felt this way back when Wendy the prom queen's father had convinced the judge not to post bail for her daughter's alleged attacker. Sam had spent the next two months awaiting trial at the state penitentiary, alongside hardened felons and child molesters. He'd been beaten, taunted, and very nearly sexually molested—all because Wendy's father's wealth had allowed him to influence the system.

Sam had loathed rich people ever since for thinking they had the right to manipulate those beneath them. Maddy's father wasn't any different. Both men had meant well. Both had wanted to protect their daughters, but to assume that Sam would give up his hard-won status as a Navy SEAL was every bit as arrogant as assuming Sam was guilty of rape just because he was Latino.

In Lyle's eyes, Sam would never be seen as Maddy's equal. He was nothing more than a tool to be manipulated, an insurance policy for keeping her safe. It had been that way from the moment Lyle clapped eyes on him. The only reason Lyle had found Maddy the job with GEF was because he'd found out through his friend General DePuy that Sam would be operating in the same location. Having noticed the chemistry between Sam and his daughter aboard the *Harry S. Truman*, he'd probably said to himself, "Now here's someone who can look after Maddy so I don't have to."

*Well, guess what, Mr. Billionaire? This is one man*

*who can't be bought. I may never make the kind of money you do, but I'm my own man. No one manipulates me!*

With a deep inhale, Sam sought to harness his runaway temper.

And what about Maddy? he asked himself. Did she have any inkling of what her father had just offered him? Surely not. She had never once hinted he should quit his job and shadow her for the rest of their lives. Sam, on the other hand, had suggested she quit *her* job. That probably made him a hypocrite, but it didn't change the fact that her father had manipulated circumstances in the past and had just attempted to influence Sam's very future. At the very least, he'd suggested that Sam and Maddy get engaged.

Hah! Like he had any say-so in Sam's future matrimonial plans.

He had *no* say-so. None at all. And there would *be* no future plans, because Sam would sooner face a lifetime of looking for a woman who made him feel the way Maddy did than bow to another man's dictates.

# CHAPTER 18

Maddy regarded the door with concern. Sam had been out of the room for more than ten minutes. She'd overheard her father's voice at first and then the sound of him walking away. Still no Sam. She could use a cup of ice water, and she was hoping the nurse would remove the little stickers on her chest so she could get up and wash her hair. Maybe Sam could help her with that? She didn't want to spend the last night of her vacation looking like something the tide had washed in.

At last the door opened—slowly. Sam edged into the room and right away, she sensed the anger and resentment emanating off his stiffly held body. He crossed to the foot of her bed and stuck his hands into his pockets, his dark eyes as inscrutable as the first time she'd ever looked into them.

"What's wrong?" she dared to ask. Her heart blipped perceptibly faster on the monitor behind her. "What did he say to you?"

Sam's chest expanded on a deep breath. His jaw muscles jumped. She knew whatever it was it had changed something for the worse.

"It doesn't matter what he said." His rich baritone

voice had turned monotone, emotionless. "Maddy, I've realized something about us."

A weight fell on her chest. Here it came. Nothing as good as what they'd shared could last forever. "What?" she whispered.

"I'm not the man you need me to be."

She hadn't expected him to say that. "Why do you say that? What did my father say to you?" she repeated.

"You need a man who's going to be there for you— maybe even travel to all the hot spots you insist on visiting." With every word, his tone grew more brittle. "You need a man who wants to follow in your father's footsteps and do everything he says. In short, you need a trained monkey, not a Navy SEAL."

Stunned by his vehemence, she could only stare at him in horror.

"I've enjoyed *every* minute of my leave with you," he continued, his tone now gravelly with emotion that she was only just beginning to glimpse in the depths of his eyes. "And you are a remarkable and beautiful woman, both inside and out. I meant what I said earlier—"

Was he referring to that moment on horseback when he'd returned her declaration of love?

"—but I *can't* give up my honor and my identity for you."

Dismay pegged Maddy to the bed. Where on earth had he gotten the idea that he needed to give up anything to be with her? "Look, whatever my father said—"

"I told you, it doesn't matter what he said. I knew this would happen. I'm not from your world, Maddy. I've fought for everything I have and everything that I am. I won't give that up for anyone. Not even you," he added with visible regret.

A knot formed in Maddy's throat, preventing her from saying anything as he stepped over to her bedside and dropped a cool farewell kiss on her cheek.

He straightened. "Now that your father's here, I don't need to stay."

"Sam," she croaked, helpless to stop the tears that flooded her eyes. "Why are you doing this to us? We were fine before he came."

The firm line of his mouth softened at her protest. He reached for her thigh, seeming to waver as he gave it a regret-filled squeeze. "Maybe I just need some time to think," he conceded gruffly. "I never saw myself getting involved with a rich woman."

The unexpected confession gave her pause. "Who says I'm rich?" she protested. "I'm an environmentalist!"

"You're the daughter of a billionaire who lives off her daddy's dime and under his thumb," he said.

The unkind words skewered Maddy in the heart.

"Well, I can't live like that. I've got to go," he added, turning and heading for the door.

Mouth agape, she watched him pull it open. He sent her one last inscrutable look. Was that resentment burning in his eyes, or was it regret? The door opened and he stepped out. It shut a second later with a *click* that seemed to echo the snapping of her heart in two.

Just like that, Sam was gone, possibly forever.

Maddy fell against her pillow, covering her mouth to stifle the bewildered sob that escaped her tight throat. How could it be? Only this morning they'd been on horseback, utterly wrapped up in each other and looking forward to a future together.

*I meant what I said earlier.*

He loved her. He'd said so himself, even if the words were softly spoken. So why was the issue of her relationship with her father such a huge deal? What in God's name had her father said to drive Sam away?

Resisting the urge to leap out of bed—she'd been told it would set off some kind of alarm—Maddy hit the call button summoning the nurse. It was either that or scream her father's name at the top of her lungs. Tears of frustration flowed freely down her crumpled face. She didn't bother to wipe them away. Her father needed to see what his controlling behavior was doing to her. She was going to lose Sam forever if her father didn't immediately address this problem.

A nurse pushed into her room and drew up short. "Is everything okay, dear?"

"Please, I need you to find my father. He went to find food. His name is Lyle Scott."

"I'll have him paged," she promised. "Is there anything I can do for you myself?"

"No, thank you. Just find him, please."

Minutes dragged by, feeling more like hours as she waited for her father to reappear. When he pushed into the room, bearing a tray of dishes for them to share, he wore a distinctly uncomfortable expression. "Where's Sam?" he asked, his gaze darting toward the bathroom.

"Gone," she said, fighting the impulse to fly into a rage. "What did you say to him?"

He kept quiet, taking extra care not to spill anything on the tray as he laid it on her raised table.

"What did you say to him, Daddy?" she repeated, her voice wobbling.

He hung his head, staring down at the food he'd brought in. "Oh, Maddy, I was out of my head with worry." He had the grace to look ashamed. "I offered to pay him if he quit his job and stayed with you."

"What?"

"I wasn't thinking," he admitted, raising both hands in a defensive gesture. "I'm just...exhausted with trying to keep you safe and running for the Senate while chasing down my brother-in-law who wants me and the rest of my family dead."

"Daddy!" she interrupted sharply. "This is not about *you.* Sam took off, do you understand? You insulted his pride by making him an offer like that. How could you *do* such a thing?"

"I'm sorry." He looked down at his expensive shoes.

"Not everyone can be bought," she continued, railing at him like she hadn't done since she was a teenager. "Especially not Sam. You should have realized that!"

"Yes, yes, I should have realized. That was—" He shook his head. "That was bad form on my part. I'll go find him and apologize." He moved abruptly toward the door.

Maddy let him go, though she knew in her heart that he wouldn't be able to find Sam. Not only had Sam had a ten-minute lead, but he'd probably fled the hospital like there was a fire under his feet.

In despair, she collapsed against her pillows and closed her eyes. *Mama,* she prayed. *You know Sam's the one for me. Please bring him back.*

Forty minutes later, Lyle Scott slipped quietly into his daughter's hospital room. He'd involved the entire hospital staff in scouring the halls and grounds for a tall, dark-haired, good-looking young man named Sam. Finally, a witness reported seeing someone of that description catching a taxi just outside the hospital's front doors. Lyle had immediately called Sam's cell phone but, of course, the SEAL hadn't answered. He left a lengthy and heartfelt apology on

Sam's voicemail. Then he called the hotel where he'd made reservations and left a message on their room phone, as well.

Except he knew Sam would never see the flashing red light. He might drop by the resort Lyle had paid for in order to pick up his bag, but then the SEAL would head straight to the forward operating base to await a military hop taking him back to Oceana Naval Air Station. He'd probably be back in Virginia Beach well before his leave ran out at noon. Maybe he would check his voicemail then. Maybe he would recognize Lyle's number and delete it.

Either way Lyle had done all he could do to rectify his mistake, and he had a sinking feeling it wouldn't be enough.

He still felt lower than whale scum as he neared Maddy's bed. To his relief, she was sleeping soundly. He was glad not to have to gaze into her pain-filled eyes and hear the accusation in her voice. It was hard enough to behold her red-rimmed eyes and accept that he was responsible for her heartbreak.

It *was* his fault. He'd gotten so accustomed to "fixing" problems with his wealth that he'd forgotten some things couldn't be bought—like a man's pride.

Ironically, he respected Sam hugely for turning him down the way he had. What had he been thinking making such a ridiculous offer anyway? He'd been too preoccupied with Maddy's welfare to think clearly. Hell, she'd nearly died today! He had every right to be concerned, especially when she insisted on fulfilling her contract with GEF, even with her crazed uncle still on the loose.

And now there wouldn't be any Navy SEALs in Mariscal Estigarribia to rescue her if she got herself into trouble again. Ah, well. With the terrorists disbanded and Paul in Switzerland, how much trouble could she possibly get into?

Knowing Maddy? Plenty.

He picked up a pastry off the tray and eased into the armchair to eat it. The treat tasted like sawdust, but he finished it anyway, licking his fingers to get the stickiness off them. With a heavy-hearted sigh, he tipped back the chair, propped up his feet and fell asleep, hoping to heaven he hadn't wrecked his daughter's love life irrevocably.

Sam's breath fogged the window on the C-123 Provider as he watched his descent into Virginia Beach. He'd been gone less than three weeks, so why did it feel like he'd left the beach a lifetime ago?

Picking out the boardwalk by the bright hotel lights, he noticed a number of cars still cruising the strip at two in the morning. He'd spent plenty of late nights there himself, mostly back when he was regular Navy. Cruising Atlantic Boulevard in his old Mustang, picking up women had been the norm back then.

But those days were long over. He was a SEAL officer now and expected to comport himself with dignity. At the age of thirty, he'd grown weary of the type of women who frequented the oceanfront looking for a cheap thrill.

He found himself comparing the shallow-minded, self-absorbed young women with Maddy, and all he could do was shake his head and collapse back into his seat. The weight on his chest made it hard to breathe.

Maddy was a one-of-a-kind woman. He'd never find another like her. The only way that could be a good thing was that many women wanted to stay home and raise a family. If only Maddy had that urge, then a future with her wouldn't look so impossible. On the other hand, she was perfect—smart, worldly, compassionate, and incredibly, incredibly brave.

Christ, he admired her so much it brought tears to his eyes.

He thought about her going back to El Chaco and a wave of homesickness rolled through him—not for Virginia Beach or Miami, but for Paraguay. He wanted to go back with her.

Maybe he should have taken her father's offer and run with it. How many times had he asked himself that in the last several hours. Double the salary, huh? Making twice the money he made now, he could buy himself and Maddy a house anywhere they desired to have a home base. He could follow her from one site to the next. Under his vigilant eye, he wouldn't have to worry so much about her safety. It sounded like fucking paradise, except for one thing: He wasn't made that way. He was his own man. He charted his own seas. His goals didn't come second to Maddy's.

*I made the right decision*, he assured himself. Just then the C-123 Provider's landing gear groaned, and for a panicked second, he was back in the Cessna-182 bracing himself for a hard landing. He looked over at the empty seat next to him and pictured Maddy in it, scared to death.

If he'd asked her to live with him in Virginia Beach, would she have even considered his offer? The memory of her hand gripping his as their Cessna went down had him curling his fingers into a fist. He remembered stroking the silky hair at the back of her head.

*We'll be all right, querida.*

Except they weren't all right. They weren't even a couple. They were two individuals returning to their very separate lives, pretending they'd never shared a deeply satisfying connection.

*Christ, I don't know if I can do this.*

Maddy looked over at the driver's seat. "Thanks for doing this, Ricardo," she said, as he maneuvered the Jeep along the narrow dirt road heading toward South Chaco. "Now that you've given GEF your notice, I know you don't really have to come to work."

"You think I'd let you drive into the wilderness on your own?" he scoffed. "Oh, no. Until GEF replaces me, you'll find me right here at your side."

A sudden suspicion pricked her. "Has my father been paying you to keep an eye on me?"

He shot her an incredulous look. "What? I wish," he retorted. "I could stand to make a little extra money. But I do have a confession to make."

"What's that?" she asked as they lurched through a pot hole. The road had narrowed substantially in the last mile. Riddled with holes and strafed by gullies created in a recent downpour, the route would have been impossible in a two-wheel-drive vehicle. Even with four-wheel-drive, the rough going was making Maddy's stomach roil. She'd never been car sick before, but there was always a first for everything.

"I was instructed by someone higher up the food chain to keep you away from certain areas of the region, like the one we're headed to now."

She gasped in astonishment. "What?"

He sent her an apologetic grimace. "Scott Oil must have bribed my immediate superior, or the next person above him, to keep GEF away from a region known to be polluted. I was specifically told to keep you from collecting samples in a certain area, the one where we're headed now."

"Are you serious?" The implications distracted her from her car sickness.

"Perfectly. At first it didn't bother me to comply with those instructions, but when I realized one of my bosses had been bribed and that the environment might be truly suffering, I decided it was worth my while to help you out, even if it gets me into trouble later."

"Oh, I hope it doesn't," Maddy exclaimed. She lowered her window further, desperate for fresh air.

Ricardo shrugged. "If someone gives me a hard time, then I'll know who took the bribe and I'll blackmail him."

She had to fan her suddenly clammy face. "I never realized what a truly devious man my uncle was. He must have a friend in the CIA. Ricardo, can you stop the Jeep for a second?" she pleaded suddenly. "I think I'm going to be sick."

Startled, he brought the Jeep to a lurching halt, one that made it impossible to keep her breakfast down. In the nick of time, Maddy threw her door open, leaned out, and vomited on a beetle scuttling across the dirt track. *Sorry, buddy.*

She waited for more to come, but her queasiness had immediately abated. She wiped her mouth with the back of her hand, sat back, and shut the door against the stench. "Sorry about that," she said. "I've never been car sick before."

Ricardo accelerated slowly, while slanting her a thoughtful look. "Maybe you ate some tainted food?"

She thought back. "No, I just had bread and jam this morning. Come to think of it, I wasn't feeling all that great this morning. I must have picked up a bug."

A hum reverberated in Ricardo's throat. His dark gaze flickered again in her direction.

"What?" she asked, sensing he was keeping a thought to himself.

"Okay, any chance you could be pregnant?" he inquired. "Lucía threw up every morning for the first three months."

Maddy's breath caught. Every extremity of her body tingled. She'd entertained the thought that she might be pregnant about a week earlier when she first realized she was late. But she'd managed to convince herself that the physical trauma she'd endured followed by two weeks of emotional despair as Sam made no effort to reach out had confused her menstrual cycle. Suddenly, with Ricardo's suspicions weighing in, she could no longer deny the possibility.

She groped for bottled water from the back seat, twisted it open, and washed the awful taste from her mouth. "I can't be pregnant," she explained to Ricardo. "The doctor in Curacao told me that the poison would affect an embryo adversely."

His sidelong glance reflected sympathy. "That doesn't mean you're not pregnant," he gently pointed out.

"You're right. I need to be tested."

He didn't bother to comment that she would then have a heavy decision to make.

God, could this really be happening now, when Sam had yet to attempt any contact? How much more time did he need? More likely, he'd already decided that they had no future together. Her spirits sank at the thought.

Her being pregnant added a whole new layer of uncertainty to her already battered emotional state. Yes, it felt satisfying to be finally homing in on the region of El Chaco being desecrated by Scott Oil, to be finally taking measures to ensure that the pollution stopped. Yes, she felt a measure of fulfillment at ensuring that Salim and his brother hadn't sacrificed their lives for nothing. But the void left in the wake of Sam's abandonment made her wonder, at times, why she was still there.

If she'd followed him back to the States, she might

have convinced him to forgive her father and to give them a second chance. The longer they remained apart, the more the rift between them seemed to widen. Then the terrible ruminations started—thoughts that he couldn't have loved her that much if letting her go had been so easy for him.

She recalled his declaration of love for her. The blazing fervor in his eyes and the ferocity in the kiss he'd give her had made the words seem genuine. But why had he uttered them so quietly that the wind had almost whisked them away?

It could only be because he didn't love her as much as she had loved him. *As much as I still love him,* she amended.

Emptiness throbbed in the region of her broken heart, accompanied by a faint tingle of hope. Would it change anything if she were pregnant? And if she were, should she even tell Sam when the doctor had advised her to abort? The awful poison her uncle had made her drink would have affected the embryo, increasing the likelihood of deformity. How could she accomplish her work as a global environmentalist with a special needs baby vying for her attention? She should probably take the doctor's advice and abort it.

In that case, it wasn't likely she could use the excuse of a pregnancy to bring Sam back into her life, nor should she. Of course, he would want to give his child the legitimacy he'd never had. The possibility that had tingled in her briefly faded away.

It was better if she said nothing, then. She wouldn't want Sam to marry her out of a sense of obligation. She shook her head, loathing the thought. *No more than I want to abort a baby conceived in love,* protested a voice inside her.

With a catch in her throat she pictured the little Maddy-n-Sam embryo fighting to thrive in her womb.

Suddenly, fervent love for their unborn child roared to life, prompting her to lay a protective hand over her abdomen. There was a baby in there. She was suddenly certain of it. Her tender breasts, her queasy stomach, every symptom pointed to the truth.

*I am pregnant. And my baby has every right to live.*

Resolve made her roll her shoulders back. She sat taller. She owed her baby the benefit of the doubt. Considering the DNA it had inherited from both parents, it was bound to be a tenacious little bundle, a fighter just like her and Sam.

All she could do now was wait and see. And then she would have to make the most critical decisions of her life.

# CHAPTER 19

"There you are."

Chief Brantley Adam's voice accompanied a crash of waves on the nearby shore, making it sound like God was talking to Sam, which he wished was the case. He'd been praying a lot lately, asking for a sign, for strength, for relief from this unending misery. His despondency had driven him to seek solitude on the deck of the Shifting Sands Club, even though the Christmas party was about to kick off inside, and it was a cold, blustery night that no one in his right mind would want to be experiencing first hand.

But Sam scarcely even noticed the cold. Compared to the desolation in his heart, it felt like nothing. More than three months had passed since he'd walked away from Maddy. He'd thought for sure he would have stopped obsessing about her day and night; stopped spying on her Facebook page, hunting for her name on the Web, following her father's political career in the hopes that the media would mention something about the Senator's daughter.

He should have pulled himself together a long time ago.

Startled, he glanced up to see Bronco and Bullfrog

pushing out of the brightly lit door to join him. The throb of a base guitar emanated from the nightclub on the lower level, letting him know that the party had begun. Starting tomorrow, hardly any training would take place until the New Year. He should be joining his platoon members and the rest of SEAL Team 12 in celebrating the upcoming holiday. Except he didn't feel celebrating, not one bit.

His teammates plunked down in the two chairs across from him, their backs to the ocean, drinks in hand. They were acting like this was what they wanted to do: sit and stare at Sam's long face. "Why are you here?" he demanded.

Light shining out of the windows at Sam's back reflected in Bronco's bright blue eyes. "Sir, we need to talk," he stated, balancing his bottle on the grooved table top.

Bullfrog did likewise, except he was drinking his own poison of choice—Macallan eighteen-year-old single malt Scotch whisky—while Sam had gone straight for tequila. Three shots later, he was finally more numb than devastated.

He nodded his assent. This moment had been coming for some time. There was a limit to how long his top NCOs could put up with his pathetic and distracted leadership. "I know," he began, forcing himself to sit up straighter and not slouch. "I've been a lousy platoon leader."

He'd pretty much continuously snarled at every man in his platoon for three months straight. He'd even leveled a punishment on Bamm-Bamm this morning for a violation he couldn't now recall, forgetting that the young SEAL had saved Maddy's life by identifying Elliot Koch as The Annihilator. "I've been an asshole," he admitted.

"Right," Bronco agreed. "And Kuzinsky's starting

to take note."

Which was never a good thing.

Sam swallowed the bitter taste in his mouth. "All right. I hear you. I'll take some time over the holiday to get myself together."

"We think you should talk about it," Bullfrog gently suggested.

Sam stiffened. "Talk to who?" he asked with an edge to his voice.

"To us," Bronco invited. "We're the guys who have to work with you," he added before Sam could summon a protest, "and I think we deserve an explanation."

"Christ, you know what's eating me," Sam tossed back irritably.

"Of course we do." Bullfrog's soothing assurance tempered Sam's black mood. "What we want to know is what you're going to do about it."

"Because we won't put up with your crap much longer," Bronco added, far less tactfully. His crooked smile took the edge off his words but, for once, he seemed completely serious.

Sam chuckled humorlessly. "So you're here to counsel me," he concluded. How ironic. As platoon leader, he was supposed to be the one advising them.

"What we'd like to suggest," Bullfrog smoothly continued "is for you to forgive Maddy's father. He did apologize, remember? What more can he do?"

It had taken Sam almost two months to even listen to Lyle's message. He'd done it at the Veteran's Day picnic at Little Creek Park, the last time all of SEAL Team 12 had gotten together for a barbeque. Lyle's apology had thrown him into such a confused state that he'd downed a six-pack in less than an hour and Bullfrog had been forced to drive him back to his apartment before he made a total fool of himself.

"What exactly did he say in his apology?" Bronco wanted to know.

Sam had to think to remember. In a fit of disgust, he'd deleted the voicemail before he could listen to it again, and now he regretted his haste because there was no way to tell, now, how serious Lyle really was.

He blew out a tequila-laced breath. "He said he should never have asked me to quit the Teams. He'd been so upset about Maddy almost dying that he'd spoken in haste. Blah, blah, blah."

"That sounds pretty sincere to me," said Bullfrog with a question in his voice.

"Why don't you believe him?" Bronco demanded.

"I do. It's just—" The fact that his teammates were siding with Lyle Scott ratcheted Sam's annoyance to new heights. "What he asked me to do was insulting. I'm supposed to give up my career for his daughter?" His temper reignited. "How could he even suggest such a thing?"

Bronco cocked his head in a considering manner. "What? You've never said anything in haste that you've regretted? He already apologized. What more can he do?"

"I heard him give a speech on TV the other night," Bullfrog added. "He's united the major parties for the first time in a decade."

"That has nothing to do with it. He's a great guy," Sam muttered, trying to ignore the guilt pinching his cheeks. He had been harsh in his condemnation of Maddy's father. "It's rich people in general."

Bullfrog frowned, sat forward, and steepled his fingers. "Do you have a basis for this assessment? Because it sounds like you're stereotyping all rich people as SOBs, which is ridiculous."

Sam scowled at him. The impulse to bite his NCO's head off morphed into the grudging acknowledgment that he really wasn't being fair. That suspicion had occurred to him before now, usually during the long, lonely hours when he'd lain in bed aching for the feel of Maddy's arms around him.

Maybe he was stereotyping. Ever since Wendy's father had pegged him as the Latino sexual predator, he'd viewed the wealthy as presumptuous and manipulative, as people who viewed him as unworthy. What if the fault didn't lie with them, but with *him* for viewing their actions in a prejudiced light?

If Lyle Scott were destitute, would he have made a similar request of Sam? Probably. It wasn't that he viewed Sam's career as unimportant. It was simply that he was overwrought with concern for his daughter's safety. Sam's stepfather had been the same way back when Sam was in jail. He'd knocked on doors and thrown himself into raising the funds needed for a top-notch lawyer. Wealthy or poor, it was a father's job to protect his off spring.

Sam swiped a hand over his eyes, "Shit," he muttered, wondering if it was too late to make amends.

A comfortable silence fell over the table, filled with the roar of the ocean and the lulling throb of the base guitar.

"So, you're going to call him?" Bronco urged.

"You should call him tonight. See how Maddy's doing," Bullfrog seconded.

Sam dropped his hand and sent his teammates a wry smile. "I'm going to call." He felt immediately better having made that decision. "Thanks, guys," he added.

Bullfrog flashed him an evil grin. "Any time you need a kick in the ass, I'm here for you," he sniggered, reaching for his empty bottle and pushing his chair back.

Bullfrog rose up after him, his scotch glass still full.

The two went back inside leaving Sam stewing in a whole new cauldron of emotions.

If he called Lyle Scott after all these months, would the man even answer? What if Maddy had given up on waiting for him and gotten on with her life? By now she ought to have finished taking samples in El Chaco. Was she busy analyzing them or already hard at work on another assignment? Assuming Sam even secured her father's blessing, would she be open to forgiving him after he'd behaved like a moronic idiot?

He drew a steadying breath. The bite of damp, winter air chased the fog of tequila out of his brain. He'd better do this while he still had the courage. Teasing his cell phone out of his pocket, he accessed his contact list and dialed Lyle Scott directly.

A bolt of lightning, unusual at this time of year, jagged out over the ocean, forking into half a dozen branches that sizzled across the sky.

He shouldn't have let the past dictate the present. Life without Maddy was meaningless. He hadn't needed any lectures or another sleepless night to know that that was true. Nothing had tasted, smelled, or felt like it did when she was with him. He'd never find another woman like her—didn't even want to try.

A chill breeze dried the sweat on his palm as the phone rang and rang in his ear. He was just about to hang up when Lyle Scott answered.

"Sam?" he said. The friendly tenor and the hopeful quality in his voice was all it took to banish Sam's apprehension. "Is that you, son?"

*Son.* The word warmed him. "Yes, sir. I'm sorry it took so long for me to call you back."

"Oh, don't worry about that. Can't blame you for not wanting to talk to me."

"No, it's my fault. I took your offer completely wrong. I overreacted, and I ruined the best thing that's ever happened to me. How's it going on your end?" he asked before Lyle could comment. "What's the latest with Van Slyke?"

"Well, Maddy's idea to get him on the poisoning worked, thank God. That's exactly how Elliot Koch died—he'd been poisoned, same as Maddy. Paul was charged, extradited from Switzerland, and taken into custody. His trial is set at the end of this month. I'm hoping you can testify."

Sam thought about the next op, which wasn't until the end of March. "I'd be happy to, sir. How's, uh, how's Maddy doing?"

"Oh, well enough."

The hesitation in Lyle's voice filled Sam with dread. "Where is she these days?" he dared to ask.

"She's right here in McLean," the Senator said unexpectedly, "taking some time off before her next assignment."

Sam's spirits rose and then plummeted. She was already headed on a new assignment. "How much time do I have?"

"Hmm, well, it's hard to say. I wouldn't dawdle if you'd like to see her," Lyle suggested.

Sam's mouth went dry. "You think she's open to seeing me again?"

"It might take some persuasion on your part, but you're not the type to walk away from a challenge now, are you, Sam?"

Maddy was going to take some convincing, then. "No, sir," he agreed. "I'd like to show up tomorrow morning." The next day was a Thursday, with Christmas Eve on Friday. "Is that too soon? Will she be there?"

"I'll make sure of it," Lyle countered. "By the way, did I get your vote on election day?"

"No, sir. I'm a resident of Florida, not Texas."

Lyle laughed. "I'm just joshing you, Sam. Doesn't matter to me if you're a Democrat or a Republican, Communist or Libertarian. You saved my life and you're the man my daughter loves. I'll make sure Maddy's here tomorrow. 'Bout what time do you plan to show up?"

"Say ten hundred hours?"

"I'll expect you at 10 A.M. sharp, then. And Sam?"

"Yes, sir?"

"Next time I overstep my bounds, you just tell me to back off, you hear?"

"Yes, sir. Thank you, sir."

*Nice guy*, Sam thought, putting his phone away. Jumping to his feet, he resisted the urge to pump his fists into the sky and holler, "Yeah!" Instead, he bounded down the steps at the side of the building and hurried toward his parked car.

Maddy was back in the states, within driving distance. He knew an urge to drive straight to her house, only first he needed to rehearse the words required to win her back and to keep her there, safe in his heart, where she belonged.

"Where've you been?"

Looking harried, Maddy's father greeted Maddy at the front door. It was quarter to ten in the morning. Her appointment hadn't lasted any longer than she'd expected.

"What do you mean? I had the follow-up on the amniocentesis, remember? You wanted to come, but you had a video conference?"

"Oh, that's right." His confusion cleared, giving way to immediate concern. "What's the news, sweetheart?" he asked, drawing her into the foyer and holding both her hands. "How's the baby?"

She managed to drum up a smile for him. "So far,

everything looks great."

"Really? No genetic disorders, no spina bifida? Nothing?"

"Nope. The baby looks healthy."

"Thank God!" Relief shone in her father's damp eyes, filling her with shame for not being overcome with joy herself. Of course, she'd been relieved to find out that Dr. Troost's concerns hadn't manifested. She didn't have to make the awful choice to abort her baby, which was all she had left of Sam and the hope of a life together. But an equally big decision now loomed over her.

Her father engulfed her in a hug that enveloped her in smells of ironing starch and aftershave. After a silent moment, he set her at arm's length and frowned down at her. "Why aren't you smiling? Something else is bothering you," he guessed. But then he answered his own question. "You're thinking it's time to tell Sam, aren't you?"

Just the sound of Sam's name had her squirming out of her father's hold and heading for the hall closet. "It's not an easy decision," she mumbled, hanging her purse on a hook and tackling the buttons on her wool coat. "Maybe if he'd shown some interest in me these last few months," she added with anguish.

She felt a sudden need for fresh air. Changing her mind, she buttoned her coat back up. "You know what? I'll be in the back yard. I need some time to think."

Turning away from her father's torn expression, she hurried through the great room at the rear of the house and out the French doors that led to the veranda.

The flagstone path, edged with flowerbeds of purple and white cabbage, conveyed her toward the tree line and the little bridge she hadn't visited since the night Elliot Koch had targeted her father. Thoughts of

Uncle Paul's upcoming trial flitted into her head, but she pushed them aside. Justice would prevail. The path ended at a fountain, drained for the winter. She crossed a bit of bristle lawn to enter the woods. Pine needles crackled underfoot. The crisp December air of winter seared her nostrils.

*Sam.* The memory of the last time she'd been here assailed her without warning. She could still recall the thrill of holding his hand, of guiding him toward the bridge arching over the creek ahead. She'd wanted so badly for him to admit she had as much right to pursue her calling as he had to pursue his, to realize that they were more alike than different.

She'd wanted him to kiss her and have that kiss transform his life. And it almost had.

He'd finally admitted—not then, but many weeks later on the night that the Cessna had crashed—that they were like a tag team. A dynamic duo working to make the world a better place. A sentimental smile touched the edges of her cold lips.

But then he'd left her because of what her father had offered. Because her father had ground his pride beneath the heel of his polished, patent leather shoes.

She didn't blame Sam for that. She didn't even blame him for not loving her enough to forgive her father, for not loving her the way that she loved him. You couldn't chose whom you gave your heart to or how much you loved someone. She'd learned that the hard way. She knew he'd felt something for her but, in the end, it wasn't enough.

Her heeled boots struck musical tones on the wooden planks as she climbed to the height of the bridge. Pausing at the railing, she studied the creek rippling below her. The rocks at the bottom glinted like multi-colored eggs.

For the longest time, she stared hypnotically at the

sinuous rush of water, her thoughts empty. A peaceful hush, filled only by the distant sound of the beltway and the wind stirring the naked branches overhead filled her ears. Loneliness swelled her empty heart as she remembered how it felt to have Sam standing next to her.

The time had come to make the next big decision. Now that she was fairly certain the baby was okay, she was obligated to tell Sam about it. And while the prospect of having him back in her life made her pulse quicken, it also filled her with dismay.

He would want to marry her out of a sense of obligation, so as not to leave her the way his biological father had left him. She had no doubt about that. But she didn't want him marrying her because he had to. She wanted him to love her, as completely and purely as she loved him. Yet considering he hadn't attempted even once to reach out in the weeks they'd been apart, that wasn't likely ever to happen.

*I don't want him this way.*

Feeling a splinter gouge her palm, Maddy looked down at the railing she was gripping. But then a fluttering in her womb tugged her attention lower to the baby whose happiness came before her own, who seemed to be demanding that she make her decision already.

"I know," she crooned, rubbing the bump of her belly absently. "I'll call him today."

Sam's stride faltered as he caught sight of Maddy through the dark tree trunks ahead of him. Her father, ecstatic to see him, had immediately shooed him out the back door with directions to look for Maddy in the yard. Something had told Sam that he would find her on the bridge where she'd led him the night of the soirée. Sure enough, there she was, swathed in a periwinkle town coat that made her look breastier than usual.

The sad, resolved look on her face as she absently rubbed her stomach plucked at his heartstrings. He slowed to a stop for a moment drinking in the sight of her. Then he scrounged up the courage to announce his presence.

"Maddy." He started forward again.

Her eyebrows quirked with bafflement as she looked over at him. Through wide, wondering eyes, she studied his approach. Sam's step slowed. She hadn't said a word by the time he reached the bottom of the bridge. He'd clearly caught her off guard.

"Hey," he said, offering a tentative smile.

Her answering smile was more of a grimace. "What are you doing here?"

It was not the warm welcome he was hoping for, but then what did he expect? Before he even got the chance to speak she proposed an answer.

"My father called you, didn't he?" Her eyes flashed with indignation and her hands flew to her hips.

The accusation reminded him so much of the words tossed at him in Paraguay—*My father sent you here again?*—that he issued a bitter laugh. "No." He shook his head. "I came because I wanted to. Because I should have come a long time ago."

The fury seemed to drain out of her. "Oh."

He took a step forward, then another one, until they both stood where they'd been that late summer night before they'd been so rudely interrupted. A mere six inches separated them now. It felt like six miles.

Maddy's eyes had locked on his face. The cold teased a vapor from her slightly parted mouth and painted her cheeks pink. She was the prettiest woman he'd seen in his entire life.

"Did he tell you about—?" She stopped talking

abruptly.

He cocked his head wondering where she was headed with her words. "Winning a Senate seat?" He nodded. "Actually, I heard it on the news. I always knew he'd win."

She sent him a faint nod.

"How've you been, *querida*?" he asked, unable to withhold the endearment any longer. One look at her and he couldn't fathom what had kept him away this long. For the first time in three months, he felt *alive, hopeful.* "Did you get the samples you wanted to take?"

The endearment softened her brittle façade only slightly "Yes. And Salim was right. The pollution there was awful. My uncle wouldn't have done anything about it, but the board of directors is implementing a cleanup and repairing the faulty containment wall." She blew out a breath and added quickly, "Daddy's got them abiding by the initial trade agreement so Paraguayan investors can weigh in on the company's decisions."

"That's great. It wouldn't have happened without you," he praised, meaning every word.

"Thanks," she said more remotely than he would have wanted. "So, how've you been? How are the guys, Bronco and Bullfrog?"

"They're good."

"You never told me how they got their names."

This was how it was going to be, he thought with an inward sigh. They would dance around the subject until they couldn't avoid it any longer. Fine, he could play this game if that was what it took.

"Brantley's a champion rodeo rider and Jeremiah swims like a fish," he explained with a shrug. "Only that's not how the song goes."

Comprehension flickered in her eyes and she

promptly supplied the familiar chorus by Three Dog Night about the wine-drinking Bullfrog named Jeremiah. Her sweet voice was exactly as he remembered.

"Nah, nah." He tacked on the electrical guitar portion, strumming the air in lieu of a guitar.

A brief smile touched the edges of her lips, but then it faded, and all he saw in her face was a reflection of the pain he'd caused her by walking out on what they had.

"Maddy, I have a story to tell you," he said cutting straight to the point of his being here.

Her forehead puckered. "Okay." She obviously thought it a strange time for him to be telling stories.

He slipped his hands into his coat pockets. "When I was in high school, I had a crush on the prettiest, richest tease in the school. Her name was Wendy, and her father was a real estate tycoon."

Maddy's expression turned quizzical, but he had her full attention.

"Our senior year, she hosted an after-prom party at her house—a big mansion in Miami, right on the lagoon. I saw her go upstairs with two of her male friends. A while later, I heard her shrieking at the top of her lungs. They were raping her."

Maddy gasped. "Oh, no."

He nodded. "I did what came naturally to me. I broke down the door, beat the crap out of the guys, and chased them off the premises."

She was astute enough to know that wasn't the end of it. "What happened then?"

"She told her father that I'd been the one to rape her."

Her eyes widened with horror. "What? Why?"

"The boys who did it were her friends."

"Oh."

"Her father convinced the judge that I was dangerous. I spent two months in jail while my stepfather looked for a lawyer who could stand up to the prosecution. When my case was finally heard, I was cleared of all charges, but I'd missed final exams and graduation. I had to get a GED."

"Oh, Sam."

He wanted to reach for her but he kept his hands firmly in his pockets. "I'm not trying to excuse myself, Maddy," he insisted. "I just want you to realize why your father's offer offended me so much. That experience taught me that wealthy people step on those who were less well-off. In actuality, I've been carrying a chip on my shoulders and making stereotypes that simply aren't true. I know that's no excuse for the way I walked out on you. I was a fool to have done that. I'm so sorry." He swallowed hard, forcing the next words past the lump building in his throat, "and I hope you'll take me back."

The burble of water was the only sound to fill the sudden silence. Sam's heart suspended its beating as he waited for Maddy either to forgive him or reject him forever.

"There's nothing to forgive," she whispered, finally.

His heart leaped, and he sucked in a breath of relief as she spontaneously threw her arms around his neck. His hands came out of his pockets pulling her closer. His eyes closed in relief as she laid her head against his shoulder, burrowing closer.

"Oh, God, Sam, I'm so sorry you went through that," she said, still engrossed in his plight.

Her selflessness humbled him. "I'm good now." The firm curves of her body captured his attention. Her breasts felt like balloons—incredibly sexy water balloons—crushed against his chest. He wanted to stay locked together like this forever, but then she stiffened and drew back. "I have something to tell you, too," she announced, wetting her upper lip with a dart of her tongue.

The vision distracted him. "What is it?"

"I'm pregnant." An uncertain smile kicked up one corner of her supple lips.

Sam's gaze dropped past her full breasts to the rounded bump straining the buttons at the front of her coat. "Pregnant," he repeated, stupidly. "How...how long?"

She arched an eyebrow. "Well, we only had unprotected sex those first two times, so obviously it was then. That puts me at fifteen weeks."

Incredulity crashed over him. "And you're just telling me this now?"

He knew his choice of words was wrong when she visibly bristled.

"Well, maybe if you hadn't walked away from me, you would have known. Besides, the doctor in Curacao warned me if I was pregnant, the embryo could have been poisoned, too. He said I would most likely have to abort."

Horrified, Sam looked back at the telltale bump. He found himself reaching out to lay a protective hand over it.

She searched his face, clearly heartened by his concern. "I got the results of the amniocentesis this morning," she told him. "No genetic defects." A sheen of tears suddenly filmed her eyes making him realize everything she'd been through since he'd selfishly walked out on her.

"*Querida*, you must have been so worried," he guessed, feeling like more of a jerk by the second. "I'm so sorry. I didn't realize."

"I didn't want you to worry about the baby if it wasn't going to make it, so I kept it to myself."

"You shouldn't have had to. God, I'm a thoughtless ass!" He lifted his hand to capture the side of her face. Awareness arced between them, and he was helpless to lower his head and gently kiss her. The familiar sweetness of her lips brought moisture to his eyes. "I love you, Maddy," he whispered, kissing her again, more deeply this time, with all of the hunger and devotion raging in through him.

Maddy's head spun at the delicious languor taking over her body, making her feel more alive than she had in months. *He loves me.* And this time he had said the words first and with total conviction.

"I love you, too," she managed between heated kisses. She stroked the crisp hair at the back of his head, measured the powerful breadth of his shoulders with her hands and arched her hips toward the hard length of his thighs, craving more.

He stopped kissing her reluctantly. "You'll never be alone again," he swore.

She blinked up at him, wanting to believe it was love and not duty that prompted those words. "Because of the baby?" she pressed.

"Because we belong together," he steadily replied. "You knew it as long ago as the last time we were here, didn't you? The night you tried to tell me how much alike we are."

She nodded. Deep down in her heart, she'd known it all along.

A worried thought creased his forehead. "Your father said you have a new job coming up?"

She nodded in agreement. She could tell by the dread in his eyes that he feared she was going to embark on another wild field assignment. "Dr. Troost put me in touch with the Amazon Conservation Team."

"You're going to the Amazon?"

She had to laugh at how horribly he hid his dismay. "No. I'm compiling and organizing the data they collected into articles for publication. Our baby won't be born in the jungle, Sam. Don't you worry."

Relief shone in his eyes. "And you're okay with that? Staying in the States?"

"I think, for the baby's sake, I can avoid the hot spots for a while and still make a contribution," she answered honestly.

He looked stunned by her declaration. "Damn, I should have gotten you pregnant a long time ago!"

She had to smile at his rueful tone. He grinned back at her, looking younger and happier than she'd ever seen him.

"There's only one thing that could make this moment any more special for us," he announced unexpectedly.

"What's that?"

Releasing a button at the front of his coat, he reached into an unseen pocket and withdrew a little velvet box.

Maddy gasped. "That's not a…"

But it was. He cracked it open, revealing a simple yet stunning solitaire ring nestled in a bed of satin. And, in the next instant, he was down on one knee, wincing when his knee cap came into contact with the sharp edge of a plank.

"Madison Marie Scott," he said, surprising her as he spouted off her middle name, "would you do me the tremendous honor of being my better half for the rest of my life?"

"Oh, Sam." The fact that he'd had that ring in his coat even before he knew about the baby was proof: He *did* love her as completely and purely as she loved him. "Yes!" she cried, leaning over and kissing him soundly on the lips.

In the next perfect moments, the ring was practically forgotten. At last, Sam slid it onto her left hand, managing not to drop it into the stream even though his fingers visibly trembled. And then he pocketed the box, swept her up into his arms, and marched all the way to the house with her locked in his embrace stealing kisses as they went.

# EPILOGUE

"Here we are, little one," Sam called to the newborn swaddled in her car seat in the back of his Charger. "Home, sweet home."

Maddy sat next to her daughter, scarcely able to tear her gaze off little Melinda's sleeping face. But Sam's proud remark had her looking up at their remodeled rancher, basking in the shade of several towering oak trees. "Oh, look!" Someone had rented a large wooden stork carrying a pink bundle that announced the arrival of Melinda Sofia Sasseville, born on July 7th and weighing in at six pounds, four ounces.

"My mother, probably," Sam said, naming the most likely culprit.

"But no one's here," Maddy observed, a bit disappointed, as he swept them into the carport and killed the engine. "I thought you said your family would be visiting."

"They'll show up sooner or later," he promised on a resigned note.

She'd come to expect unpredictability from his large, boisterous family. His mother Sofia and stepfather Raúl had given him three half-brothers, all in their teens. Maddy found them hysterical. She'd rather hoped they would be here now to see the baby.

Sam had opened the rear door and unlatched the carrier before she'd even taken off her own seatbelt. "I've got her," he said with a grin.

They'd been fighting over who got to hold the baby ever since she'd come into the world, hiccupping but not crying. Maddy had taken her first peek at her daughter and gasped, "She has my mother's nose and eyes!" making the name they'd chosen for her even more fitting. "It's fate," she'd marveled, tingling from head to foot with the certainty that her mother's spirit had found a way to be with her again.

Sam held the carrier in the crux of his arm while inserting the key into their front door. "Wake up, little one," he called in the sing-song voice he reserved for his daughter. "You're going to miss it."

"Miss what?" Maddy asked, eager to get out of the heat. "I hope you left the air-conditioner running."

Pushing the door open, he stepped into the foyer holding the door ajar for Maddy to join him. She dove with relief into the cool interior only to startle back as bodies materialized out of the living room and kitchen bellowing "Surprise!"

The baby's arms flailed in a startle reflex. Her eyes flew open but she didn't cry.

Sam's younger brothers were the first to swarm them, followed by his mother and stepfather. Sam's teammates, Bronco and Bullfrog, hung back, as did her father, who'd already visited them at the hospital. This was Sam's family's first contact with the newest relative. Baby Melinda returned their rapt stares with slate-gray eyes that held the promise of lightening to a blue-gray.

"*Qué linda!*" Sofia exclaimed, throwing up her hands in rapture. "*Mi hija*, you did a beautiful job!" she praised, plastering an effusive kiss on Maddy's cheek.

"Good thing she don't look like you, Sam," fourteen-year-old Jaime ribbed with a smirk.

"Next time you need to have a boy," said Jaime's twin brother, Javier. He looked disappointed not to have a nephew to play ball with.

"Give Maddy a break." Frank, who was older by two years, did his best to keep the twins under control.

"Take her out so we can hold her," Sofia begged, rubbing her hands together eagerly.

Sam put down the carrier and Maddy leaned over with a grimace of discomfort to unbuckle her. "I'll get her," offered Sam, attuned to her limitations. "Everyone go wash your hands first," he ordered.

As his family sought out every sink in the house, Bronco and Bullfrog made their way over. By then, Sam was holding baby Melinda in both hands, preparing to pass her off. "You going to hold her?" he asked Bronco.

"No." Bronco eyed the baby as he might a live hand grenade and fervently shook his sun-kissed head.

"I will," Bullfrog volunteered holding out his large, gentle hands. "I just used hand sanitizer."

Maddy suffered no qualms about letting Jeremiah handle her tiny infant. One look at his wondering features and she hoped one day he'd experience the privilege of raising his own child. Brant, too, for that matter. Her attention swiveled to his wondering blue eyes. With reluctant fascination, he watched Jeremiah croon at the baby. Melinda studied them both raptly. Already, her daughter promised to be a serious and authentic child.

"Wow," Jeremiah said. "Just...wow."

Slipping her hand into Sam's, Maddy gave it a squeeze. He turned his head to look over at her. "I love you," she mouthed.

He sent her a wink and a satisfied smile. It didn't get any better than this.

And being the tag team that they were, she would always have his back, just as he had hers. Whenever work took either one of them away temporarily, they knew the other would be waiting, with arms wide open, for the other's return. Together they'd only begun to make the world a better place. With little Melinda, they were off to a fabulous start.

# THE
# ECHO PLATOON SERIES

Danger Close
Hard Landing

*Turn the page for an*

*excerpt from*

# HARD LANDING

## The Echo Platoon Series
*Book Two*

Marliss Melton

———◆———

Brantley Adams stepped out of his 1996 Ford Bronco, clutching his contribution to the party—a twelve pack of his favorite beer. Checking that he'd cracked the windows of his old truck to counteract the sweltering Virginia Beach heat, he locked it up and plodded toward the sprawling white brick ranch-style house where his commander lived.

Commander MacDougal—Mad Max, as all the Team-guys called him behind his back—headed up Brant's task unit. He didn't command all of SEAL Team 12, just Brant's unit, but he carried a great deal of influence and enjoyed throwing his weight around. Hosting parties on every national holiday was just one of the ways he did that. Brant grumbled under his breath. Here he was, forced to make an appearance at another of the CO's parties when he was supposed to be enjoying his day off.

Approaching the man's whitewashed house, Brant had to admit Mad Max owned a lovely piece of property, about an acre in size and situated on Rudee Lake, surrounded by other million dollar homes. He had a custom pool shaped like a seashell in his back yard, his own fishing pier, and a three-car garage that housed his Tahoe and his kit car. Mad Max loved his toys. He also laid claim to the prettiest, most pleasant wife on planet Earth, who happened to be Brant's good friend. Unfortunately, the way he saw it, the CO treated his wife as just another of his possessions.

Brant had considered playing hooky today. These social functions weren't mandatory, just suggested. But if you wanted to stay on Mad Max's good side, you showed your face—and no one wanted to get on the CO's bad side. Not that it really mattered in Brant's case. He'd achieved the status of chief petty officer in the eight years that he'd been a SEAL. He didn't particularly care whether he made senior chief one day, or not. But he did want to see Rebecca, Max's wife.

As usual, he would have to be careful not to spend too much time alone with her. Max watched her like a hawk—not that he needed to. She seemed as true blue as apple pie, and Brant had no intention of making any moves on his commander's wife. Who would be that stupid? He just wanted to hang out with her—period, the end. Was that asking too much?

Blowing out a frustrated breath, he coursed the paving stones that bisected the lush front lawn and brought him to the wide stoop. Framed in pretty flower beds, the entire front area showed evidence of Rebacca's caring touch.

He didn't bother knocking. The inner door had been left ajar, and through the storm door, he could see straight through the great room and out the wall of windows to the throng gathered around the pool out back. The interior of the house looked deserted, with the exception of the one dark haired woman he was hoping to see, standing behind a counter in the kitchen—Rebecca. His spirits abruptly lifted.

He slipped into the air-conditioned foyer and cut through the formal dining room to keep himself out of sight for the time being. Pausing at the back of the kitchen, he leaned against the door frame to watch her slicing celery for the veggie plate.

What was it about Rebecca MacDougal that made him smile inside? He wasn't attracted to her sexually—not much anyway. She wasn't his type, which tended toward blondes with big knockers. Rebecca projected femininity, but she didn't ooze sexuality. She represented everything that was honest and considerate and well-thought-out. He liked the way her glossy brown hair, caught up in a ponytail, brushed her shoulders when she moved. The angle of her jaw and the slight scoop of her nose made her profile so interesting to look at.

"Hey," he said unwilling to waste another minute just staring at her.

To his astonishment, she jumped like a startled cat. The knife in her right hand came close to slicing her cheek open as she whirled to face him, lifting up her hands simultaneously as if to ward him off. *Whoa, sister.*

"Brant," she breathed, visibly relaxing. "God, you scared me."

"Sorry." He stepped closer taking in her strained smile and the way she broke eye contact almost right away. She looked stressed, he decided. Hosting these enormous parties couldn't be easy. The skin of her face, usually soft and incandescent, looked like it was pulled taut over her forehead and especially around her mouth. "How are you?" he asked.

"Good." She glanced at him again, her dimples flashing, but they promptly disappeared as she looked down at the box of beer hanging from his left hand. "The cooler's out back, if you just want to stick those in there." She turned her back to him them and started slicing another stalk of celery.

Brant didn't move. Everything about her greeting struck him as off. She hadn't asked him how he was doing, for one thing. She'd never once *not* shown an interest in what was going on in his life. But then she asked a question.

"Where's your date?"

"Couldn't find one," he replied, lying through his teeth. Truth was, he was dating two women at once, both of them SEAL groupies, and the probability that one would find out about the other if he brought either to the party wasn't worth the inevitable drama. Besides, he'd come here to see Rebecca, which neither of his playmates would understand.

"Oh, please," she scoffed. The blade of her knife struck the cutting board at regular intervals. *Thwack. Thwack. Thwack.*

"No, I'm serious." He hoisted the box onto the countertop so he could lean a hip against it and watch her work. "I'm going through a dry spell right now. In fact, I'm going to try celibacy for a while."

She slanted him wry look and snorted at the gross fabrication. "Sure you are."

"You don't believe me?" Her lack of faith wounded him. "You think I can't handle celibacy?"

"Maybe for a day," she said, "but I bet you couldn't last a week."

---

## HARD LANDING

**available in print and ebook**

Marliss Melton is the author of ten gripping romantic suspense novels, including a seven-book Navy SEALs series and continuing with The Taskforce Series. She relies on her experience as a military spouse and on her many contacts in the Spec Ops and Intelligence communities to pen heartfelt stories about America's elite warriors and fearless agency heroes.

Daughter of a U.S. foreign officer, Melton grew up in various countries overseas. She has taught English, Spanish, ESL, and Linguistics at the College of William and Mary, her alma mater. She lives near Virginia Beach with her husband, tween daughter, and four young adult children.

You can find Marliss on Facebook, Twitter and Pinterest. Visit www.MarlissMelton.com for more information.

CPSIA information can be obtained at www.ICGtesting.com
Printed in the USA
LVOW07s2120150215

427160LV00001B/7/P